Founders Less Than Three

Halley Suitt Tucker

This is a work of fiction. Names, characters, places and incidents are either the product of the author's imagination or are used fictitiously, except for the following enterprise sponsors:

Pixability, Innovation Nights, Speek, Franchises Unlimited, KindleNation.

Print Edition

Version 1.0

For every entrepreneur and entrepreneuse
who dares to dream about
the next big thing.

Please, keep dreaming!

Dedicated to:

Critt Jarvis
Social Strategist
who is always so far ahead of the rest of us.

Guy Kawasaki
Thank you for turning me into a real APE.
(Author, Publisher, Entrepreneur, that is.)

My husband
who makes everything possible
but never likes to be acknowledged.
<3

Special Dedications:

To all my Kickstarter supporters
who need to take a bow, right now!
You made this happen.
Thanks so very much!

Special thanks to my creative supporters
who invented startups for me:
Brad Feld, Todd Randolph, JP Rangaswami, and Gary Turner

Special thanks to my brilliant enterprise supporters:

Matt Biskup (Franchises Unlimited)
John Bracken and Danny Boice (Speek)
Bobbie Carlton (Mass Innovation Nights)
Bettina Hein (Pixability)
Steve Windwalker (KindleNation)

Special thanks to Kickstarter:

Launch date: August 22, 2012
Successfully funded: September 24, 2012

Founders Less Than Three
Published: August 2013

Founders Less Than Three

PART ONE

Chapter 1

Getting In

Once upon a time there was an accelerator named Celery. No, I suppose that's not quite the way to start my story. But there really is an accelerator program in Boston called Celery. It's a jumping joint where geeky folks come together to start new companies, meet mentors, find financing. But the best stories start with boy meets girl, don't they?

So, it all started when I met Nick Belden. He was a nerdy geek with big glasses who never thought any girl would give him the time of day, until he founded a start-up company, then suddenly he was famous.

But I didn't know who he was. I was just being nice. I nearly ran into him on my bike on a side street, off University Avenue in Palo Alto, California. He had a flat tire and was holding the wheel in his hands, examining it as if it were a mysterious invention. He turned to look at me as I rode by, my blonde braids hanging out the sides of my helmet. I was wearing a red polka dot dress and going to a birthday party. He was blocking the path in an annoying way.

"Hey! You nearly slammed into me," he said.

"Hey! You're blocking the whole road," I said. "What happened to your tire?"

I got off my bike and took the wheel away from him. I spun it and found the problem pretty easily.

"Here," I pulled out a nail and handed it to him.

I got my Park tools and patch kit out of my backpack. My dad had taught me to fix bikes and I always carried my tools with me.

"You'll need a patch," I explained and made him one. I worked quickly and silently. He seemed amused to watch me work.

"Who are you?" he demanded in a rather confused way.

"What, you've never seen a girl fix a bike? My name is Monica."

"Monica What?"

I ignored him as I finished what I was doing. I got the feeling people jumped when he asked them questions.

"I asked you, Monica Who?" he said.

"I'm just Monica. Monica, the girl who fixed your bike. Who are you?" I said returning his bike to him. I wiped my hands on a rag I carried.

"Nick, ah, Nick Belden," he said.

"Nice to meet you Nick. Take it to a shop soon and get it trued up," I told him and rode off.

An hour later, he walked into the same party he'd made me late for. The birthday girl introduced us.

"Monica Kroy, this is Nick Belden," she said.

"You mean, Monica the girl who fixed my bike? Let me see your hands," he said. "No bike grease. Impressive."

My friend was looking at me strangely, like this was a big deal that he was talking to me.

"Nick's running a hot new startup," my friend, birthday girl gushed.

"Monica wouldn't be interested," Nick said, "It's got nothing to do with bikes."

"Actually she's a whiz at coding. She went to Caltech," she told him.

"Really? We're hiring. Here's my card," he said.

I nodded, slipped the card in my jeans jacket pocket.

"Gotta go fix another guy's bike, catch you later," I said and ducked out. Later I tossed his card in the trash on the back porch.

I was in full crush mode on some other guy, so I ignored Nick most of the evening. It ended up crush guy worked for Nick, and as I started hanging out with him, I kept running into Nick, at his company, at a local coffee place, at parties.

Nick was charming, but no prince. I was 20 and he was 40. Nick was becoming Silicon Valley royalty and kept calling me and trying to convince me to come work for him. I finally agreed. A week after I started, he fired the guy I liked. Nick didn't know that things had already cooled down with the crush guy and we were just friends. He actually did me a favor, letting the guy go. I settled into my job and kept ignoring Nick.

Other guys asked me out but I said no. I had changed my mind a little. I was kind of getting to know and like Nick. But I didn't want to lose my job over an affair with the boss that could end. Girls did dumb things like that all the time. I didn't want to.

I'm a girl who grew up believing it was okay to be a totally nerdy blonde girl on a farm in Manteca, CA, who would some day start her own high-tech company. Manteca isn't the cool part of California; it was the hot, inland part. My dad made me believe I could do anything. It was an unlikely place to start believing in that dream, but he was good at making me believe in anything.

I had a Cinderella story going, in a way. I grew up on a farm, not rich, but in a working-class family. We even had chickens. But instead of waiting around for some Prince Charming to show up, I decided to take things into my own hands, learn how to write some code, go to school in computer science, create a company, and change the world, even though I was from an unknown town like Manteca, which by the way means "lard." It's a crazy thing to name a town. Bad branding. It's an agricultural Garden of Eden in a way, a part of California with peach orchards and almonds trees and tomato fields and grape vines, which makes it feel as far away from Silicon Valley as the moon.

Nick was getting bolder, texting me funny messages and leaning over me when he was showing me stuff on my screen, teaching me Agile Programming, you know, romantic stuff like that.

So I guess, he just talked me into it. He decided he was going to make me love him one way or another. He did all the romantic things geeks are good at doing. Engineers are seriously sexy and very romantic. They have the best brains anywhere and that's the way to turn a girl on. Nick knew how to get me smitten. He took all the time in the world to listen to me and teach me things. We talked about every new company, every programming language, every new device and we stayed up late with good California wine many wonderful nights talking about the future. I really fell for him. It was a fun time. Riding the roller coaster to the IPO for his startup and getting to be his main squeeze was a thrill.

We founded a second company in 2009, but it wasn't taking off as fast as the first. That was more about being early in mobile and the lousy economy. By 2011 things at the company were getting a little better, still, it hadn't been a piece of cake. We'd had a few years of slogging along, the regular hard work of it, not at all glamorous, but necessary. And lately, my now famous husband was getting tough to deal with. He wasn't very nice to me any more. He didn't seem to have the time. Didn't seem to want to bother. I was beginning to think Nick was the wrong guy for my story.

By now, I was 32 and Nick was 52 and I'd always wanted the same thing he had, the same thing most of the guys in the Valley wanted. I wanted my own company. But I also wanted something he didn't have and didn't want. A baby. I guess I changed my mind one day between 20 and 32. It happens. But Nick hadn't changed his mind. He made it clear he didn't want one.

So over breakfast one morning, I saw a blog post about accelerator programs around MIT and I thought I might like to try one of them out. The article explained what accelerator programs were, a kind of summer camp for entrepreneurs, but not necessarily in the summer, giving them money and mentors and six months to try to launch their company. People knew Celery; it was getting some good press. It wasn't as famous as Y Combinator or TechStars, but it was respected.

I showed it to Nick. He seemed politely encouraging. So I applied to the program and waited to see what happened. I thought I might have a chance. I needed a chance. I applied in September and they said we would be notified by the last day in December.

It was two weeks before Christmas and the Bay Area was having a heat wave. I remember what I was wearing that day, a blue cotton summer shift, knee-length, and a tiny white tee shirt underneath. I was dressed for a day at the ocean. But this would be no day at the beach.

I remember the weather in Palo Alto that morning; it wasn't breezy and fresh as usual, but actually hot. I had my blonde hair up in a ponytail, to keep it off my neck. I was wearing grey Converse sneakers and white gym socks.

I went into the office early, leaving Nick home to meet one of his "guys." He often worked at home to meet one of his many house buddies: the plumber, the roofer, the electrician, or the contractor. I could never keep track of them.

I was at my office. It was about 7:30 a.m. and there weren't many people at work yet. My lead programmer Puff was already in. The rest of the team had just left, after working all night. I was waiting for a special email. Today could be the day. Nick was getting on the conference circuit, getting famous since his first three startups had done well. People knew the name, Nick Belden. He could get a table at a cool restaurant. It might help me get into the Celery program. It might not.

Lately, he was complaining a lot about stuff I did. And he was realizing I might actually get in and then really go to Boston.

"How the fuck am I supposed to manage without you?" He loved to use the F-word.

"Nick, relax. What are the odds … ?" I'd said.

I was the CTO of our current startup. Hell, it had been my idea and I had done the pitch that got us funded. That made it tricky if I actually got into Celery. Who would replace me? My top three coders, Puff, Sanjay and Ranji were seriously fine coders, and Sanjay was almost ready to step into my shoes. But not quite. The VCs had invested in Nick and me. It would get them nervous if I left.

We had gotten some good press just last month, hinting at a big valuation, so suddenly my husband had his old Berkeley buddies hanging around the office looking for jobs. At a party the other night, his friend Steve had "volunteered" to take my place, when the two of them were very drunk and being stupid. Steve didn't have the chops. No way.

When I thought about it, Steve was suddenly hanging out at our place a lot. He was showing up at our office parties, dragging along that stupid model-pretty PR chick he was dating. Her name was Cindy, but she spelled it "Sendi." He even talked Nick into hiring her.

On his birthday, Nick had promised me we'd go out alone, just the two of us, to a new place in San Francisco I'd wanted to go to and somehow we ended up with those two, Steve and Sendi, crashing our birthday dinner date. I didn't want to spend Nick's birthday with them. I wanted a dinner date with my husband alone. It wasn't a lot to ask. Sendi the PR chick was telling another name-dropping story about someone she knew at Facebook. The hostess brought over a blue birthday cake for Nick. Blue, hmm, it reminded me of a free Viagra sample he tried a few months back. That didn't go so well. The cake had a straight line of candles, some on, and some off.

"I asked them to do it in binary for you, Nick," Sendi gushed at my husband.

Yes, it was supposed to be fifty-two in binary — 110100 — six candles with the first two lit, then one off, then one on, then one off, but the last one was lit which actually made it fifty-three. Do the math, as they say. But she didn't know crap about coding. She couldn't have figured it out herself. Wonder who explained binary to her… they had done a great job.

Nick thought it was cute.

He actually said that word, "cute!" He never says that word.

I leaned over and blew out the ones digit.

"Now it's fifty-two, it was fifty-three before," I said.

I didn't enjoy the birthday party. I really didn't like the idea of Steve trying to take my place at work.

The office was surprisingly dead the next morning. Lately it was the place I'd rather be at dawn than in bed with Nick. This wasn't a good trend.

The email from Boston had arrived overnight and was sitting in my inbox when I opened it. It was a YES from Celery! I read it, then jumped up and shouted, "Yes!" I printed it out. Old School, I know, but sometimes, nothing beats paper.

"And that means?" my coder pal Puff said. His turban looked sharp this morning.

"I got into Celery!" I said.

I handed Puff my phone, "Here take my picture." I stood at the screen pointing to the email, as if you could see it. "I can't wait to tell Sonya!" Sonya was my best friend and I wanted to talk her into going to Boston with me, to join me at Celery.

"Lovely," Puff said, handing me back my phone.

"I gotta go tell Nick," I said and headed for the printer room.

I headed out the side door, and took University Ave at a gallop. It meant I was going to Boston for five months, starting in January and ending in May on Demo Day when we would show off our companies and try to snag financing. I was so excited.

I ran up the street on that sunny hot morning, already hot even though it was early. It was more like half running, half skipping and half jumping up and down. I was going to run my own company!

Yes! It felt so good to run. Just like I used to feel when I was 12 and I spent the summers at the beach with my family, my dad giving me projects, asking me to invent stuff with him and we'd both try to build something with junk we found on the beach and see who came up with the better product. We were builders. We were makers. We were prototypers. My dad always made me feel like I could do anything, as long as I could just start building it.

My feet were strong and sure in my sneakers, flying up the street. I got to our driveway in about 10 minutes. I didn't see any workman's truck in the driveway, just a shiny little red VW beetle. The house was looking good.

I realized I'd be a little sad to leave it behind. I flipped on my video and did a quick selfie video to show Sonya.

"Sonya, I got in, I'm going to Boston, but look at the house, I'm gonna miss it!" I panned over to the addition we'd just finished, past the red car, to the patio.

I teased Nick that he had bought the house just so he could have some real guy-type guys to hang out with, instead of geeks. Working men. Real men. Men who looked like they belonged on the covers of romance novels, tan buff hunks, sporting cowboy hats, carpenters' belts, and big biceps. I couldn't remember any of them having a red VW beetle; they were more the pick-up truck type. I ran into the house.

Nick wasn't on the first floor. I called his name, no answer. There was a dull pounding noise on the second floor, but not like a hammer, more like furniture moving or maybe they were fixing a wall. I ran upstairs. I burst into our bedroom, "I got into Celery!" I yelled. Then I saw them.

There was my naked husband in our bed, with Steve's alleged girlfriend, Sendi, the PR chick. What the hell? She was all tangled up with him, her skinny tan legs wrapped around his white butt and the soft pounding noise was him, my husband, on top of her, up to the hilt, maybe banging her head against our headboard.

Her toenail polish was bright blue.

She saw me and knew enough to make a squeaky gasp and some words that sounded like, "Oh my God!"

He didn't see me at first, but then turned to look at me, his face hot, red, interrupted. I remember things — little things — like his expression. He didn't look embarrassed or sorry. He looked mad.

"What the fuck?" he said, to me, his wife, like, *"Why are you interrupting me while I'm busy screwing the PR chick!"*

His red face and her bright blue toenails. It made me sick. I would remember those colors.

I turned around, took a few zombie steps, stunned, leaving our bedroom door wide open and then turned back, gripping my phone.

"Out! I want her out of here!"

"Shut the goddamned door," she growled at Nick, pulling the sheet up around her.

He walked towards me, naked, slammed the door in my face.

I was dazed, seeing her, seeing him. And then a red-hot bolt of anger went through me. I turned to get out of there, just get out and get away from both of them and the slightly dank sexy smell to the clean, sunny street below.

I ran out the front door and across the street to my best friend Sonya's place. I was in tears that left splotchy marks down the front of my sundress. I had the crumpled-up piece of paper in my hand.

"Oh my God, what happened?" Sonya said, at the door.

"I got into Celery," I was crying.

"I know, but then why are you crying?" Sonya hugged me because she always knew when people needed hugs. She was short and came up to about my shoulder.

"I just found Nick in bed with the PR chick," I said.

"No! The PR chick? I hate her!" she said. "He's a bastard! They both are!"

"Yes! I'm going to kick his ass," I said.

"Los traidores sucias!" Sonya went all Spanishy on me when she was pissed off. Her mom was from the Dominican Republic, her dad from Puerto Rico.

She brought me into the kitchen. Her computer was on the table. She got me a glass of tap water.

It was dawning on me. I said to Sonya slowly, "Oh my God, do you think that's why he was wanted me to go to Boston… "

"You mean?" she said.

"Yes, that's why he pushed me to apply to the Celery!"

"Crap! Like he wanted to get rid of you?" she said.

"She has blue toenails," I said.

"That blue OPI color? Called, 'What's With The Cattitude?' I do love that color," Sonya said. "Seeing them, Senorita. It's like a bad YouTube video blowback thing. It might be stuck in your brain like forever. Yuck!"

"Yeah. And a fake orange tan! Who does that in California?" I said and then I sort of stopped breathing. "And he's gonna put his idiot friend Steve in my place at work!"

"This is bad."

"There's only one thing to do," I said.

"What?"

"Hit him where it hurts!" I said.

"There?"

"No, I mean start another company that's about a hundred times better than his. I'm leaving tomorrow," I said. "You have to go with me."

"Boston? It's freezing and girlfriend, Latinas don't do freezing," she said, "and I'd have to quit."

"Then quit, I can pay you. I can pay you whatever Google's paying you," I said.

"Quitting Google is cool now," she said.

"It's like quitting Harvard used to be," I said.

"But what about that cute cook in the gluten-free café?" she said. She was kidding. We liked stalking that guy for fun cause he was so hot. And we liked eating his excellent polenta.

"Please go with me," I told Sonya.

I grabbed my phone. I had to move fast.

"Ok, but I can't leave for two weeks at least," she said, "Monica? What are you doing?"

I was using my banking app on my phone, transferring a little money from our joint account to my personal account. Okay not a little, a lot of money. "Nick loves investing in startups. He just gave me a little bon voyage present," I said. "We're going to Boston."

Chapter 2

Getting Lost

Sometimes people make it easier to leave. Nick did. Cheating with the PR girl was bad, but in the morning on the way to the airport, I had four new discoveries. A close friend sent me an email telling me Nick had tried to get into her pants too. An ex girlfriend of Nick's texted saying he'd been with her a week after we got married. The receptionist from his first company DM'd me on Twitter reporting he'd also slept with a different PR girl there and as if all that wasn't enough, some girl at an accelerator in New York sent me Facebook pictures of her and Nick at CES the past January that were really pretty gross. I was mad, sad and glad I was leaving him all before 7 a.m.

Sonya drove me to the airport and headed into work. She planned to quit and join me in Boston two weeks later. She was usually good at cheering me up, but I wasn't feeling too cheery. I didn't tell her about the four new revelations. I just didn't want to get into it.

It was a beautiful day out my little airplane window as I buckled in and started thinking about Nick. I was trying to understand how I had missed what was really going on with him. We'd worked so hard at the last company. I really wasn't watching.

The pilot announced that it was 74 degrees out, but that we were heading into a snowstorm in Boston. Great. We were up and over Nevada by the time I started thinking back on how Nick and I met. I was just looking out the window as I crossed from west to east, trying to figure out how I'd married such a jerk. I'm not one of these women who think all men are jerks. I like men. I thought back on early days, how much I loved learning geeky things from Nick, how we'd talk until nearly dawn about Hex and Python and Android. We used to tell jokes about the Fibonacci Series, for goodness sakes. Those were the better times, when he took me seriously, helped me get into the startup world, showed me the ropes. So was it all just crap? Had he just been stringing me along (and all the other girls, too) not because he thought we were smart, but just because he wanted to sleep with all of us?

Sendi had staked her claim. That was the thing that bugged me. There were articles all the time about how women didn't know how to compete like men in the entrepreneurial world, but no one ever pointed out the obvious. Women definitely knew how to compete. Unfortunately, they were competing against one another. When it came to fighting it out for the attention of certain alpha males, we never shied away from a good battle, without thinking twice. We could be cutthroat and shrewd, but why were we cutting each other's throats instead of helping one another get ahead? Why didn't we help other girls get inside startups and make sure we all got promoted to the important jobs, with seats on the executive team and finally, made room for one another in the boardroom?

And Nick? Had he encouraged this kind of thing in his company? I'd never thought of Nick as a philanderer. A cheater? I'd never believed he could do that. He wouldn't do that to me. "Nick was no cheater," I remembered saying that to a friend. Ha!

We'd been gaga for each other in the beginning. He asked me to marry him the first weekend we met. It got to be a joke, him proposing to me all the time. Then later, when he sold his first company and gave me a new Porsche, his lawyer thought it might be a good idea to draw up a pre-nup, just in case. I had a friend who went to law school at Berkeley and she reviewed it, adding in one of those cheating clauses, so if he ever cheated, he owed me big bucks. It was enough to really piss off Nick at first, but he finally agreed to put in a mutual cheating clause, which he insisted on calling the "good for the goose, good for the gander" clause.

I wanted to think bad things about him there on the plane that morning, I certainly was getting encouragement from all round to do so, but I couldn't. I kept thinking of nice things we had done together. It seemed so sunny when I strolled down Memory Lane and turned the corner onto University Ave in my mind.

Bright yellow sun. And dark black sunglasses. That's what I think of when I think of meeting him in Palo Alto. Blinding sun. Or maybe I was blind. Sunny happy Silicon Valley where the cool kids in black sunglasses and shorts and tee shirts roamed like wild animals imagining new ways of doing things. Kids who happen to be founders of companies you've heard of, builders of software you use every day and you probably think some adult invented. Well, an 18-year-old is legally an adult, right?

The bike shop. The Apple Store. The coffee shops. The rat-a-tat-tat crunch of a skateboarder tearing up the sidewalk. We were all so casual and cool and killing ourselves working 24/7 out there. Startup city. Even the names — try "Sand Hill Road" — it sounds like a day at the ocean, just bring your shovel and pail. Not exactly. More like, "Bring your A game." A phrase I hate. The people who use that phrase seem to come from the camp where A stands for Asshole. It all looks cool and fun, sun and sand and silicon.

But don't start thinking founders are having all that much fun. They are intense, serious people burning their brains over the next new thing, the perfect app, the big data mega-solution, even if they look all relaxed and casual in their cute clothes, madras Bermudas and the famous Adidas beach sandals with the black and white stripes. Don't be fooled, they aren't so relaxed.

Getting into Logan Airport, Boston looked grey and cold, the snow had ended and was deep, but Boston had one wonderful feature not noted in any guidebook — it was a town my husband wasn't in! Yes, December in California meant I was wearing flip flops the day before, and now I was exhausted after a night of bad sleep and worry, but bundled up in wool and GORE-TEX, wearing my L.L. Bean boots ready to fight the elements and win in a town where Nick didn't rule.

The pilot announced the fact that it was 20 degrees out, but with the wind chill, it was more like 12. One day ago Sonya and I were wandering down the street to get some frozen yogurt. Now this. I didn't know from "frozen" yesterday.

I stood in the cab line, half freezing to death, and then finally got a cab into Cambridge. When we got to Kendall Square and I tried to pay the cab driver with my credit card, it was declined. That never happened. Maybe Nick had been up to no good. I scraped together enough cash from my purse, paid the guy and dragged my stuff into the lobby of the Marriott and stood near the concierge desk, as I pulled up my banking app on my phone.

My wonderful husband had emptied my account. I was broke. Great. I guess he figured, two can play at this game. I found an old credit card that was an individual account of mine and paid for the hotel. After I'd checked in and my stuff was settled in the room, I went swimming, hoping to forget the day. It almost worked. But even the pool was a bit cold and so was the air, nothing like my good old home sweet home of California, which suddenly wasn't my home anymore.

I was thinking of how broke we were growing up and how I'd been given one of those pre-owned dresses for my senior prom. All night, I thought any minute some mean girl might come up to me and say, "Hey, that's my dress!" I'm tall but it made me stoop a little. I don't like the word "broke." It makes me think of an old man in tattered clothes with a back nearly breaking.

After swimming, I felt a little better so I'd bundled up in all the clothes I could drag out of my suitcase and made the other plunge, out into the snow, in fact, into a full-on snowstorm. I made my way into Kendall Square, weaving through the streets of partly shoveled Cambridge to an ATM, where I could get some cash out of my personal account.

Kendall Square in January. Snow swirling up, snow blasting down the street, slapping the back of your neck, doing rude things up your skirt, if you were stupid enough to wear one. Nothing gets the heart racing quite like icy rain and having to leap chunks of snow every time you tried to cross the street. A chill that thrills some people perhaps, but not me. It only warns me to button up and keep moving.

It was like some video game set on a distant planet with whiteout conditions, but this was real and really cold, and you weren't feeling like any Halo hero in this mess. It was "Beam me up, Scotty!" weather. Get me back to the ship or give me a new planet for God's sake. Any planet. This one's a loser. Bone chilling, wind whipping, seriously!

I rushed back to the hotel, not keen on doing much exploring. I was looking at the room service menu, thinking about the genius who invented that concept, wishing I could thank them when Sonya called.

"I did it," she said.

"You quit?" I said.

"Yup and they didn't like it. But Marissa said she understood."

"I forgot you know her."

"Duh, yeah," Sonya said.

"What did you tell her?"

"I told her I was going to Boston to be a co-founder in a new company," she said. "She said that was awesome." Sonya sounded so cheery.

"She's right. Co-founder, shit, of course, I'm sorry I didn't say that when I asked you to join me," I said. "Sonya, will you … will you be my co-founder? It sounds like 'will you marry me?' "

"Don't mess with me girl! Of course, I'll be your co-founder!" she said.

"Crap, I can't even pay you. Nick took all my money," I said.

"Yo, Monica, girlfriend! I've got money. Don't you think Marissa treats us right? She showed all us girls how to take care of our pretty little assets?"

"Your assets," I goofed.

"You betcha," she said. "I'm buying in and you need money honey, you ask me. I don't want you talking to that idiot Nick."

"You're the best, Sonya," I started crying.

"Don't be crying! You cry at anything."

"I'm just happy and I'm freezing. It's so cold here, I have to warn you, it's insane," I told her.

"What time is it there?"

"Already 10:30."

"So just take a bath and go to bed!"

"Now you're my friend, my co-founder and my mother?"

"You need all three, girl!"

She was right. I was wiped out and a bath and bed sounded good.

The next morning I woke late, thanks to the jet lag and the dark sky getting ready to dump more snow on my new city. I got bundled up again and by the time I got downstairs the snow was falling heavily. I asked the hotel doorman where MIT was. He pointed straight ahead.

Welcome to Boston. I headed towards MIT, thinking the offices of the Celery program were near there. I was outside the Stata Center at MIT, beautifully designed by Frank Gehry with that stunning slanted roof, corrugated and crazy, decidedly out of the box. They were surprised the slanty roof leaked? I was surprised the roof was still attached to the building in this weather! I checked out the local geeks going by like Inuits sporting fur-rimmed hoods and puffy coats in many colors. This town had great hats.

But who the hell named these streets? There were no simple street addresses. Instead, there was 1 or 2 or 3 Cambridge Center or 800 Technology Square, or on the MIT campus which stretched across many blocks, you'd have an address like "E39" as if that made it easy. How about a number address with a real street name, something simple, like 367 Addison Avenue?

I was twenty-four hours from a sunny Palo Alto afternoon, now lost in the Star Treky ice of Planet Kendall and an hour away from pitching my startup idea to the other new kids on the block— God knows which block— at Celery, the coolest accelerator program in the MIT hood. Cool. Or more like FRIGID! Except I can't find the block and my GPS is doing me no good.

Next to me, outside the Stata building, I asked a guy waiting for a bus for directions. He looked like a professor. He was happy to help, pulling out his smartphone. He assured me, "It's right here on my phone."

But all his phone said was LOADING.

Great.

He started shaking the phone. Who shakes their phone, like it's a saltshaker that's gummed up? So maybe he's not an MIT professor. There's something poetic about thinking you can shake a piece of gorilla glass to get more data to fall out of it. Hello, Sir, it doesn't work that way!

I said thanks and ran inside, out of the beastly weather. The building was warm and welcoming, beautiful spaces to study or meet, all curving around a cute café.

I stopped to ask another stranger — a tall, skinny Indian guy in shorts. Wait, shorts in a blizzard? I was dreaming of Palo Alto and he's jones-ing for Punjab I guess. He showed me his cool tablet phone, I played along, like I'd never seen one, but I knew the guys who invented it.

He looked at the address seriously.

"Wait, are you at Celery? You in the new winter class of startups?"

"Ah, yep, except, I'm not there and I can't find it."

"My roommate applied but didn't get in. Three thousand, nine hundred twenty-five people applied. Ten got in."

"Sorry," I said, trying to sound humble. "He probably had a great idea. Tell him not to give up."

I sounded like a parent. This guy must be about 16. I'm 32 and he probably thinks I'm about 1000 years old here on Planet Wunderkind.

"It wasn't such a great idea really. He kind of did give up, but he's got a great gig now at Pinkberry."

More frozen yogurt. All Artic, all the time, around here.

"I know where you're going. I'll take you. I'm Vivek1412. I mean, I'm just Vivek, but there are a lot of us at MIT, so I'm Vivek1412 now. "

"I'm Monica. Monica Bel… I mean Monica Kroy."

Jetlag. I can't remember my own name. Back to my maiden name after what my idiot husband did. Monica Kroy was easier and she sounded like a hot chick in a video game dressed in a black latex cat suit. I don't look like that, but apparently I'm relatively hot for 32, since some young Android programmer told me so the other night at a party in Soma. Nice to know. Wasn't feeling that way. He was likely very drunk.

A pretty girl in a bold blue sari wanders by. She's sporting one layer of baby blue azure gauze and three gold stripes across the hem. Perfect for this weather. "Vivek, we're gonna be late!" She is very beautiful, almost mythic. A goddess.

"Oh no, I forgot. I can't take you over there, we're busy doing something, um, wait, almost here … there, look at this map. It's right opposite the post office, up on Main Street. Do you know where the Kendall T station is? It's on that street."

Oh great, that's where I started. "Yes, actually."

The goddess is impatient with him.

"Sorry I have to go. We're getting married," he says.

"Wow, okay, congratulations," I said.

I head back out the door. Vivek is dragged off in the other direction by the goddess, but he pivots and points toward the T.

He forgot he was getting married today. Forgot? So all the MIT engineer jokes are for real.

The snow was getting very serious, blowing sideways, but occasionally falling in straight steady lines. I got back to Main Street and asked someone where the post office was, they say right, their friend says left, a girl with them tells me to ignore them and points toward the river. "Next to the flower shop." It's the first tip to orientation here. Just like Californians base things on where the Pacific Ocean is, this town is about the Charles River and the Atlantic.

I trudged along, feeling snow bunching up between my boots and socks, melting on my ankles. The streets were fairly empty. No one wanted to be out in this. There's a nattily dressed guy in a black cashmere coat, double breasted, like a fancy lawyer, looks expensive. Handsome guy, dark skin and short close-cut afro like President Obama. He's heading my direction. I was trying to read my smartphone again and there was snow falling on the screen. I nearly ran into him.

"That's not going to work," he said taking the phone out of my hand and brushing off the snow. "What are you looking for? You look a little lost." Touch screen in a blizzard. And you have to take your gloves off to use it. Do California designers think about that stuff?

"Got that right," I said, really sick of being cold and lost. "It's called 1 Cambridge Center, whatever the hell that is. I can't believe this place has no street names."

He laughs. He pointed to a kiosk, not three feet from us with the large letters that read DIRECTORY on top. There's an actual map behind the glass.

He points to 1 Cambridge Center on the directory map and then points to the building about 10 feet to the left.

"Ever get the feeling, thanks to all these geolocation apps, nobody knows where they're going anymore?" he asks me.

He was right about that and I laughed, "Yeah!" He smiled a friendly smile. I liked this guy.

"I'm Marshall," he shook my hand.

"Monica. Thanks," I said.

"You're freezing!"

"Palo Alto yesterday. Hard to get used to this kind of thing," I say.

"Ah, yes. So it's right in there. See you later, Monica from Palo Alto," he turned the other direction, then took a quick left into a café called Cosi. I went into the office building.

I'm wondering why he said "later" when I'd likely never see him again. But mostly I'm rushing into a warm building and glad to be there.

It's hard to start anything from scratch. And this is a cold start for sure. I could walk into a party of entrepreneurs in the Valley and know about half of them. But I was about to enter Celery pretty much cold. I'd have to meet and remember 10 startup ideas and 10 new CEOs at a minimum and their co-founders and their teams. I aimed for remembering three after this first meeting. Unless I write them all down, that's about all I could hope for with my mixture of jetlag and frostbite. And no team yet. Sonya wouldn't be there for two weeks and my coders are now likely stuck slaving away for Nick, since I never got a chance to talk to them about joining me.

I took the elevator to the sixth floor, see a sign with the word "CELERY" then head down the corridor to a large conference room with glass along one side and take my seat for the first meeting.

I'm too tired and frozen to be nervous I suddenly realize. The leaders of the program Suzy and Walt, are the only people I've met before, just once in California and even these guys aren't all that close to me. I go up to shake their hands, sit toward the front and we're ready to begin. There's an empty seat next to me and after about five minutes, the same guy who gave me directions in front of the building comes in and sits next to me.

"Marshall," he reminds me and reaches to shake my hand.

"Monica. I guess you said you'd see me later," I say.

"Yes. I try to say what I mean," he says.

He pulls out a business card, it has the Dr. Seuss lines on it from Horton. "I meant what I said and I said what I meant, an elephant's faithful 100%."

I have to laugh. Suzy and Walter walk to the front.

She's Samantha Bewitched 1960's TV housewife pretty. Suzy's a tall skinny blonde of the country-club-and-equestrian-team-Connecticut type. She even wears her hair in that 60's style, shoulder-length and curled up at the bottom. I met her at a cocktail party in San Francisco through friends at Y Combinator. She and I had a bet, that a class that's half men and half women CEOs will be their most successful yet. I'm glad she took me up on the challenge. The bet is dinner at Legal Seafoods at Kendall, which is downstairs and a few blocks away. Just don't make me try to find it, after the kind of day I've been having.

Walter is even taller and skinnier than Suzy. He plays the bass fiddle in a jazz trio and makes that instrument look about the size of a ukulele. He's a brilliant Ph.D. from MIT in something — I don't remember — lasers, optics, security? He was a millionaire at 30. Does this for fun now. He actually wears a black beret like a jazz-playing beatnik.

"Welcome Class of Winter 2012. No speeches, let's just get into it," he says. "Who's ready to give me their pitch?"

I heard a slight gut punch of air coming out of most of us. I guess many of us didn't expect to be pitching our startup ideas for at least a few weeks from now. I have to give my philandering butthead of a husband some credit. It's something Nick taught me — always be ready to pitch.

Marshall and I both raised our hands at the same time. We looked at one another and laughed.

Chapter 3

Pitch or Die Trying

"I'm Monica Kroy from BrightLight. The world is all about mobile now. But there's one big elephant in the room when it comes to mobile. You're only as mobile as your battery life. Battery life stinks and with each new version of the iPhone or Android, or the iPad or any other tablet, we need more battery not less. We're solving power source problems for cars. We're building windmills. We're going green, but we still haven't solved power problems for mobile devices. Battery life still keeps us tethered to an outlet and we'll never really be mobile until we fix that. BrightLight solves that problem." I wasn't telling them how it solves it quite yet.

"And do I need to tell you I had to ask three people in Kendall Square for directions and two of them lost battery power as they were trying to load their geo loco apps to help me out?"

I went on a little more, probably too long.

"We need power sources for our mobile phones, but what do we do all day? We run around, so we are nowhere near a convenient power source. We're more mobile than our devices, until now. BrightLight is a power-generating fabric you can sew into clothing, backpacks, anything you wear or carry, that has micro solar-collectors, which are wired to charge your device as you go about your day. My co-founder and my team's heading here from California soon."

Thank God for Sonya, because my "team" was non-existent, thanks to a very quick exit on my part.

I saw someone make a face and I knew it was about using that dirty word "California" in Boston. Note to me: Whatever they say, they hate California here. Don't mention it. And never say Silicon Valley, ever. I mean, "evah."

I sat down and Marshall popped up, like we were on a seesaw or something.

"Yo!" he says.

The room is still a bit chatty.

"Yo!" a little louder this time. He commands attention. Quiet now.

"Yo," he says in a very ghetto voice and then with a charming British accent, "Hell… O!"

People were won over by this goofy opener, by his smile, his presence, by his insistence they should listen to him. Also his excellent tailoring which fit his trim body perfectly.

"I'm Marshall Plum. My company is … "

We waited.

He punched a key on the computer and two very large words appeared on the screen behind him.

"KNOW HOW!" It says.

"Time to change geolocation forever," he said.

"It's not about getting there – it's about HOW you get there."

He didn't show any other slides, just the big name of his company. Then he jumped right into it. KnowHow: a contextual app for geolocation. I sure picked the right guy to help me find this place. He was all about maps and what they mean and how to make good choices with them — not just let the GPS babe (Carmen Garmin he calls her) tell you what to do. His app lets you pick routes by context: scenic, fast, cheap, historical, big picture, shortcuts. If you're taking the scenic route through the mountains or need to get from Vermont to Montreal by the fastest route or cross the border where the guards are easy-going or your crappy car can't make it up an incline, his app gives you that kind of detail. Traffic overlay, sure, but lots more. Where did he start this project? As a Harvard Ph.D. student in physics. It's got government and DARPA written all over it. He's ex-Navy (and ex-CIA I'll bet) and hails from "the DC area" which I figure means Northern Virginia more likely.

Marshall sat down.

"Thanks for the map reading skills, sailor," I said. He winks.

We're going boy girl boy girl in the intro pitches. Next up is another team led by a woman. Women in high tech is a sore subject since there are so few of us. Even for me, it's so damned weird to be in a room of startups where half were led by women. It's long overdue. I don't think I can take one more innovation conference where every speaker is a man with the exception of one woman founder who comes from Asia, who happens to be married to one of the organizers. Promoting this kind of gorgeous exotic woman, via nepotism is apparently okay, but getting plain-talking American women running startups and being heard continues to be a challenge. Not okay with me.

I'm also sick of every startup accelerator program with nine male CEOs from California, except for one fashionista woman from New York who's pimping a shopping app. Snore. She's always hot and you get the idea she's just eye candy for the VCs to check out, when they are sick of looking at male geeks. God forbid they take on a serious woman with a serious idea who might challenge their franchise.

Suzy stood up to introduce Barb. I'd heard about her. She's a girl-next-door type redhead married to an MIT professor. He's twenty-five years older than her, gossip has it (sounds familiar), and he's a Nobel Prize winner. They must have some amazing dinner conversations. Her startup was called EverGrow. The "green team" is the way I'll remember them. She's got bright green skinny jeans on and an expensive well-ironed white button-down shirt. Green lace-up Converse basketball sneakers. No jewelry. Big black nerd glasses, likely from Chanel, they are so cool. Great sharp angled bowl-cut red bob haircut. Her team is Chinese — Bing, Bin and Lincoln, all grad students from MIT. EverGrow was a biotech research effort that's "yielded an environmentally safe resin that allows trees to grow a new superwood that has steel-like strength but bamboo-level flexibility," she explained, as if you hear about things like that every day. I made a check mark on my score card. Evergrow / Red China / Green Jeans.

After Evergrow comes MortalWarriors. They're hard to miss.

MortalWarriors was a startup founded by ex-military guys. It's some sort of video game interface for training new combat troops, which already had some nice funding from InQTel, the CIA venture capital group. Mortal still wants and needs to find big money, like we all do. The warriors of MortalWarriors wear camo fatigues. They have buzz cuts. Today the MW team is in green camo face paint in splotches.

They brought their whole team and start cranking some music and all three start dancing. It's Michael Jackson. Actually, wait … it's Jackson Five. They have a PowerPoint that has three big letters on it: A, B, C! Now they show a slide for each of them: Adam! Bill! Chris! Their CEO Adam literally looks like a GI Joe action figure. He's just about the most buff, wholesome, shiny clean American-looking Mid-Westerner I've ever seen.

"Seriously Caucasian, eh?" I scribble and pass the note to Marshall. He does a long, slow, up and down head nod.

After MortalWarriors danced their way into our hearts, no, more likely our minds, they explained their startup and then they're off stage in a whirl of male military energy. "Sir! Yes! Sir!" Gaming software for military training.

After the ultra-American soldiers, we went to the Russians, then the Israelis.

The Russians are led by a very pretty woman named "Irina Tovarich." I jot "Irina Comrade?" in my notebook because it sounds completely made-up. Gotta remember to ask about that. The company was called Slotnik, some kind of slot machine gaming interface to help people manage their finances. Maybe their target market is all new Russian billionaires. And Irina's the one to deliver the message in a leopard-print mini dress and tall black suede platform pumps.

Slotnik's CTO was a guy named Slava. He was big and sweet like a bear and has a round face and thick black hair. I wondered if Irina was his wife or something. He was giving her one thumbs up after each sentence she delivered. She looked very nervous, and with the very high-heeled platform shoes she was wearing, it looked as if she might just topple over. The dress was wool, maybe cashmere, very clingy in a good way, showing off her curves. The belt was wide black vinyl with a big buckle, cinched tight, as if to keep her together and keep her from exploding with nervousness. She held onto the buckle like it would save her life.

Next up is CrowdTrial, the Romanian-American team. We'd all been hearing about the many brilliant programmers in Eastern Europe and how Bucharest is the new Bangalore. The team has a CTO named Alex and a senior developer named Alexander, and another developer named Alexandre. Okay, but a little confusing. They went by the names Alex, Alexander and Dan (since his name is Alexandre Daniel Somethingescu.) Conveniently, Alex with the shorter name had very short hair, Alexander with the long name had long hair, Dan fell somewhere in between. All three were very good-looking guys. They explained how they use big data, with social networking and crowdsourcing to develop new ways to conduct clinical trials on medicines and therapies with their advisor, Craig MacDowney, an American guy who was a researcher at Mass General Hospital. They called him Mac.

The French team is supposed to be next, but their CEO had not arrived. Strange. The most important meeting of the session and the guy's not here. Suzy gets up and explains Jean-Claude is stuck in customs and may be here later. Makes me think of Trey Ratcliff's killer photo blog, called *Stuck in Customs.*

"Jean-Claude. He has a unique approach to solving an interesting problem," she says rather seriously.

Maybe he's curing cancer, solving world hunger or ending global warming. She went on and on about how great the missing-in-action Jean-Claude Longrée was. I asked Marshall what he knew about the French guy.

He showed me the results of a Google search and a picture of him.

"He's hot," he told me in a whisper.

Yeah, I could see that. Looks arrogant.

We moved on to the Israelis.

PatientPal was the Israeli team. They had a male CTO, Solly and a female CEO, Johanna. He started feeding her lines like she's an understudy actress for the leading role and had only just arrived on stage.

Suzy made an exasperated expression, then interrupted.

"I know certain teams did a shuffle to make sure they had a woman CEO because that might help them get into Celery this year. It's no big secret. But here's the deal, guys. If she's the CEO, she's the CEO, not you, so let her be that. I don't want any male CTOs running the company and turning their woman CEO into a figurehead, or just a puppet. Forget it. I still have a list of startups that want to get into the program and I can replace you. So

Solly, you can sit down and let Johanna finish. I'm sure she's more than capable."

Solly looked a little crumpled and sat at the end of the first row. Johanna stood even taller and already looked about 100 percent happier to be free of him. This will be an interesting team to watch. Their product is "PatientPal" something for hospitals that keep patient records secure in the cloud, with security and redundancy software as well as a payment system that sounds a lot like PayPal. It ran on mobile devices and was actually way further along than the rest of us. It was built, working and they had … customers!

PortMoney was the next team. Named after a spin on the French word, "porte monaille" which meant "wallet" and the idea of it being portable. I think instantly, who's going to get the French word? Nobody. This is America. Nobody speaks French. Nobody speaks any other languages, except Spanish. I only happen to speak French because I did a junior year abroad program there in Grenoble.

PortMoney was run by a pushy girl named Victoria from New York. I'm wondering why they didn't wait to apply to the New York Celery program that starts later in the spring. You can see she's pitching her biz to the guys in the room. At one point I catch her eye, I smile, she doesn't smile back, but rushes on to talk in a flirty stupid way about her digital wallet app. "Yes, guys, I want to get into your pants and slip that leather wallet out of your back pocket, and put PortMoney in it's place. You can trust me."

I wrote a note to Marshall, "Didn't Jack Dorsey already kill the payment space with Square?"

He tilted his head in a gesture like "you bet."

Don't forget the Aussies and XStream. They had a sports app to share and track extreme sports results, which they claimed was just so much better than RunKeeper or Gympact or a million other sports mobile apps. Their CEO was an adorable guy who would rather be jumping off cliffs with any variety of glider, wings, parachute. He was wearing a rock climbing helmet and harness, carrying one of those big ropes. His name was Chris Mooney. I wrote the "XStream / Chris Mooney/ Aussie Hunk" in my notes.

"Always handy to look like Hugh Jackman," Marshall said to me quietly.

I agreed and rolled my eyes a bit. Didn't seem fair to have to compete with someone like that.

We were winding down and they were going to serve us dinner in the main room, when the French guy Jean-Claude actually arrives from the airport.

"Nice of him to bother joining us," I said to Marshall.

He was dressed in a black leather kimono-type coat and skin tight black leather jeans with a long studded chain from belt to a D ring above his knee. And you could tell, the stuff he was wearing was really expensive and looked amazing. He had a Louis Vuitton duffle. He was tall, very thin, with dark brown sleek hair pulled back into a ponytail, bangs in his eyes, and big black sunglasses at night. He carried it off, like someone just threw the clothes on him but he'd also be fine in a crappy tee shirt and jeans. Marshall leans over.

"Runway model in Paris before this," he explained, like this is what all geeks did before starting companies.

I don't like him. Looked just like that guy in the Chanel ad. What's that eau de cologne by Chanel? Oh yeah, Égoïste!

"No way," I said.

"Yes way, Suzy's assistant, Roan, told me and he knows fashion."

Things were seriously upside down. So there was a style and fashion startup in this group, but not run by a woman. It was run by a guy.

Jean-Claude did his pitch. Not too much of an accent. For a guy who looked so cool, he wore a big sweet smile, which was not the usual expression of boredom and ennui guys like him often wear. His app let designers geolocate, buy and sell fabric from distributors all over the world, but especially in France, Italy, the UK and China. It's an arbitrage system for silk, wool, cotton and leather. The app was up and running, with customers. It was very beautiful. It was already in English, French, Spanish, Italian and Chinese. He called it BSpoken4.

Jean-Claude talked about his company and also about the volunteer stuff his team did to help improve conditions for workers in factories in Asia. This guy was too cool for school. I might like him, if I didn't dislike him so much. I know there must be a word for cocky in French; I just don't remember what it is. After his presentation, he sits down across the room; Suzy starts talking about our pitching talents.

I scribble to Marshall. "And his boyfriend is Karl Lagerfeld?"

Marshall giggles, "Nah, he's straight and married to a woman, but he does know Lagerfeld."

"How do you know that?"

"The gay part or the Lagerfeld part? Honey, you understand that's my tribe, right?"

"Marshall, I kinda thought you might be gay."

"Not kinda, more like totally. So my gay-dar is finely tuned. I met him and his wife at LeWeb in Paris last month anyway, when Lagerfeld spoke. She's from Bangladesh."

"You don't know Löic Le Meur, do you?"

"Honey, everybody who's cool knows Löic," he said and looked at me like this was obvious, "and I love Geraldine."

I turned to check out fashion boy and he turned toward me, as if he could feel me looking. He looked directly at me, then burst into that big smile, like a big puppy dog, surprisingly sweet.

He raises one eyebrow at me, as if to say, "What are you looking at, lady?"

Zing!

I looked away.

Chapter 4

Boys Are Back In Town

Winter in New England is best left glued on Christmas cards with cheesy little glitter for snow, one horse here and one horse there with their open sleighs dashing toward Grandmother's house. They can just keep it. You couldn't help wondering, how do people even do business here? There's no running to the corner to grab coffee easily in this weather. Casual encounters like you had in Silicon Valley on a regular basis required a dog sled team around here.

After a few days in Boston, I was already sick of the freezing weather. Glad I liked hats. I found one in the local Nordstrom that looked more Russian than the Russians' furry flap hats.

I'd been lucky as hell about finding an apartment. An old friend who was going to grad school at MIT was getting married and moving in with her fiancé, so she let me have her apartment in Porter Square near the T station for the next six months. The dash between the T and my place was 8.5 minutes if you ran at top speed to avoid the weather. After being in a hotel for too many days, it was good to spend the weekend unpacking and getting settled in. Finally, on Friday of the second week, the blessed day of January 18, Sonya arrived. Thank God.

I don't think anyone at Google expected her to quit. Surprise! I put her up at my place for a few weeks until we had a chance to go look for another apartment for her. I didn't like living with anyone I worked with, but was willing to do this for her for a while. We spent the weekend "slushing around" as Sonya called it. She knew from slush, having attended Harvard.

On Monday, we headed back to the Celery offices and I introduced Sonya to Marshall. I showed her the kitchen and gave her a new MIT mug, just to annoy her snobby crimson Harvardian heart.

We were seated next to MortalWarriors on one side of the cubicles and Marshall's team on the other. He took his diversity seriously; his team was two African-American guys and two African-American girls. As noisy as Marshall could be, they were very quiet, glued to their monitors. Jean-Claude's French team was at the end of the hallway. The Aussies were next to them. We could see them if we stood and looked over the barrier between our desks and the team next door.

We suddenly had been gifted a pretty girl intern named Sarah, whose's style was Wellesley Girl meets Central Square Goth. Whoever was paying her tuition at Wellesley probably didn't love the purple streak down the back of her blonde hair. She was a nihilist she informed us, but also completely boy crazy.

"The view in that direction is certainly sweet," Sarah said, standing and faux-stretching just to check out the

Down Under guys and the Frenchmen. "Do I look like totally casual or what?"

Suzy, our director, came out of her office and walked down the hall to talk to the Australians.

"Stop looking casual and look busy, here comes the boss lady," I said.

"She's my aunt," Sarah said.

"Interesting," I said. How did I miss that?

I took Sonya over to meet Suzy, then showed her around the rest of the office. I was thinking of my idiot husband again. I was remembering when Nick and I set up our offices in Palo Alto, for the first company, before we were married. There were seriously cute interns, always hanging around him. I never worried about it in those days.

I would go see my lawyer at three o'clock. She was based in California, but they had an office here as well, doing a lot of IP and startup work. I was lucky as hell she came to Boston about once a month.

Sonya and I looked at the one Ping-Pong table as we took the tour. "Only one?" she said.

"That's exactly what I said," I told her.

Celery had a big reputation, so you'd expect it to look as good as our cool crazy bright green offices in California. Our old place looked like some wing of a museum of modern art, with amazing spaces popping with color and mega-kitchens full of free food, all the soda you can drink, all the candy you can wreck your teeth with, anything you could dream up and courtyards with real art and fountains and eight Ping-Pong tables and six pin ball machines and ours even had the massage rooms and a sauna … okay, it was a little out of hand really.

But this is East Coast, not West. It's Boston, and it's a serious place. Packed with universities and brainiacs, here since 1620 on the colder, more sobering, Atlantic Ocean, not the surfer-dude my-girl-wants-to-party-all-the-time Pacific.

Boston is just never going to be as sexy as Cali — thank goodness. I've had enough of that for a while. Cambridge had things that California would never have — like MIT on one side of our offices and Harvard on the other, to mention only two of two hundred amazing schools in the area and add to that, New York four hours south. And there's something about the fact that East Coast Time, aka EST, is always three hours ahead of California that I was already noticing that fact made this place somehow more … authoritative. Of course, we Californians think we are ahead of East Coasters in every cool way that matters, but they really are, literally ahead of us. I liked that about Boston.

Celery's got a big office space, but it's not fancy. There were cubicles with the usual funny stuff on the walls, superhero posters and glowing light sabers and street signs (Mass Ave) that someone stole and hung up on wires, but there's nothing as super designy going on in Boston like there is in San Francisco.

On the other side of the floor, where the conference room is, you could look out the big windows and see down the street into Kendall Square to the MIT buildings and even steal a glimpse of the Charles River. It was a serious and cold, blue and fast-moving body of water dotted with crew teams slamming ahead of the waves, in their skinny shirts and shorts, showing off their narrow shell boats with long thin oars synchronized in the morning sun, reminding you, this is New ENGLAND. It's not called "Cambridge" for nothing.

As for the inventory of cool stuff: Ping-Pong table yes; kitchen but no endless food, no soda, just coffee, yes. And of course, the requisite graveyard of old coffee mugs with startup logos featuring names of companies that have gone bust. Odd bright green long couches that should make you think of celery. As for candy, I don't see any.

I let Sonya in on new details of my husband's hijinks.

"Remember that idiot Jimmie Dunhill I told you about? He was the venture shark guy Nick turned down. That evil girl worked for him," I told Sonya.

"The 'evil girl' means the idiot who you found in bed with your idiot husband?" she said.

"Yes, Nick Belden's dream girl," I said.

"So you think Dunhill connected them?"

"One way or another," I said. "And get this, he's here this month at one of the Pitch Meetings, talking about how to get great co-founders."

"You already got one, baby!" Sonya said.

"True, but we should watch this YouTube interview of Brad Feld talking about founders. The guy wrote the book on this stuff and I don't expect Dunhill can add much to the subject."

Our intern pulled up the Brad Feld video. She was good at that, finding videos on YouTube and queuing them up so we could jump the ads. She hit the play button, but I stopped it to tell her who Brad was, that he was a co-founder of TechStars and an amazing entrepreneur. She hit play and then the three of us watched, stopping and starting it to discuss stuff Brad was explaining.

"So what about a business guy?" Sonya said, "Feld says a coder plus a business guy is a good team," Sonya said, looking at her notes. "That two or three business guys without a coder is not a team. Co-founders give each founder backup, a new way to see things and a way to take it easy, also bring the other side of the brain to the mix. So what's ideal number of founders? Fewer than three, but it's the mix that really matters."

"I know a lot of the business stuff," I told Sonya and Sarah, who was grinning at me strangely and looking past me.

Sarah seemed a little distracted. She was sitting in a weird way, like a bird perched on a limb, about to fly away, trying to look over the cubicle partition.

"You're checking them out," I said, "aren't you?" I looked at Jean-Claude who was standing talking to his lead coder François. They high fived and François took off to the far side of the office.

"Look at the French guy. He's so hot who wouldn't check him out?"

"Not my type," I said. Jean-Claude was doing some sort of yoga stretch with his hands over his head.

"I like the Russians," Sonya said.

"Watch the video, you'll actually learn something," I said to Sarah.

I looked back at Jean-Claude's desk. The Frenchman wasn't there anymore. Good. Maybe Sarah could focus on something other than his butt for a few seconds.

Sarah sat down, settled in and watched YouTube on the big monitor.

Someone came up from behind and put his hands on the back of my chair and started watching with us.

It was Jean-Claude.

Sarah the intern noticed him and got all squirmy.

"He's … un génie," Jean-Claude said.

"No speaka da language," Sonya said.

"A genius, Brad Feld, he's a smart guy," Jean-Claude said. He had very little accent, but just enough to sound pretty sexy. Poor Sarah.

"I agree," I said.

Sonya turned to shake his hand.

"I'm Sonya," she said.

"Jean-Claude," he replied.

"I think I'll call you J-C or maybe Jean-Cloud from now on, as the Cloud is the coolest thing and you look mucho cool," she said. "This is my co-founder, Monica Kroy."

"I know," he said, holding his hand out to mine.

What did that mean? Did he know about me from the blogs? We hadn't really met.

I shook hands quickly, but he put both his hands around mine.

"And our intern, Sarah," I said, pulling my hands away. Sarah was trying to look tall and cool.

He said a polite hello to her, but didn't shake her hand.

"I know who you look like!" Sarah suddenly burst out.

"And who would zat be?" he asked. Was he cranking up the French accent for her benefit?

"Search for that French DJ guy, David Guetta," she told me, pointing at YouTube. Now I was working for her I guess.

I paused the Feld interview and pulled up a Guetta video. I found the Usher song with Guetta, called "Without You" showing the sun coming up at dawn on a beach, but then Guetta made it stop, using his turntable in reverse, and then it was not coming up or something.

"Genie aussi," he said.

"Aussie genius?" Sarah said dumbly, pointing toward the Australian CEO, Chris.

I said, "Didn't you mean, this guy is ALSO a genius."

"Usher?" Sonya asked.

"Non," Jean-Claude said, "Guetta."

"Oh, he is, you're so right," Sarah the intern said.

"You speak French?" he asked me, not looking at me directly.

"I lived in Grenoble when I was in college," I said.

He nodded my way, but was watching the video like it really mattered.

Jean-Claude did look a bit like Guetta, tall, skinny, jeans tight, cool demeanor, shaggy sexy brown hair. He had that EU Skater Dude look. Europeans who tried to look totally American, dressing just like us, knowing our slang, wearing knit caps that boarders wore, in the end, looked even more European.

I wanted to hear the rest of Brad Feld's interview and I also had work to do, I didn't feel like DJ'ing Usher videos.

"I love fashion and love your startup idea," Sarah said, getting closer to him, but he didn't look at all interested.

"Thanks," he said, but turned away from her.

Rather rude I thought. Or just French.

"Monica, what do you zink of it?" he asked me.

"Think of what?"

"My company," he said.

"I don't really know anything about fashion," I said, "But it sounds like you found a problem to solve and you have a unique way of solving it."

"Thank you, I hope you're right," he said and turned to leave, "Enchantée," he said to me as he left.

Crazy Sarah made a little growl noise.

"Enchantée," I mimicked with a gutsy French accent like some drunken gendarme.

"He's amazing," Sarah said.

"Amazingly arrogant," I said.

I had to admit, I liked looking at the back of his low-slung pants, as he headed down the hall. There was a thin bright red polka dot line of boxer shorts cotton above his belt.

Marshall came by. "Improving Franco-American relations?"

"Hardly. Shit, it's nearly 3. I have to go see my lawyer in Harvard Square," I jumped up.

"Already?" Sonya said.

"I'll be back by 5 and we'll leave from here."

"No problemo," she said.

The snow and slush made the trek to Harvard an arctic adventure. They could take the Winter Wonderland set away now. I had had enough of this movie.

The law offices were warm and dry with dark red carpeting and nice heavy mahogany furniture that looked like it had been there since 1620 and wasn't going anywhere for the next three hundred years.

Mary had done some digging for me and with the documentation I'd sent her — the pre-nup and some other details — she was direct and to the point.

"The cheating clause is clear. If he cheats in the first ten years of your marriage, he owes you big time. And it's inside the ten years, and he was cheating. He probably owes you $10 million dollars for that and half the business."

"Wow, that sounds like a lot, a day after he cleaned out my checking account."

"Of course, he'll try to make this go away, by dragging it out, but it won't be easy. Since the ten years ends in a year from now," she said.

"January 10," I reminded her of my anniversary.

"But of course, we need evidence if at all possible," she said. "Do you have any pictures of him at the office with her, even group pictures."

"Wait, let me look," I said, flipping through my photos on my phone. "Here's one of the whole team. That's him. That's her," I point out the perp.

I saw a few group shots. He was looking rather friendly. I showed her.

"Hmmm … nothing terribly scandalous," she said.

"Let me look for anything else."

I fiddled with the camera roll on my phone and then realized I'd taken some video that morning.

"Wait …" I was suddenly there running down University Avenue.

First there was the picture Puff had taken of me with my Celery admissions email, and then I had taken video of the house outside by the red car.

"I thought I was taking a picture but it was switched to video, I didn't realize, it's her red car outside our house," I said, "but wait, there's more."

We both watched as the video went on.

I had not clicked it off that morning.

It was jerky and shaky, but it was them, in bed, together.

"Oh my God, there was video," I said. "Wait, let me listen."

I heard the PR girl yell, "Shut the goddamned door!"

And there he was, naked, in all his glory, easy to recognize as Nick Belden, and her in the background, slamming the door in my face.

"Whoa," the lawyer said.

"Whoa is right," I said.

"That should certainly help us. Would you feel terrible if this appeared in *Gawker* or Valleywag?"

"I wouldn't love it, but if we need to use it, we should," I said.

"Yes, there is still the possibility that he might try to catch you cheating, so you need to be absolutely nun-like until it's over."

"Hanging out in freezing Boston with all geeks? Being a nun with this group shouldn't be a problem," I said.

"Seriously, even the most casual group picture where there's a man next to you, leaning toward you, they might try to smear you with." She looked over the picture. "If he catches you doing anything similar, it all falls apart. Do you have her name?"

"PR chick?"

"Is that what she did – I mean, she did PR for your company?"

"Yes," I said.

"That's good actually. There will be lots of pictures of her online at parties. Email me her name and info," she said.

"Will do. Her name is Sendi." I spelled it.

"Interesting. Let's meet next month after I get a chance to check in with a senior partner I know in our LA office, who does a lot of these pre-nups," she said.

"That works," I said.

"And you have a safe place to back this up? You're sure?"

"I'm a nerd. I know what to do," I said.

"Just remember to be careful. Seriously, even casual photos or Instagrams should be avoided. If you are seen with anyone in video, the papers, social media, looking romantically involved, he could make a case," she explained.

"Even with what we've got on him?"

"Sure, his lawyer will be telling him the same thing, encouraging him to make you look bad."

"And there's nothing I can do about him taking all the money out of my account?" I asked.

"I can file something with the court. He really can't do that and it doesn't make him look good to deprive you, so we'll see what we can do."

"Got it."

She was looking at her iPad, "Speaking of *Valleywag*, did you see that three programmers walked out on your ex and filed a protest."

"Oh my God, really?"

"Check it out," she handed me her iPad.

"It's Ranji, Sanjay and Puff! They are my best guys. He must be freaking out."

"Looks like he has. He's blaming you, saying you stole them," she was reading.

"I wanted them to join me, but never had a chance to even talk to them," I said.

"Make sure you document that. Send me anything you have that's written on the subject. And listen to this part. 'The three senior developers left in protest at the way women were treated in the company. This led to a strike by over fifty women in front of the company's headquarters on University Avenue.' Look at that scene."

"Jeez, let me see." Yep, there they were outside Nick's offices with a lot of women I knew, including Ranji's six sexy older sisters!

"This should be fun. By the way, if they did quit, you can certainly feel free to hire them. Keep in touch and if anything strange is going on, let me know. Don't trust anyone."

"Thanks so much," I told her, "I will be in touch."

I hopped on the Red Line in Harvard Square and rode back to Kendall. The offices were still humming with people working. Sonya was looking over the code. I went over to let her in on some of the news. Without saying anything, I pulled up the story on *Valleywag*.

"Jesu Christ!" she said. "BTW, Sarah the intern quit."

"That's a world record. Wait, did she work for us for five hours?"

"Six. She got a new gig with Google. Our fearless leader, Suzy, who's also her aunt was making her do her homework and that pissed her off, so she quit."

"Here comes the French Guy," I said, flipping to the Google home page so he didn't see what we were doing.

"Mademoiselle," he bowed to Sonya.

Who bows? I thought instantly, The Three Musketeers? This guy was a total nut.

"Madame," he bowed to me. "Are you going to the party?"

"What party?"

He showed me a flyer, then showed me the same flyer that was on the floor next to my chair. They'd given one to every team. Silicon Valley Bank was throwing a party at a local nightclub.

He was very close to me now and I could tell he was about half a foot taller than me. He was a good-looking guy, I had to admit it. And his cologne was fine. But I still didn't like him. He was so cock-sure of himself.

"I think Sonya and I are doing some testing tonight. No partying for us. Have fun," I turned to head down to the kitchen for some tea.

He sauntered off the other way and I came back to see Sonya reading the rest of the *Valleywag* blog post about my coders having quit on Nick.

"Wow," she said. "Read this part about the girls outside the office. It has to be Ranji's sisters. They are a force of nature."

"Do you think everyone reads this? I mean, do you think the investors in Nick's company read it?"

"Nick's company? Girl, you built that place, don't start calling it Nick's company," she said, crossing her arms in a little burst of anger. Sonya could be a fearsome small tornado when she put her mind to it.

"You're right. Do you think our investors read this?"

"The VCs? Of course, they do. They are more gossipy than a bunch of little girls!"

I got a text.

"Huh?" I said, sitting up. "Sonya, Puff just texted me."

"And ..."

"And, I don't know what it means," I said, "They said something about being in the castle of the queen."

"Hmm …" she looked at it.

"What the heck does that mean?"

"Let's go get some coffee or something – the code base is a mess and I need a break before we dig into it."

We walked to the elevators and front reception area.

Puff, Sanjay and Ranji were standing right there with suitcases.

"Oh my God!" I actually started to cry, I was so happy to see them.

"We come to serve the queen!" Ranji said and bowed deeply.

More bowing?

"Hurray!" Sonya said. "You can come serve the cloud and this effing code!"

Hugs all around.

"He did a bad, bad thing, that Nick," Ranji said to me.

Puff added, "You should have seen his face when we quit!"

"It was slightly … purple," Sanjay said looking pensive, trying to pick the exact word for the color. "Perhaps, lavender."

We walked into the office and the other folks started clapping when they came in. I guess people really did read the blogs. The three of them held their hands high like champions ringside.

"Let the games begin!" Ranji called out. He was rather dramatic.

Marshall was cranking up some YouTube of Rocky and the music poured from some crappy speakers — old car speakers — which were Velcroed up to the wall.

We dumped their stuff by our cubicles, then we all went to get coffee in the Celery kitchen and catch up. I was getting good at giving tours. Now the boys were here and we were ready to kick some accelerator ass. It was time for a Code Party! Take that Nick Belden!

Chapter 5

People Know Nothing

By the next day, everyone had seen the *Valleywag* piece about Puff, Ranji and Sanjay quitting Nick's company. Correction, quitting Nick's and my company. Our programmers were getting high fives and fist bumps everywhere we went.

Notice how gossip works. It seems to thrive in environments where people know nothing about what really went on in a given situation. Whatever. The office was abuzz, but my boys were back and that was what mattered. My little code monkeys, Sanjay, Puff and Ranji were in Cambridge and I had a way to pay them a decent wage thanks to my co-founder.

I loved my team. They were all amazing entrepreneurs. That had to be one of the best things about being a CEO. You had the rare pleasure of hiring people you wanted to spend lots of time with, people who you could learn from, people who were just excellent at what they did. Compare this to taking a "job" where you signed on with strangers you might not like at all and they might only be in their positions because of politics not smarts. In startups the work was always tough, but the people were a pleasure, if you hired the right way.

Sanjay was tall, very dark, gorgeously so and grinny, with a very upbeat personality. He did amazing research at Caltech on what makes people adopt a given application, how to increase engagement and making apps lethally addictive.

Puff was shorter and rounder with a concerned, always worried look. He was a walking motherboard that guy, processing non-stop, truly a brainiac and he never liked people very much. He hated the way their emotions always mixed everything up. He was an engineer through and through, liked things being black and white, not grey, emotional, touchy feely and unpredictable. We'd joke with him that most of the time the expression on his face read loud and clear, "This is a goddamned disaster! We'll never fix it in time." But he always did.

Ranji was very American for an Indian, a skateboarder, a charmer and grew up in a family of six pretty Indian girls and was happy to be their spoiled baby brother. He loved riding bikes and fixing them, just like me. Ranji was a bit of a "surfer dude" to me. He wore his long black hair in a braid down his back, to the dismay of his proper mother, and looked a bit more like an Asian guy, not a South Asian. Also, he's the loudmouth. You'd be too with all those sisters telling you what to do.

They were so good as a team and so excellent at teaching me things, making me a better coder. I had a high level of admiration for these three. And other thing I had, but never shared with them and never would, was a giant global crush on all Indian men. You might get the idea

I like men. And you might get the idea I like engineers. Guilty as charged, and I had always been seriously turned on by Indian guys. It was one of those things you just didn't tell anyone. God forbid I ever made them feel uncomfortable. Losing three good programmers over such a thing would be crazy, just unacceptable. I always forced myself to think of them as my brothers. That was another reason I knew all of Ranji's sisters and liked to hang out with them. They kept me from crossing any lines.

Sonya was from the Dominican Republic (she says "DR") and very short and curvy and wore dresses, almost all the time in warm weather. But even in this freezing artic wilderness of Boston, she'd come up with a winter Boston style of Peruvian hats, wool skirts, leggings, cute boots. She has full gorgeous mane of black hair and wore big geeky frame glasses in bright orange. You couldn't miss her.

And then there's me – long blonde hair, taller than Sonya. I'm not thin, but not fat, but spent most of my day thinking I looked fat, but then, didn't most women think that? I looked healthy, even robust. I have a round German face and like to wear braids like Heidi and a lot of odd hats, baseball, skater dude knit hats, sun hats, and jazz musician porkpie hats. I've always loved hats.

But you learned pretty fast that a lot of other women don't like you if you have great long blonde hair, loose, flying around – and mine is real. Even some blondes made a point of telling you that they hate you. Bottle blondes, that is.

And one at the program already had it in for me. I overheard her the day after Sonya arrived. I heard her dishing gossip about me before and now I heard her again, and it was time to stop her.

Some days I see pictures of Randy Zuckerberg on Facebook and I feel sorry for her because any success she ever has will be summed up by, "it's only thanks to her brother ... "

And I had the same problem now. People knew me one way. "She's Nick Belden's ex ... I mean, come on! How hard could it be for her?" Surprise, it's not so easy, especially since he'd really been just plain mean to me. I'm thrilled NOT to be Monica Belden anymore. I was happy to return to plain old Monica Kroy, just what I was called when I was 12.

But I'll never really get away from it, like this morning, when I was trying to make the stupid copy machine work and that girl is in the kitchen next to me and I heard her talking about me again. Christ.

And once they figured out that Nick was my ex, they figured that meant they knew a lot about me, but they really knew nothing about me. They knew Nick Belden hit it big with the startup he sold to Google that lets you cut the development time between a desktop app and a mobile app to just about nothing. But what they didn't know is that I did the original architecture for it and "shared" it with Nick. And they didn't know Nick couldn't code for shit. By the way, and I can.

So I heard the PortMoney team's blonde CEO in the kitchen talking trash about me saying, "She thinks she knows everything, she's just Belden's ex ... " in such a catty way and she's a girl Suzy was not going to let in to Celery. Another group dropped out at the last minute and Suzy actually emailed me to ask what I thought about the team's idea and I gave her a "thumbs up." Silly me.

So I leaned over past the doorway and said, "Actually I don't think I know everything and I really don't know how to get this copier working, maybe one of you could help me?"

The CEO chick blushed ten shades of red and her CTO, who's a very cute Indian guy rushed over to help me out.

"I can help you. I can help you," he rattled on.

"I'm so sorry," the CEO chick actually had the good sense to apologize.

"It's cool. Let's have coffee and I'll tell you about how Suzy didn't want you at Celery but I told her to take you. Okay?" I said this really sweetly. I was all sugar.

"Oh God," she stammered.

"Get lost," I told her. "It's all good. We'll talk later."

The kind young Indian guy helped me out and I went back to our desk area. The team had left for lunch. I'd asked Sonya to take the three of them out and show them the area since she'd knew her way around.

I needed some quiet time to think about what we were going to do next. Having the team here was the best thing ever. I was tired carrying the thing by myself. I was thrilled by the sudden arrival of coding talent.

That girl was very young. At the ripe old age of 32 she probably thought of me as a senior citizen. The sexism and the ageism of the high-tech world were profound. It's only a little worse in Silicon Valley than it is in Boston. Being a straight white boy Ivy League genius is the name of the game. All the rest of us need not apply.

It's hard to even join a high-tech company if you're over thirty because you've worked long enough to get used to the old ways. That is, working with folks in their 30s and 40s and treating them with respect. When I was twenty, the people who ran things — including Nick and his friends who were more likely in their 40s and 50s — expected you to defer to them, respect them, not question them and work your ass off for them.

Everything has changed. It's like some crazy boat we're on and the thing starts going sideways and everyone flies off one side and the young, fit 18-year-old kids replace the 65-year-old seasoned salty sailors, and now some kid is the captain, and maybe he knows something or maybe he knows nothing. But he looks great in the blue blazer with the gold buttons and tight jeans.

I looked up from my monitor, the place was empty. Except for the French guy. He was looking intently at his monitor, but I could have sworn he had just been looking my way. I ignored him and did a Google search on Y Combinator.

My team appeared, done with lunch and covered with snow. Sonya came back over to talk to me. It was hard to even look at blogs without seeing something about Nick. Today Mashable had a piece on him. It wasn't about me and him, for once.

"Hey, are you okay?" she said.

"Thinking about Nicky Nick again," I say, looking very unhappy to be doing that.

"Uh oh! You gotta stop that, girl. You need a trigger phrase to get you away from that."

"A trigger phrase?"

"Yeah, something to remind you what a bum he is," she said.

"Okay, okay," I said. "Could it be any word?"

"Sure, let's just pick something random."

"How about … 'who ya gonna call, Ghostbusters!' That work?" I said.

"I don't get it. What's that have to do with him?" she said.

"Nothing. I just love that movie," I said, "And he would never watch it with me."

"It's a little long as a trigger phrase," she said.

"It'll work. If you notice I'm thinking of him, just say that and I will stop thinking of him."

"Deal. Show me your pitch for tonight."

"Ugh. Now there's something I really don't want to think about."

"Just do it."

Chapter 6
Mead Hall

Celery has a pretty amazing network of alums, mentors and éminence grise types to help their startups get to any investor they want or need. That's the thing about accelerators. They come down to clout — the best ones have a network that you can plug into and within hours be sitting in the office of some of the best known entrepreneurs, advisors or money men. And, unfortunately, it's mostly men. But that is changing.

Now that we were a few weeks in, we got to meet alumni folks from a bunch of Celery programs who came before us. Chill Factor was interesting. Their CEO, Javier Pena, was building devices that ran on chili peppers. Sonya was very suspicious of this team since she's deeply knowledgeable about all variety of hot, spicy cuisine. Another cool female alum from Alaska named Tiffany Magill was the founder of Teleportation, where they were creating portable teleportation systems.

And then of course, there were mentors and alums visiting from Pixability, Innovation Nights, KindleNation,

Franchise Opportunities and Speek. They were very well-known now and did the good and loyal thing as alums of investing in upcoming companies at their alma mater, Celery.

We met amazing people during the daytime schedule of networking events at casual lunches, lectures, tours of other facilities and co-working spaces like The Cambridge Innovation Center.

And there was an evening party circuit too, come nightfall. It wasn't less serious than what we did during the day either. In some ways, having casual contact with all these folks and having it over drinks and food and more drinks made it even easier to get into the right circles fast.

I was a spoiled brat this way, since Nick had dragged me along to all the West Coast parties for years. I had gotten to know the big players out there, like they were just kids from the neighborhood. We'd grown up together. Hanging with Robert and Maryam Scoble, Jeff Clavier, Cathy Brooks, and Steve Jurvetson was a serious treat. California was all about who you knew and these folks were the kind who welcomed all newcomers. Unfortunately, there were other rock star players in Silicon Valley who did everything to keep the newly arrived ambitious folks out of the circle.

But now I was sick of those kind of parties, since I realized it was where Nick had been scoping girls for years. His network of male friends and founders were happy to point him in the right direction of new cute girls whenever he said the word. So I wasn't keen on going out at night and wasting time anymore.

There was a great party one particular night, but I had enough work to keep me from attending. Sonya and I were working together as the time for the event rolled by. She and I were laughing and hitting our heads with our open palm as we saw an obvious fix for a bug that had been making a lot of trouble.

I looked over and saw J-C trying to get my attention.

"Alors?" he said and pointed to the clock. I turned to look. 5:30.

"What?" I asked him on instant messaging since all the teams were using it to connect at Celery.

"Going?" he IM'd back.

"Where?"

"Party" he IM'd.

He came over to my desk, as Sonya headed off to the kitchen.

"There's was a party at 5," he said not quite looking at me.

He must be tired. The "there" sounded like "zair." He usually spoke so well, but sometimes our "th" sound tripped him up. It didn't exist in French.

"Oh, the thing sponsored by Travis, McGill? The one at Mead Hall?"

"What is Mead Hall?" he asked looking at me.

It sounded just like "Meat Hull" or something. I almost laughed but stopped myself.

"It's just a bar, on the corner of Broadway and Ames. There's an accounting firm hosting the party, free food, free beer."

"You all love beer here in Boston, I have been noticing. I don't love beer as much as you all seem to love beer," he said.

I had switched my screen to the Google homepage so he didn't see what I'd been doing.

"And you like … ?" he said.

I sucked in a little air.

"Like?" I didn't know what he was asking. But suddenly I was thinking I kind of liked looking at him.

And then I was remembered I was supposed to be a nun. Nun, think Nun.

"Like beer?" he said. "You like beer?" He was turning now, looking right at me and he was serious, as if this question were very, very serious too.

"Beer?" I said it in a lazy way, like I hadn't really been listening. I hadn't. "Je préfère de la vin."

"Du vin," he corrected.

"Du vin," I said.

"Non, 'DU' vin," he was correcting my vowel.

His lips curled into a kiss shape to say, "du."

"Je préfère du vin," I said, making the same shape.

"Parfait."

"Why is your English so good?" I asked.

"My mom was an English teacher in France," he said. "She married a Brit, before she met my dad. Is Marshall going?"

"Marshall's in New York," I said.

"So, " he said, like it was obvious, "Shall we go look for some wine?"

"I really should finish this," I said.

"Alors," he said again. He liked that word.

He stood up, crossing his arms impatiently. "You should go."

"Because?"

"Because I asked you."

"Hmm, then look at this and help me," I got up and he took my seat.

He looked at my code. I'd been trying to figure out a particularly intractable bug for a while.

"What about this?"

I looked at the line of code he pointed to and his fix.

"Let me try it."

It worked.

"Thank you, I guess I'll have to change my mind and go with you."

"I guess you should," he said, standing up and just being there very close to me. Not stepping aside.

"All right, but I have to be back here at 6:30 to meet with Suzy."

"An hour? Ce n'est pas parfait, mais ça marche." Not perfect, but it'll do.

He caught me looking at his jaw. It was more stubble and whiskers than the other day. It looked very sexy.

"Une barbe," he said to me, "Do you think I should l grow a beard?"

I turned back to my monitor. At least, I knew enough to leave this alone. "Hmmm, no idea. Is it very cold out?"

"Not too bad, but wear your Russian hat." He said, showing me he had been noticing what I wore.

"I'll get my coat," I said.

He would look great with a beard and why not in winter, when it was so cold and the wind off the Charles River was so harsh.

He followed me down the hall, trotting like a happy puppy.

I wasn't feeling as annoyed by him. Something strange was happening. Maybe he wasn't the arrogant twit I thought he was. I liked him walking a few steps behind me.

When a man was following you like that, he was probably stealing a view of your legs and your butt. And any man who really wanted any woman could be seen looking directly at her backside, every now and then. It was evolutionary. I don't know where I learned that, maybe in some women's magazine, or in some anthropology seminar or maybe I'd overheard it shopping at Anthropologie. It was always good to keep them behind you looking at your behind, in classic "cherchez la femme" mode, like they were hunting you down. A woman always needed to be just a few steps ahead of a man.

We headed out and kept running into others from our group going to Mead Hall, so it was all work chatter, nothing personal. It was snowing in a beautiful way and I noticed his shaggy hair getting covered with snow, like a thatched cottage roof.

When we arrived at the party, it was upstairs, but he told me to hold back so we could sit together downstairs, before going in, like a date. He got us each a glass of red wine.

"I just don't know why they waste so much of our time," he said.

"You mean, with all the meetings?"

"Yes, I went to university, I don't need more school and I know what my company needs, I don't need to learn more about setting up an American bank account or such nonsense."

"Maybe one of these days you will need to know it," I said.

He was in that mood Nick would get in often as not. He needed to vent and just complain about things that he had no control over. It happened when Nick was having trouble writing code, which was something he felt he should have been able to execute with no trouble. So when he couldn't, he lashed out at all the things he couldn't control. I knew it was best to let him talk and just listen.

"Tell me what's bugging you," I said, as we sat at our table away from the others.

"I'd rather talk about you," Jean-Claude said, quite unlike Nick. "Or just hear you talk. You sound like California. Like sun. Like ocean."

"You're a much better talker," I said.

"Non," he said. "Tell me about when you were a little girl."

He was a good listener. I told him stories about my dad teaching me to fix things. And about a tractor we had on the farm. About my dad promising me if I could fix it, I could drive it.

"He let you drive at 10 years old!" he was laughing.

"I was good at fixing things," I explained.

"Your dad is a good man," he said. "He's still in California?"

"Yes," I said.

"Maybe he treated you like a boy. Not letting you give up."

"Yes! That's the best thing he ever did for me. That's how you learn to fix things. If your parents let you give up, you never realize how to just keep trying. Some parents let little girls just cry and give up. It's not good for girls."

"And they don't do that for boys," he said.

"That's right," I said.

"So your baby girls will have to have a hammer and a spanner," he said.

"What?"

"It's called that in England, shit," he said. "Je ne me souviens pas ce qu'ils appellent cet outil. Une clé à fourche."

"Show me what it looks like or what it does," I said.

Jean-Claude twisted his hand in a gesture.

"Not a screwdriver?" I said.

"Non, ça c'est un tournevis," he said.

He took a cocktail napkin and tore it into a shape.

"A wrench! Yes, it's a spanner in the UK, I forgot," I said.

"You never realize how much American English is another language until you learn English in England and then come here."

"Yes," I said, wanting to know about his life in other places.

"So your baby girls will get a silver wrench instead of a baby rattle," he said.

"My babies?" I said, raising an eyebrow. How did he suddenly hit so close to the one thing I wanted.

"Yes, you will have two baby girls. And, Madame, may I say, you will make beautiful babies," he pronounced the word "Madame" in a very sexy way.

"No, you may not say that, but yes, they will have wrenches. Wenches with wrenches." I said.

"What's a wench?" he said.

"Like a bar maid. Let's go upstairs and join the Celery party."

"Not yet. Tell me what you love to do when you can do whatever you want. If you had an extra day tomorrow to do anything you wanted to do."

"Is that a trick question? You know the answer. The one thing we all want to do is sleep. We never get enough sleep."

"Good answer. Yes, sleeping would be wonderful," he said grinning.

I wasn't going to touch that.

"Let's go up," he said.

We finished our wine and went up to the party and even then, he managed to side step the work talk and gave me some serious attention, asking me about my team and how it was going.

They were pouring the free wine and he gave me a glass, and then took one for himself. He took one taste then spit it out, like he'd been poisoned.

The hosts saw this, and he grinned at them.

"I'm French," he said with a boyish smile, like he couldn't help himself and this was apology enough.

We went over to the real bar and he ordered two more glasses of the good, expensive red wine we'd had before.

"A l'avenir," Jean-Claude said.

"Yes, to the future and to new ideas, new friends," I said.

We stood back watching the others. He asked me about Sonya, how we met.

"She was my next-door neighbor, worked at Google. We met one day when I saw bubbles coming out her front door. Washing machine malfunction. My coders? They used to work for my ex and me in California. When

I got into the Celery program and then my ex … well, anyway, they all quit working for my him and came here."

"Wow!" he said.

"They were mad at him, well, I don't know, maybe you saw some gossip about it in *Valleywag*."

"Non," he said.

"I found my husband in bed with the PR person."

"Not okay," he said.

"Right, not okay."

"And it's hard to find a good PR person who knows how to write," he said thoughtfully.

"Ah … yes, that's true," I said.

"I mean now he needs a new PR girl and a new wife. Stupid guy."

Sonya wandered by and I decided it would be good to let him go off with the other Celery guys. They had all been passing by, trying to get his attention.

She and Jean-Claude chatted in Spanish. I didn't know he could even speak it and they ended the conversation, both laughing about something.

"Hey Chiquita," I said, "I need to ask you about the code review. Mind if we talk some code monkey business?"

"See you later geek girls," he said and left us.

We watched him leave.

"Code review, my ass, or his ass," Sonya said, noticing what I was looking at.

"I don't even like him," I said.

But she caught me, smiling, "Yeah, right."

She and I found a table, grabbed some veggies to munch on and started talking about accelerator programs and how they worked, who they actually benefited. There was a whole new circle of recidivist accelerator guys, who just kept applying to one program after another and never actually starting a company. That seemed nutty to me. Failure to launch. We decided to make bets on Celery's new incoming class, who would win, who would lose. As we looked around the room, I said that you could almost predict it, just by watching who was schmoozing whom at the parties.

"It's so much about how you look and if people like you and if you're ... just plain cool," Sonya said. "Look at Irina, they are all crazy about her, the lawyers."

"True," I said.

"And she sure looks like the kind of girl who might need a lifetime of lawyers," Sonya snarked.

Jean-Claude did just what I expected. He was quickly dragged off by the hosts of the party, a bunch of clean-cut boring lawyers who thought he was cool. They were not his type but they could tell Jean-Claude had a high alpha male status among the others and they were keen to claim him, talk him into their plans and their future. Everyone in tech was out to buy coolness in any form they could get it. For the lawyers and accountants, J-C was the kind of guy who could bring other cool guys from other hot startups around, as if he possessed some magical magnetic property.

I figured he was always attention-getting when he walked into any room. He certainly got my attention walking into this bar with his dark hair dusted with snow, then the way it melted once we were inside, making his hair sleek and wet like a seal, the way he smoothed it back, you wanted to pet him. He just looked very handsome and fresh, just born, just born into a world where he could do anything, a world where he could be king, but he might pretend to be the jester too. He just didn't give a shit.

If I liked him a little more now, for some reason, this was the reason. He had this "I don't give a shit" look of ease and elegance he sported. The way he sauntered, better than any swagger, with his dark hair a little shaggy but chic, and his natural coolness, which was just homemade and organic, not bought or manufactured in any way. He was handsome. Most girls would want to do one thing with a guy like Jean-Claude — take all his clothes off, every last garment, and take their time doing it.

We'd had two glasses of good wine. Was I a little drunk? I was watching him and trying not to get drunk. Okay, maybe I was a little drunk and even though I was supposed to be a nun, I was seeing why someone might like him. He was a very sexy guy.

He was the kind of guy you expected to do it with, in many places — the back of a car, a field of tall wheat, a friend's bathroom during a quiet dinner party, a private jet, a broom closet, a boat, then on a deserted beach — before you ever made love in an ordinary civilized bed with linens and pillows. The kind of guy who would never make you feel shy or embarrassed or awkward making love. He was just naturally sexy.

The other guys had surrounded him and that was annoying and boring. I couldn't see him now. Sonya had wandered off to talk with Irina. I got up to leave and even though he was two tables away, he lifted his head, as if to ask with no words, "You leaving?" He had that natural way of noticing women, like they were animals he was hunting, deep in the woods, at long range, but he never missed their smallest movement.

I nodded and then he did something I didn't expect, just got up and came over and took my hand, like he was leading a little kid to school for their first day.

"I'll go back with you," he said and he pulled me through the crowd behind him. Go with me? More like drag me off. The place was packed now. I was a little worried all the people from our group would see him holding my hand. I hoped they weren't watching too closely. Maybe they did notice. But then again, they'd all had a lot of wine and beer, so maybe nobody noticed at all.

I noticed though, and I didn't want to give up his hand and then we were on the street and he still had not let go of it.

"Wolves and bears here," he said, as if to explain.

"What?"

"You need my protection. There are wolves from Harvard and bears from MIT and other dangerous animals here tonight in the forest, I don't want them to get you," he said and pulled me closer.

"Wait, the wine wasn't that strong, I still remember a few things," I said.

He laughed. "Yes?"

"Like you're married."

"And so are you, Madame."

"Hell, I guess that's true, but I'm trying not to be."

"Good."

"And I don't like getting friendly with people I work with," I said.

"You won't be my friend? Not very nice of you. I thought California girls were the friendliest girls in the world."

"You're not flirting with me are you, Jean-Claude Longrée?"

"You know my name, good," He pulled me close, but then slipped his arm around me in a more friendly than sexy way, "Frenchmen never flirt, Monica Kroy. It's a rumor. Let's go back to Celery," he said.

We walked back to the office. I liked the way he held me, his arm around my waist. His uninvited intimacy was very sexy and I liked it.

"Just don't do that then."

"Flirt?" he asked.

"Yes."

"I won't flirt with you ever, I promise," he assured me. "Jamais, jamais plus."

Something about these European guys, they never needed an invitation to touch a woman. And they did it in a very comfortable way. American men, sometimes you could feel their sheer clumsy panic when they attempted to get close to you. They fought against their own gyrating sexual energy, being thrown off, while French and Italians gave right into it, knowing how to surf the cresting wave of sensuality like pros.

Between sexual harassment training, feminism and the damned Puritans, sex in America was a mess. We were hopeless. You could feel American guys really worrying about how or if they might touch you. You'd sense a slight tremor in their confidence, as to whether they could pull it off at all. It was discouraging and disorienting for all parties. They seemed to need to ask permission.

Then there was something awful like a campus shooting, not necessarily even on your campus, and it was hugs all around. So much hugging and so little romance. Some guys were just all hugs and no action.

This Frenchman certainly didn't need to ask permission to seduce a woman, he just knew how. I liked Jean-Claude's proximity, his gallantry. This kid was 20 and he already knew lots more than most American guys who were 35. Think of it. The French invented romance. They came right out of a history book just chock-a-block with knights and swords, and kings and queens. They invented chivalry. They made chain mail look stylish. They knew from velvet britches, troubadours, and damsels stuck in high castle towers. They knew how to play the game. Cherchez la femme and carpe diem and seize the lady too.

And Jean-Claude's closeness and his height were appealing. Our bodies were knocking into one another as we walked. Was he doing that on purpose, all this slipping in the snow, gripping me tighter? I needed an antidote. Maybe if I asked him something really boring, it would put sex out of my mind. It was like getting sober fast. There must be a way.

"What do you think of Agile Programming?" I asked as we took the corner of the building.

He laughed out loud, "Is that what you're thinking about right this very minute?" he said grinning at me, looking even sexier than before.

So he could read my mind too, goddamned French guy. No I really wasn't thinking about programming. We were a block from the office. He stopped me dead in my tracks and said two words.

"Come here."

He pressed his back against the building, pulling me close to him, close enough to kiss. But he didn't kiss me. He just held me and looked at me like something wonderful to eat. If there were wolves and bears out tonight, he was surely one of them.

"So, what were you really thinking about?"

"I don't know," I said, dodging the question, looking away down the street. I knew I was a goner if I looked into those eyes of his.

Sheesh, he was so close to kissing me. Why didn't he just do it? I didn't believe for a minute that he didn't know how to kiss a woman. He was French for Chrissakes.

"I'm thinking about Suzy," I said.

"Suzy? Oh, yes, she's very hot," he said, looking surprised I said this.

"She'll be hot, like pissed off, mad, angry, hot, if I'm late," I pushed him away.

"Yes," he said, standing up a little straighter, looking rather serious now and not so sexy as before. "I'll go up with you. I have to work to do too."

We entered the building. The security guy, John, the one we liked and joked around with during the daytime hours was gone for the day. There was a very dark skinned guy from Nigeria named Christopher there. Stylish guy for a security guard.

He had a low tone as he said, "Good evening. Celery?"

We showed our swipe cards, "Yes."

We entered the elevator, the doors closed and J-C started waving at the video camera.

I pressed our floor. Six.

"See, the camera?" Jean-Claude said, "No privacy and so many people think elevators are private," he said. "Did you know that, people even kiss and make love in elevators thinking it's private. Did you know that?"

He winked at me.

"You're flirting, and you said you wouldn't."

"No, I was winking."

I just looked away. I was hiding my grin.

The doors opened on 3, two men got in, well dressed. We'd call them "suits."

The elevator stopped on 4 and they got out.

"See here, under the camera," he said, "only safe place to … you know … kiss."

And then he did that silly kid thing, wrapping his arms around himself like someone was hugging him and making a big silly kissy mouth and wet smooch sounds and had me laughing like an idiot.

"You would do anything," I blurted, "wouldn't you?"

He gave me a drop-dead look. "Of course," he said, "So would you, we're founders. We're building a new world. They want us to be daring. To think up anything. To do everything."

"Everything?"

He looked at me. No words.

And this time it was an even deeper look – a solid beam into my eyes that said he would do anything at any time, and do anything WITH ME, if I felt like letting him do it.

After a bit, he did speak.

"Yes. We must try … everything."

I said nothing.

"Voilà, Madame!" he said as the elevator stopped on our floor.

The door opened.

"Après vous," he said, gesturing to the hallway.

I marched past him, very close to his body, but pretending to ignore him. I left him behind, as I walked briskly down the hall, he sauntered. I turned down Suzy's hallway and he went past me, down the hall to the other side of the building where his desk and teammates waited for him.

I went into the Boss Lady's office.

Suzy was in a rare mood. I could feel her tension.

"Sit down," she said. "Your pitch sucks."

Chapter 7

Rooms With No View

When I first moved from California, I thought all the cool kids must live in Harvard Square but figured out fast it was too expensive for students and there were better places to live on either side of "the Square" as Harvard Square was called by the real estate people I met.

If you looked at the subway T map and moved your finger along the Red Line toward downtown Boston from Harvard to Kendall, where MIT was, you saw Central Square was right between them. It was a little rough and tumble as a neighborhood — older, poorer, but cool when it came to student apartments and hangouts and dance bars, and super convenient to a bunch of universities.

If you moved your finger the other way, heading out of Harvard Square towards Tufts and the suburbs, you saw Porter Square. Porter was a bit fancier than Central Square and was a good neighborhood for restaurants and shops. They had an excellent bookstore there, the greatest mark of civilization I know. Also right by the T station,

Porter Square had a cool metal sculpture that looked like a bunch of red kites spinning in the wind, or maybe like the petals of big metal flower.

I was waiting at Porter Square Books for Sonya on Saturday morning to start her big apartment hunt, but I wasn't optimistic. I'd found my apartment easily because a friend gave it to me when she ran off to get married. Finding a good place in Boston wasn't easy, especially "off-season," which was September 1 when all the students moved in. Leaving Google wasn't so easy after all, because she had this crazy boss and she also had an even crazier boyfriend who didn't want her to go.

"Do you miss him?" I was holding a copy of *He's Just Not That Into You* up for her perusal.

"Him? No, I think he was just TOO into me. I feel like I can breathe again. Thank God you dragged me out of there," she said.

"I'm so glad you're here," I said.

"Remember when Nick tried to hire me?" she asked.

"And we're talking about my evil ex and his first company … for what reason?"

"Just remember how he asked me all those questions about startups and funding and everything," Sonya said. "I won't make you talk about him, I just wanted to remind you of that time and how crazy it was and how fast it was growing."

"Yes, I remember," I said.

"And then I went to Google. So I don't know shit about startups and I really want you to take it slow and explain all this stuff to me this time and let me ask you a million questions. Like what a 'tranche' is and stuff like that."

"Wait, come over here," I said, leading her to the section labeled Business Books. "See all these books, nobody else knows anything either, that's why they sell these books."

"But it always sounded like … " Sonya said.

"Do you think we knew all about it? We didn't know shit either. I don't think anyone does," I said. "Wait, this one is great and so is anything else Brad Feld has written. Read it." I held up *Venture Deals: Be Smarter Than Your Lawyer and Venture Capitalist.*

"But that's the thing, you had Nick to ask and you already knew a lot more than any other females around there and I just don't want to be one of those geek girls who doesn't know any of the business part, so I'm going to ask you everything today. You don't mind?" Sonya looked a little emotional and even teary.

"No problem, but all in one day, is SO not gonna work. And there's other places to find it all, like blogs."

"I know, but even after reading a bunch, I still have questions on things like stock options and valuation and how they dilute the value of stuff, so can I ask you stuff as we walk around today?" Sonya asked.

"Sure, but dilution is just how they screw you and water down your shares," I said.

"You know that, but it's not so clear to me and I want to know exactly how to keep from getting screwed," she said. "I'm seriously in and I'm gonna take the time to learn all this, because after we're done, I want to do a startup on my own." She said, standing tall, which is still barely five feet, but she's a force to be reckoned with, or will be some day.

"Way to go girl!" I said. "So here's just about everything you should know. Build something people need and want."

"That's it?"

"That's Y Combinator's mantra," I said. "Wait, I think it's 'build something people want."

"Cool," Sonya said.

"That's the problem. As things start getting crazy in a startup, you can forget that. You start thinking too much about features and details. So you need to stop and ask yourself, 'Is this something people want?' and if you can answer that, thinking that way can get you back on track."

I hadn't seen Sonya looking so determined or serious about this stuff before.

"Repeat after me, 'Is this something people want?' go for it." I said.

"Is this something people want?" she repeated.

We sat down at the Children's Section in the back. She almost fit in one of the kids' chairs. I did not. My legs made me look like a stork.

"But the better question is, 'is this something people want … ready … want to PAY for?' that's the big one."

"So, the simple version is, 'Build Something People Want.' " Sonya said.

"Yep! There are three blogs you have to read for starters — *AVC*, which is not an All-Terrain Vehicle, but it's Fred Wilson's blog. And for what's going on in startups every day, just read Sarah Lacey's site, *Pando Daily*. And of course, like I said, Brad Feld, the TechStars guy has a great blog at www.feld.com, called, *FeldThoughts*. Show me the maps."

"Here's the list," she said. There were four apartments to visit around Porter Square on a Google map printout.

"As for getting screwed, seems like everyone does, and even if you know everything about dilution, if they decide they don't want to play with you, make you an outsider, there's nothing you can do."

"So it's not about knowing the right stuff?"

"You need to know stuff, but it's also about knowing the right people, it's always about that. Remember that fight I had with Nick about my shares before we were married. Remember how Darrell came in and kicked Nick's ass about it? Darrell was standing up for me, so Nick wouldn't screw me. Darrell fixed it for me," I said.

"He always liked you," Sonya was smiling.

"Yeah, I guess so," I said, knowing there had been a lot more with Darrell, remembering how jealous Nick was of him, and for good reason, but I'd never acted on it like Nick had.

"Here's the first listing. It's at 2 Cypress, fifth floor, two bedrooms, one bath. Let's go look."

As we walked past the shops and over to Beacon I told her everything useful I could think of.

"If you build a great product, that really helps. I mean, it's not the only thing but it's a big deal. Remember when we first saw Instagram. We knew it would kick ass, right?"

"Yes, but remember too, how messy it was, that first beta we played with," Sonya said.

"Yep, but it was simple and easy to use even then. So you get the feeling when you see something simple and useful. You just know the good stuff."

The apartment at 2 Cypress wasn't the good stuff. It wasn't even two bedrooms. It looked like one bedroom and some room you could barely fit a baby crib into.

"Who's supposed to live in there? My little pony?" I asked Sonya.

We headed off to see another apartment a block away. It was a dungeon, basement level, dark.

"Oh, Chica. This sucks," Sonya said to me.

"Looking at apartments on the East Coast after living on the West Coast is pretty scary, isn't it?"

"Californians are so spoiled. I mean there's no place to live, but if you find something, at least it doesn't look like a broom closet like this," she said.

"Let's go look at the other one. What does 'first round' mean? And 'A round' and 'B round'? And why is it called that?" she asked me.

"I can answer what it is and what it means, but no way do I know why it was called that. It's been that way for a long time."

"It's confusing. Ever get the feeling they make it confusing on purpose?" she asked.

"Yes, it's the language of the high priests. They don't want everyone to know it just means a bunch of money they give you, or they can't be the priests then. The first round just means the first round of financing and the Series A, B — all that means is later rounds. What you really want to know is what happens in a Series A that would never happen in a Series C, for instance, right?"

"Exactly." She said.

"It's about timing and growth. Other founders will explain it to you when you need to know."

"Because founders have so much time on their hands and nothing else to do?"

"Hey, they should make time for others, like people made time for them," I told her. "With Series A, Series B, just think of trolley cars. They are kind of like trollies. Like one will get you to Market Street but no farther – that might be Series A – and some of the passengers, some angels, some VCs who rode with you for the first trip get on or off for the next round. That part is important and WHY they are staying on or getting off. Do they still believe in you? Have they lost confidence? Some go with you and jump the trolley down to Fisherman's Wharf, and if things are going well, some new ones get on and they get the better seats, that might be Series B. But remind me, oh wise one, what really matters?"

"Is this something people need and want?" she was right on it.

"Bingo!"

"And which is better need or want?" she asked.

"Need. But then there are a few amazing people who can build products people really want and need. Stuff they don't even know they needed or wanted until you built it."

"Like?"

"Steve Jobs, RIP," I said. Sad, sad, sad to remember he was gone.

"Right."

The next apartment was a few blocks closer to Harvard Square and it was a two-bed, two-bath sublet by a girl who went to Harvard's Graduate School of Design and she was going to Italy for a year. Lucky girl.

It had an actual view. We'd gone from a fifth floor walk-up to a basement dungeon to this nice place with a view and an elevator. Sonya and I both loved the place.

"Look at the French windows," I said.

"Girl! I know who you're thinking about," Sonya teased.

"No, no, I wasn't' thinking about him, come on."

"Seriously, girlfriend. I'd better teach you Spanish, so you can stop thinking about that French guy."

"Listen, these are called French windows, everyone know that, because the hinges are here on the side and they open out. Christ!"

"It is great, but too much dinero, dear," she whispered.

There was a yippee little dog that jumped up and down on Sonya's leg. Sonya didn't like that kind of nonsense.

We told the girl we would get back to her.

"Sheesh, I loved that," Sonya said out on the street.

"Well … way too expensive, but a great place," I said.

"You know in the Facebook movie how they diluted that guy's shares and screwed him?" Sonya was back to our *Startups For Dummies* walking lesson tour.

"Yep."

"Why didn't he see that coming?" she asked me.

"Well, wasn't it after Sean Parker joined and Facebook moved to California and that guy wanted to stay back East?" I said.

"I think so. Hey, I know where Zuckerberg lived at Harvard! It's near here. Wanna go see it and we can take pix there?" Sonya was jumping up and down.

"Sure," I said, so we turned left at the end of Everett and headed for the Square. "So YOU tell me, why do YOU think that guy got screwed?"

"I guess, for those reasons you said, that new investors came in and he stepped off the trolley and then he wasn't inside enough to see where the thing was going," she said correctly.

"Yes, so it's about politics too, often it's all about politics — power and money that is — and who wants to run it. But you're still a kid and you have some years to make mistakes and if you got pushed out of something, you leave knowing a lot more and also you leave with real experience in a startup at a young age and that's pretty valuable, especially for a woman entrepreneur," I reminded her.

We were in Harvard Square in about 10 minutes.

"He lived in … " She was reading the results of a Google search off her phone, "Room D11 of Straus Hall the freshman dorm, right there," she pointed up to a stately brick building right next to the Johnston Gate in the Harvard quad.

"Good view of the Coop," I said. It was right across from the Harvard Coop Bookstore.

"And he was in a dorm called Kirkland as a sophomore," she said.

"You got all the dirt, eh?" I was surprised she cared so much.

"My mom wanted pictures of the buildings," she said chagrined.

"Your mom is … interesting," I said.

"That's a word you could use," she said.

"When's your next appointment to see apartments?"

"In about an hour," she said.

"Let's go do lunch then at that sushi place I found," I told her.

On the way we heard from Irina. She needed a place to live; did I have any good ideas? I told her Sonya was probably looking for a roommate, I'd have her call.

"Awesome," she crowed when I hung up.

"She's kind of a drama queen, you really want to live with her?" I said. "Think about it before you jump."

"Hmm, you're right, but I love that place we saw on Everett."

After lunch Sonya had gotten the design student at Everett to see us again and also called Irina to have her come by to take a look.

"And what are preferred shares compared to common shares?" she asked me as we walked back up Mass Ave.

"You really want to know this stuff, doncha?" I blurted.

"I want to know it, so nobody can mess with me and try to blow me away in a meeting because I'm a short, sexy girl. You know they never take me seriously!" she nearly yelled.

"Okay, okay, I get it. I'm tall and have done three startups and they always take me really seriously," I said sarcastically. "Never."

"They take you a lot more seriously than me."

The Harvard Law School buildings were under construction on one side of the apartment, which meant it probably had lots of noise problems. It was noisy today.

I got back to her question. "What do you think sounds more valuable – preferred or common stock?"

"Preferred?" she said.

A cement mixer right next to us started to spin with so much noise.

"There's the Starbucks, across the street," I said.

"I'll text Irina to meet us there."

We headed over.

"So if there is a VC and a founder with shares, who do you think gets the preferred stock and who gets the common stock?" I asked her.

"I guess the VC takes the preferred and the founder has the common," Sonya said.

"That's it. Do you know what an exit is?" I asked her.

"Like when you and Nick sold Strandly?" she said.

"Yes, but remember we were talking about other things that could happen too."

"Oh crap yes, that you could go bankrupt?" she said.

"Yes, that's an exit, but it's one you don't want to take, most of the time," I said.

"And the IPO thing, but you didn't think it would work," Sonya said.

"Yes, that's called going public, you sell stock in the company. Sometimes it's a big win," I said.

"Are there more exits than that?" she said.

"How about what happened to Strandly?"

"You sold the company to another company," she said.

"Yes, so let's go back to preferred and common. This is really the simple version. When you exit, the preferred stockholders, usually the investors, get paid back first. The common stockholders, the founders and the employees, come second."

"Wait, you'd think the guy who had the idea first would be paid first," she said.

"Yeah, you mean the GIRL with the idea?" I insisted, as it was MY idea, not Nick's.

"Yes!"

"You would think so, wouldn't you?" I said, "but … you'd be wrong."

The Starbucks was packed, but by the time we stood in the line to get our drinks. There was a table with three chairs over by the window and we settled in to wait for Irina.

Sonya held up her coffee, "Is this something people need and want?"

"You tell me," I said.

"People really want the coffee and the time they spend here, but do they need it?"

"Some people really need it," I said.

"And they pay way too much for it."

"True," I said. "So back to stock. What I told you was still more basic than it is in real financing, but it's good to remember that usually investors have preferred stock and founders have common stock. And preferred means they have a chance to cash out first and usually can pick better terms. It matters a lot if the company has raised more than it's sold for. Right?"

"Not sure what you mean," she said.

"Well, say you borrow money from a bank like $2 million to build a house and you make it a beautiful house, but then the neighborhood ends up full of drug dealers or something and no one wants to live there. So in the end, you can only sell the house for $1.5 million, who takes the hit?"

"The guy who owns the house takes the hit, and still has to pay the bank."

"Yep. But it's not a perfect analogy because a mortgage is debt. VC money is an investment in you and your idea and your company. If you raise a lot of VC money and then you sell the company for a bunch less, the VCs get their money back first, which might be what they put into the deal, or even as much as three times what they put in, and then the rest of the people, like the founders and employees get what's left, which might be ZERO."

"Ouch!"

"Yup, it happens."

Irina showed up, all in purple suede today. Who owns thigh high lavender suede boots? We headed over to the apartment on Everett by 4 as arranged. She loved the place. It was a great apartment and they could move in the next week.

"This is something I need and want," Sonya said to me as we left.

"And you'll have to pay a lot for it," I said.

"Half of a lot, thanks to Irina."

As we walked back to the office, I got Irina into our conversation.

"Sonya asked me about exits, what would you say about them?"

"Well, there are four kinds, by sale, by IPO, by bankruptcy, by stock swap," she said with her sexy Russian accent. She knew her stuff.

"I wouldn't call it four – stock swap is still a sale, but for stock instead of money," I said.

"Yes, and of course, you know they decide on the terms of the exit way in advance. They don't leave things to chance. Almost like a pre-nup."

"Don't say that word. What other exits did I forget to mention?"

"Also exit by murder or poison," Irina said seriously.

We both looked at her with big eyes.

She laughed at us.

"Gotcha!" she grinned. "You Americans think Russians are capable of anything."

"If you can deal with Slava," I started, "you certainly are capable of anything."

"Yes, that's true, he is not so easy sometimes," she said.

"I know where we can lease some furniture cheap," I said.

"Let's do a moving party and make all the guys do the heavy lifting," Sonya said.

"Yes, I know an invitation on Eventbrite with a picture of lots of champagne bottles and blondes. It always works," Irina said.

"I think this is going to be a memorable apartment," I said to them.

PART TWO

Chapter 8

Pitcher Up

I was not in a good mood. It was Pitch Night again. I'd read accelerator programs described as, "Pitch Eat Sleep Pitch Eat Sleep Pitch Eat Sleep" and that about said it all. I thought it was cute before, but now all of us were "exiting" the honeymoon period at Celery.

"Fucking idiots," I said to no one.

"Hey, hey girl," Marshall was behind me and I didn't realize it. "What the hell are you talking about?"

"Fly fishing," I said.

"Oh yeah, that makes everyone really, really mad," he said.

"No, I mean, VCs and angels and all the suits and stupid shit they say and we're supposed to look at a list of fifty mentors and know who to work with. And they all went to Exeter and Harvard and HBS and love fly-fishing. All I want to do is get time with my team to code something real, make something, prototype something, instead of taking 800 meetings with these guys talking about dry flies and there are no WOMEN MENTORS! Look at this list!" I scream at Marshall.

"Oh yeah, and *my* calendar is just bursting with meetings with my VC brothers of color, my nigger angels, yes, that's the ticket!"

"Oh my god Marshall, you are SO BADASS!"

"It's hard to be so cool, but somebody's gotta do it."

Marshall put his hand on my forehead like a doctor.

"Wait a minute, baby. You're coming down with something. Uh oh! I know what you got. You got a bad case of Pitch Night Fever!"

He was right. I was glad he was my friend.

"Pitch Night Fever and you got it bad!" Marshall started singing. "And did you see the pitching order? Can you believe I'm first and you're last? You poor girl!"

"I hate last, but I hate first more," I said, "Maybe the email was wrong."

"Yeah, and *I'm* your Aunt Lucy, an Episcopalian from Greenwich, Connecticut, drinking gin and tonic on my cottage porch in Nantucket," Marshall said.

"I mean, do you think they look at us and think …"

"Who they?" Marshall hated pronoun problems, "who you talking about?"

"The white boys in the blue shirts – the VCs! The money boys," I nearly shouted.

"You think they even *look* at us at all? Are you kidding?" he says.

"It can't be that bad!"

"It's worse, baby girl. We're barely on their radar. They just figure, I'm not trusting my money to some woman girly bitch," he said, "or some well-educated snotty African-American from Hah-vard!"

"Marsh! Don't say that!"

"Girl, the problem is … they don't LOOK at us, and they don't even SEE us. They look at the young white boys, who remind them of their favorite person — themselves, you know, when they were young and white and not too wrinkly. A long time ago in a galaxy far, far away, when ugly hair did not grow out of their nose holes!" Marshall said.

"Stop, you're killing me," I said.

Now Marshall was in full throttle. He used his "professorial" voice now.

"That's exactly why I discerned, that it would be advantageous in the extreme, to co-brand myself with the esteemed educational establishment known as Harvard University," Marshall explained. "They can SEE Harvard! And as long as I got Veritas on my backpack, that's all good. In fact, they no longer see me as a black Negro but as a crimson Negro!"

"Yeah, right," says I, "that shit cray."

"What she order?"

"Fish Fillet!" I said.

Jean-Claude came by and picked up our rap lyrics. With a French accent he recited the rest of Kanye West's song. It was even funnier with a French accent. Hell, just the way he says, "FRANNNNCE," is deep, dark, and delicious.

"Excuse my French," J-C says.

Marshall gives him high and low five. J-C gives him a fist bump in return.

"Lah-di-da," I say, "Just go over there and get in your zone! Get outta here!" He heads over to his desk.

"Nous allons gorillas tonight," Marshall says.

"What's that mean?" I say.

"I have no idea, it's just supposed to be, provocative," Marshall is looking at someone coming down the hall. "You know I sent my team home tonight."

"I noticed. They always look like they're working so hard."

"They are, but not on my product."

"What?"

"They are my little experiment. They have zero experience in high tech. They've never coded, never been in a startup, never done computer science," he said seriously and very quietly.

"Are you kidding me?" I said, really stunned.

"Sheba's a manicurist, Sidney is an auto mechanic, Gloria is a bartender and Franklin is a garbage man. I'm trying to seed the startup community with African-American entrepreneurs. I'm hoping even if they start from scratch, they can get in. My team spends every day learning to code while I get them ready to join other accelerator programs next year and have them hire five more folks of their own," Marshall explained.

"Is that why they don't hang out with us?"

"They have too much to do. They are doing a crash course. Sheba's really a good coder already."

"I know. She's great. She asked me a really tough question the other day. We both sat down and figured it out, but she did most of the figuring," I said.

"Have you read about the Indian community and how they committed to generating a new bunch of Indian entrepreneurs?" he asked me.

"No," I admitted.

"Girl, just Google 'Vivek Wadha.' He's done the research on building out the Indian entrepreneurial community. They needed Indian VCs and Indian mentors and Indian CEOs and CTOs. They turned it around. It took twenty years, but they changed everything for their community."

"You're a piece of work Professor Plum," I said.

"Yes, honky white girl, I am."

"You really ARE changing the world," I said.

"And you have to do the same for women entrepreneurs. You women are not invited to the party either. You've got to get into the mud and fight it out. You know Rachel Sklar and the List, right?"

"I've read about her."

"You're here now, you're in Boston, she's in New York, go meet her! Take the $10 bus. She kicks ass."

Suzy sends Roan around, her new cute gay guy assistant, to give us the warning.

"Girl and boys! We're on in 15!" He says, prancing. He's wearing a pink wool suit, tight as hell, very Chanel, with white piping, skinny white pants. He looks like someone from the circus or a high school performance of *The Music Man*. The outfit probably cost a fortune.

There something about accelerators that's theatrical. Something about performing. Something about entertaining. Something about seduction. I haven't pieced it together yet, but all those parts come into play.

I slogged through my PowerPoint one more time. I was getting so bored with it, I couldn't tell if it was boring, I was boring, or my pitch was just plain stupid anymore.

Apparently Roan pressuring us wasn't enough, so now here comes Suzy for the five-minute warning.

"Wednesday Pitch Night, let's go, five minutes!" She called out.

She droned on about Pitch Night through the halls like she's selling seashells down by the seashore or bouquets like Eliza Doolittle in Coventry Garden. Does she honestly think we might forget what night it is? We wake up every Wednesday morning in a cold sweat grabbing our pillows, teeth chattering and whispering, "Pitch Night tonight!"

I ran after her, "Suzy, are you okay with my team missing the pitch tonight? I'll be there, but they were up all night. I want them to just take it easy."

"You're the boss of them. It's okay with me this time. But they can miss things that get said. They should try to pull all-nighters any night but Tuesdays, okay?"

"Gotcha," I said, and texted them that they can all bail tonight.

The rest of us dragged ourselves down the hall and into the big glass conference room to see the list of the presenters on the board has now been… reversed!

I just pointed at the list and made my eyes wide crazy, scared.

I was first and Marshall was last!

I made a sound like I was being strangled and choking to death. I fell on the ground demonstrating this. Marshall's laughed. Founders love big drama. Marshall dumped his computer on a chair and yanked me up from the carpet.

We sat in the first row; the seat next to me was empty. I noticed the room is filling up but Jean-Claude was nowhere to be found. I put my stuff on the seat next to mine hoping to save him a spot.

Suzy came in with Jimmie Dunhill.

I say quietly to Marshall, "Holy Fuck."

Chapter 9

Fewer Than Three

Jimmie Dunhill. I can't even believe it. Dunhill was doing the hottest deals going now. Not a bad-looking guy either. Suzy looked all excited she'd snagged him for evening's event. He was also an old acquaintance of my ex, a guy I never did get around to meeting in person. I'd only seen pictures of him in all the big tech blogs, the typical ones with pretty girls and nerdy geeks at parties, looking really drunk with my darling ex. I was trying to remember if Nick hated him a little or a lot. My ex hated everyone really. The guys he hated a little he called "friends" and the guys he hated a lot he called "assholes." And, of course, I knew the adultress Sendi used to work for him.

Dunhill looked at me. "Hello Monica."

I got up and shook his hand.

Marshall texted me, "So you know this guy?"

"Oh yeah. More California past life hallucinations."

Jimmie Dunhill was a Brit, but a cool one, not one of these super shy goofy nerdy ones. He lived in some castle in France. Very smart, very rich, used to mentor at Y Combinator until he got bored. Then he went to teach at INSEAD, the French Harvard Business School. Of course, in the British tradition, he said dreadful things about the French and how they have no startup culture whatsoever since they are so "Mediterranean" (aka, lazy, sybaritic, pleasure-seeking do-nothings).

Suzy introduced him and talked about how critical he is to the startup ecosystem or something. And she's told him he should feel free to shoot us down if he wanted. Great, this should go from fun to a complete fucking disaster fast.

There was a bunch of beer and wine on a cart in the front and many of my Celery colleagues went right up there, after this comment. I stay away from that. Drinking and driving is at the top of the list of stupid things to do, but drinking and pitching comes in a close second.

Then he looked at the board, "Let's shake it up, let's take the list the other way." He thinks this is cool. Marshall grunts a funny laugh like a sneeze.

Suzy jumped in. "Well, actually, we started with the list the other way and then we turned it around, so it's already upside down."

"Hey, they need to get used to things changing in a New York minute. Marshall, you go first."

I looked at Marshall and semi-rolled my eyes back in my head.

He's grinning. He loved going first.

Marshall got up and started setting up his computer to show his PowerPoint.

Jean-Claude came out of nowhere and touched my arm, "Is that seat free, Madame?"

I pulled my stuff off the seat. He sat next to me. He looked good. Hell, he always looked good to me. And he smelled very good. I was almost too nervous to look at him.

Marshall looked over at me, gave me a tiny, almost easy-to-miss thumbs up, noticing I had the Frenchman next to me.

"Shall I start?" Marshall asks Jimmie Dunhill.

"Oh yes, by all means," he said.

Marshall says, "Good evening … "

Of course Jimmie had to interrupt him right off.

"I wanted to just jump in a minute and talk about co-founders."

He stood there very quietly, as if he were a high priest about to recite mass, looking sideways at Marshall, who's standing next to him trying to set up the computer. They exchanged glances. It's Silent Alpha Male language they're speaking, Dunhill was essentially saying, "I'm in charge, I'm going to share my profound wisdom. You're annoying me. You don't matter. Go sit down and shut up."

Marshall sat down and grinned the most fake grin ever.

"Thanks guys, so let me tell you about the most important decision you will ever make at Celery. The intensity of this program is renown. The mentor network is extraordinary and exclusive. The colleagues you'll make here are invaluable and likely will be lifelong friends and a source of the best advice and inside information about technology you'll ever get. Just don't make the mistake so many people do. You need to have co-founders. A one-founder startup is a non-starter. No one should go it alone."

He's talking about co-founders? This is a "déjà lu/ déjà vu" moment. I've read and seen this before. Like on YouTube when Brad Feld from TechStars said it. So Dunhill's stealing Feld's stuff. We nodded politely, since we all knew this and have heard the spiel before many times.

"You need more than one founder," Jimmie explained, as if he's Einstein or something, "and when it comes to founders, the quick rule is more than one and less than three is best."

I raise my hand.

"Isn't it 'fewer' than three?" I corrected his grammar.

"Doesn't matter," he said, "I said, you must be sure you have less than three founders but more than one. Any other questions?"

"Monsieur Dunhill," Jean-Claude interrupts him, "Monica is right, ze grammar is 'fewer' than three, n'est-ce pas?"

"I'm sorry, what's your name?" Dunhill said in a really snotty way, like you are SO wasting my time.

"Jean-Claude Longrée," J-C says like everyone knows him.

"So, this is lovely. I'm getting English grammar lessons from a Frenchman?"

Everyone laughs. Cheap shot.

Dunhill said, "Marshall let's go," ignoring us and turning to Marshall to kick off his pitch.

As Marshall began, Dunhill came over and took the seat Marshall left, the one on the other side of me. J-C on my right, Dunhill on my left.

He ignored me when I spoke to him, but then sits right next to me?

Dunhill was wearing a black leather jacket and black leather pants. He looked like the inside of an expensive sports car. Were you supposed to want to sit in his lap, shift his gears? He was a cologne guy like a lot of Europeans. But his was too heavy. J-C smelled better.

Marshall, always the minimalist, put his one slide up. He always uses one slide only. His slide is a very large version of his company logo. That's all. He didn't show anything else. I knew he'd do this. That just he way he works it.

"There's more to geolocation than Google maps or simple apps," Marshall started.

Jimmie interrupted him, "Marshall, show your next slide."

Marshall clicked.

The next slide was red like the first, but with no text or logo..

Jimmie said, "Brilliant. Go on."

His presentation was smart and short. He's just a great presenter. You'd listen to anything he said. Marshall's ten points were simple and direct.

Jimmie loved Marshall's presentation. He got up and talked about how simple it was, why it was good. He explained why Marshall was such a good presenter. How Marshall opened up to the room and used the energy of the audience. He asked him if he's had theatrical training. I didn't listen to the answer. I turned to check out the room. People looked either bored or scared.

When Marshall was done he came over and swapped seats with Jimmie Dunhill who was back up front again telling us stuff we already knew.

Next up are the MortalWarriors and they were better than the last time they pitched. Their style was REAL actual Boot Camp. They stood at attention. The CEO said loudly, "Team ready?" The team shouted back, "Sir, yes, sir!" at the CEO.

They went through their loud and shouty PowerPoint. They were handsome and interesting, always fun to watch all those muscles. Still the presentation was a little boring.

Jimmie said, "Rather dull I'm afraid and too long. Love you guys though and your style. Go through it fast as hell and I'll raise my hand when I'm interested."

He didn't raise his hand until the tenth slide.

On the eleventh slide, he lowered his hand.

Marshall got up and left the room, leaving an open seat next to me.

Well, surprise, surprise, Dunhill wandered back to sit next to me again.

I turned away and took a quick glance at Jean-Claude, not expecting he'd be looking right at me. But he *was* looking right at me, with a slight grin and then, he took my phone out of my hand.

He sent himself a text message on my phone, since he must want me to have his number. Or have mine.

He slips my phone back in my hand, whispers, "Voilà."

His text says, "Drink with me after?"

"Too tired already!" I text back.

Dunhill was trying to see what we were doing, I could tell by the way he was leaning forward, down the row, looking at J-C.

Every founder in the place probably wanted Dunhill's money. So when Dunhill asked the Warriors to do their pitch a second time, they were happy to oblige.

Dunhill went up front and gave the Warriors a hard time, but told them what to fix in an astute manner. He's arrogant and obnoxious as a person, but he's smart.

Jean-Claude leaned over and said, "You were right. He's a shit," about Dunhill.

Dunhill saw the Frenchman talking to me. He got up as the ABC team sat down.

"Suzy, let me pick the next team. You go next, Monica Belden," he announced, pointing at me. I nod. He thought I wasn't listening to him, but talking to Jean-Claude.

"Monica Kroy," I say.

"Let me go next," Jean-Claude says, gallantly, standing, offering to take my place.

"No, let's hear what BrightLight is about. Monica you go." He reached for my hand, as if to pull me into his car. He walked me up to the front of the room.

People cheer me on, chanting my name, "Mon-i-ka!" I hear the Russians in particular.

"Okay, okay," I said, setting up my laptop.

Jimmie Dunhill sat in my seat next to Jean-Claude.

This meant he'd blocked me from sitting down next to J-C when I'm done.

I delivered my thing smoothly, and thanks to Marshall, it was good. Each time I showed a new slide, I saw Dunhill moving forward, as if he were just about to rip it to shreads, but then, he would sit back and say nothing.

I finished. People clapped in a friendly way.

"Well done," was all Dunhill said.

"That's it?" I said.

"Well, slide three was boring as shit, but we can chat about that later," he said in front of everyone, like we had some rendezvous set up.

He tapped the empty seat next to him, as if to tell me, come sit, like a puppy.

I found that creepy and ignored it.

I went past both Dunhill and J-C and sat three rows back with the Russians, next to Slava who's shaking my hand and telling me I did a good job.

Dunhill was watching and didn't seem to like this. He pointed at Slava, "Your team next."

I gave Slava's arm a squeeze. "Just relax, you'll be great," I whispered in his ear.

When Slava waddled to the front, Jean-Claude got up and came back to sit next to me.

I'd been helping Slava with his pronunciation and especially with the word, "leverage." It was hard for him to say and he was saying it like "overage" or something. I told him it rhymes with "beverage" and we were practicing that. The sentence was, "This allows you to leverage … " I don't remember the rest. I rehearsed his pitch with him for about two hours, but in the end I wasn't sure it was really ready for prime time. I told him to drop "leverage" and rewrite it to "This lets you use … " to make it easier.

Slava stood up there, ready to start.

Dunhill said something to him in Russian – and it sounded like he actually knew Russian. And he had a really good accent. I was impressed. Slava looked surprised, answered him in Russian. Then they talk a little while in Russian as Slava sets up.

"Ready?" Dunhill asked.

"Da," Slava said.

He starts his intro of the team and the product. So far, so good.

Then he says, "This will allow you a beverage … " but then stops.

People stared laughing and held up their beers and wine. "Da, da, beverages," one of the ABC team said, with a phony Russian accent. People were laughing and loving this.

Suzy had to tell the room to shut up and let him finish.

It all got serious again and Slava continues but he looks nervous. He's definitely rattled.

I suddenly realized he's about to hit the other part of the pitch he had trouble with. It's something about how this app will blow you away.

He said, "This will blow you away… "

He clicked on an icon and the whole office goes dark.

Power outage.

"Oh Christ," Suzy said, "Now what?"

"You certainly did blow us away Slava," Dunhill said.

Everyone laughed.

It was not too dark, but dark enough to stop the Pitch Night.

Everyone started hooting and making silly noise. There was always a locker room feeling around an accelerator. Even this one, with the best ratio of men to women ever.

It was dark enough for no one to notice that J-C has taken my hand.

"J'ai peur," he said in my ear. Afraid? Yeah, right. He was very close and I liked it, but wasn't sure this was the best time or place.

"Really? You don't look like someone who's afraid of the dark," I said, taking his hand and putting it back on his leg.

Suzy got up, "All right you brats. Everybody just calm down," and headed down the hall.

Slava came over and plunked down in a chair next to J-C. He looked like a big unhappy slouching Russian engineer who was extremely frustrated with how things were going.

The lights went back on.

Slava got up and went back to his computer.

Dunhill was up front. "Slava's back, good. Come on over here. Let me tell you what to do if you are up on stage on Demo Day or in front of investors and you say something you didn't mean to or something crazy happens. Perhaps apologize but more likely, ignore it, just go on. They don't know what you planned to say anyway. Of if they find it funny, laugh, and then go ahead. Just say, 'I see I got your attention!' and that's all you want anyway, right?"

I got up and went to the back of the room. I felt the need to take a bit of a breather from J-C. I just wasn't sure what he was thinking and I needed everything to slow down.

He called me "Madame" reminding everyone I'm married, but funny how there's no word for a married man in French. It's all "Monsieur" all the time.

Slava finished his pitch and joined me in the back of the room. Marshall and Jean-Claude did the same. My

Frenchman calmed down a bit. He wasn't leaning all over me, or whispering to me.

We sat through about four more pitches. Everyone was really ready for dinner. I was trying to remember what Roan told me about what type of food he'd ordered. Then I remembered. Indian. Excellent.

The elevator opened and a very short Korean guy dragging a wagon with lots of containers appeared. Everyone cheered and retired to the Ping-Pong lounge and kitchen area to chow down. It's where we eat most of our group meals. I've imagined some of the more aggressive founders just using the Ping-Pong paddles to load their plates with food some night.

They all stood up to leave, I did too, but I didn't want to leave yet.

They went in. I stayed.

I didn't want to be near any of the guys or Dunhill and looked down at my phone.

It was a text from Jean-Claude, a room away.

"U were right, it is FEWER THAN 3 FOUNDERS."

I texted back, "Thx"

He replied, "But less than 3 is more sexy = Founders <3 "

The "less than 3" rotated and turned into a heart as I read it.

I decided not to reply.

Chapter 10

Flowers

I went into the lounge, filled my plate and sat next to Barb from Evergrow.

"Do you get sick of this place sometimes?" I asked her.

"Sure do," she said, "Even with half the house being female, doesn't it feel like it's all run on testosterone?"

"You betcha," I replied.

We talked about Dunhill. We both decided he was a bit of a showman, all ego, but smart. We talked about our teams, how they could get so down and how to rally them.

"Glad I have some sons, they remind me of them," she said. "These guys are like a bunch of silly little boys half the time."

"Meaning?"

"Sometimes you just need to take them to the park and let them let loose to run wild," she said.

"I'll remember that," I agreed.

J-C wandered over, making the most amazing eyes at me.

Dunhill appeared before J-C could even talk to me, trying to cut him off.

Barb asked Jean-Claude, "Youwere in that accelerator in Paris, right?"

"Yes, Le Camping," he told her.

Barb asked, "Why is it called Le Camping?"

"You spend six months living there, you know, camping out with your team," he said.

"It's the best accelerator in Europe now," Dunhill explained.

I knew some friends in Berlin who would not agree.

J-C mentioned the French guys who started Le Camping. He pronounced their names so well in French, most of us missed them completely. It just sounded like a bunch of expensive French wines.

"Yes, they've invited me to their place in Juan-les-Pins," Dunhill jumped in. He liked to name-drop and beach-house-drop.

"Ah oui," Jean-Claude said, sounding unimpressed.

"Monica, care for dessert?" Dunhill asked me.

On the far table there were pieces of cake, some white, some brown.

"Sure, maybe something chocolate," I said, hoping this would send him off for a while, leaving me with J-C. It worked, Dunhill left to fetch me cake, but all the other Celery people surrounded him, asking him questions.

"Catch you later," Barb said, also leaving us.

J-C was standing right next to me, not looking directly at me. We both were looking at the teams in the other room. He leaned closer to me, the side of his thigh touching mine briefly, then he pulled away. I felt warm around him now. I felt like I wanted to touch him and there's nothing good about that. A girl could get in trouble.

He was chanting something. "Choco, chocolate, choco, chocolate," he said quietly under his breath. It sounded more like, "show-ko, show-ko-la."

I just laughed.

"So drink with me after?"

"Drinking with Frenchmen late at night, hmm, sounds like… a very bad idea," I said, putting my head on my chin like Le Penseur.

"Au contraire," he said.

Dunhill was back with my cake, a slice that was ridiculously too big for any modern woman who's constantly on a diet, as most of us are.

"Thanks," I said taking the plate.

"How's Nick?" he says.

This idiot was asking me about my ex?

My body went tense. J-C must have noticed it. He sort of pulled back a bit from me.

"Fine, I guess."

What was I supposed to say?

"He's a fucking idiot," Dunhill said, "What he did was reprehensible."

"Umm … thanks," and how about, I really don't want to talk about it.

Suzy came by to rescue us, "We're starting again."

"Really, if you need anything, come to me," Dunhill says, then heads back to the room with Suzy.

I nearly dropped the cake and noisy plate on a table. J-C caught it for me.

J-C, "Was he talking about your stupid husband?"

"Yes. Christ, let's go sit down."

"I-dio," he says. French for "idiot" I realize.

"Which one?" I say.

"Both."

We went back into the big conference room and Dunhill's messed with the order again and Jean-Claude was up. Now Dunhill introduced him and they chatted in French and joked a bit as he set up. They seemed very friendly. No big surprise that Jean-Claude handled it with aplomb, but I got the feeling it was all "politesse" and he couldn't stand him.

"I hacked together something new since last week," he said.

His "something" sounds like "some-zing." Okay, it was just plain sexy. I wondered if he did it on purpose.

Apparently Jean-Claude had pivoted big time. I hate the word "pivot," stolen from basketball to say you stop and turn and go in a whole new direction with your start-up company. I found it was used most often by people who didn't know what the hell they were doing.

He started up his presentation with blaringly loud rock – it was Guns N' Roses' rock anthem "Sweet Child of Mine." He took a scarf and wrapped it around his head like Axl Rose and danced like him, swaying in a sexy way. Behind him on the screen, the music video was embedded in a large screen of music mash-ups – very creative and amazing graphics like you took LSD or something.

But, weirdly, it had absolutely nothing to do with his company, BSpoken4, that let you buy and trade fabric for couture design.

His PowerPoints were actually gorgeous and interesting – very '60s flower child Haight Ashbury and weird. His app was a music app that let you pick music based on photos that matched your mood. You could go the other way too, upload the pictures you'd taken lately and then it matched them to music you might like.

"Let's do some music mashing for Mr. Dunhill," J-C said.

There was a photo of a sporty red racing car.

He splashed a picture of a sexy woman in a corset across the screen. Every male cheered. The women groaned.

The last photo was a lovely one of a tropical beach at night, palm trees, moon.

This last click brought up a merry-go-round of music, the first one loud and disco.

J-C started to dance and pulled up Roan, the oh-so-gay guy to dance with him, then he got a few other girls up to dance as well and they were all going crazy. I was hanging back.

People cheered.

"Okay, okay, there. Ballroom, we make music easy to find and experience."

He ended the presentation. The last page said, "bAll-rOOm" in an up and down logo.

All great, but HELLO, this was not the startup J-C started with, at all.

I looked over at Marshall with a quizzical stare. He raised an eye brow as if to say, "Whatever!" knowing the same thing I knew. This had nothing to do with what he'd been working on.

"Well," Dunhill said, as he started his critique.

I was not really listening, since it was all crap anyway. I'm watching J-C, who was looking fascinated by what

Dunhill was saying, but I knew he couldn't care less. He was just pretending to care, just to mock him.

"Merci," J-C said.

Suzy called up the next crew and J-C came over and actually asked Marshall to move out of the seat next to me, so he could sit down. What was this, breaking in on my dance partner to take me for a few twirls around the ballroom?

"Ballroom?" I just looked at him "You can't call it Ballroom."

"You like "BallerRoom" better?" he said, deadpan serious.

"Yeah, right," I said.

"It's all sheet. I just don't want him knowing about my real company. I don't trust him at all," J-C said quietly.

The last two pitches were surprisingly dull and everyone in the audience was unsurprisingly drunk and tired.

Suzy thanked Dunhill and we were dismissed around 9:30 or so. I was dying to get out of there. All I wanted was my room, silence, nothing. Lots of sleep.

J-C left before I could politely dodge his drink invitation a third time. I saw him take the elevator down.

I also saw Dunhill at the end of the other hallway on the phone, away from everyone, looking a little agitated at whatever someone was telling him.

I had texted Marshall to meet me downstairs by the subway entrance. He agreed to walk me home to my place in Porter Square, which was on the way to his apartment.

We went back to our desks to gather our stuff and Marshall looked at me and gestured with his chin, over my shoulder to silently point out Dunhill coming my direction.

"Here comes Jimmie," he said, quietly through his teeth.

"Oh God," I responded.

Marshall peeled away, heading out, "See you downstairs or text me if you get waylaid."

"Way laid. Very funny. Shut up!" I said.

As he headed my direction, Dunhill was stopped again, by one of the Romanians, asking him questions. He looked impatient.

Hurray, I'd be able to escape.

I turned to leave.

"Monica?" I heard his British accent.

"Yes?" I said eagerly, but I really didn't want to talk to him.

"Listen, a few of us are going down to Mead Hall. Why don't you join us?" he says.

What? He doesn't even have balls enough to ask me out alone?

"Sorry, I can't. Thanks though," I mumbled. No explanation or excuse.

"Well, I think you need some help with that pitch, happy to rehearse it with you. Shall I call you?" he asked.

This would have made any other founder jump for joy, I suppose.

"Sure, yeah, great idea," I said, but I was seriously insulted.

Arrogant twit. I left.

Downstairs it was cold and windy. Nice way to sober up fast although one beer hardly had me drunk.

"Let me guess, Mister Wonderful asked you out," Marshall said, as I caught up with him.

"Oh no, man. He doesn't have the balls for that," I say.

"Don't tell me, he wants to help you with your pitch," Marshall said, laughing.

"Bingo. Actually, he needs help with HIS pitch," I said as we disappeared into the Kendall T station.

The trains were slow and it took a while to get one headed in our direction. At Porter, more snow was falling. Cold dry snow. We crunched our way toward my place. Marshall was the best, just what I needed tonight. Brilliant and ironic and reassuring. He could put things in perspective better than anyone. At the door, he hugged me good night.

I was so tired climbing my three flights of stairs. Tonight they felt like thirty. As I turned the corner toward my apartment, I saw a big bouquet tied on the doorknob with my name written on it. I untie the flowers and take them inside.

It's late and snowing and someone got here before me and left flowers? What the hell?

I closed my door quickly, since I didn't want my nosy neighbors seeing the flowers and asking about them. The crazy blue-haired girl group across the hall would want to know what's up, I just knew it.

I open them. Purple irises. Beautiful and expensive, since they're out of season. And no card … hmmm. I'm guessing Dunhill. I'm hoping not Slava. I'm wishing Jean-Claude.

Chapter 11

Park Your Heart In Harvard Yard

In the morning, Marshall and I had a secret meeting to keep track of how the different pitches went over the night before, based on no data, just gossip. He'd heard the PortMoneys might be out and reapplying for the New York Celery program since they were from the city and Suzy doesn't think they are ready for our group.

I only told one person about the flowers—Sonya.

My new game plan was to make every effort to ignore Jean-Claude. I'm avoiding him but thinking about him all the time. I'm thinking about him in general and about him touching my hand specifically.

The next day was Mentor's Day. Or as Marshall calls it, "Mentors Make Me Mental" Day. We had to decide on which mentors we wanted to work with and ask them if they would work with our company. It's like inviting someone to the prom or something. They can turn you down. My short list includes John Bracken, the CEO of Speek, Laura Fitton aka Pistachio, Dave Balter from BzzAgent. They are all spectacular entrepreneurs in their own way, and I waited to hear if they would consider working with our team.

New rule, we ask them by 10 a.m. and they have to answer by 5 p.m. Bracken says "yes" early in the day and I'm so excited that I've got Speek behind me, I don't care who else says agrees to being my mentor. He used to work at a company a lot like mine. I jump up and down and yell, "yes!" when I get their email. They are so cool and I love their monkey logo.

Laura at Hubspot was likely being bombarded with hundreds of requests. Same goes for Balter. Balter sent a nice note explaining he's already got his dance card fully booked, but suggests I talk with Sarah from Intelligently. Ends up Sarah was overbooked too. Laura actually called me and we chatted. She agreed to take me on when she heard that Speek was in. That was the best news ever.

Late in the day I heard from the guys at Franchises Opportunities who have been recommended by a friend of mine in Atlanta. He works at CNN now as a business reporter and can't say enough good stuff about them. They were doing cool things and I liked that they were not in Boston, but willing to visit anytime. I get a commitment from their CEO and I'm thrilled.

It had been a stressful week. By 6, everyone was a little tired and a lot crazy.

"Marshall, we need to get out of here and eat and drink something, anything," I told him, as I sat on the side of his desk.

"I can see that, yep, I could do that for you, Miss Lewinski," he says, still not looking away from the screen.

"Do NOT call me that, smart ass. I'm Monica, but not *that* Monica," I say.

Marshall's gotten in the habit of calling me Santa Monica Freeway too, or just the route number for short – Ten.

I pushed him a bit. "Make an announcement, come on, let's get everyone out of here and hit that noodle shop in Harvard Square."

Marshall had his computer rigged up with microphone and disco music app so he could crank up different tunes and make announcements like the guy from Soul Train, Don Cornelius.

"Attention hipster boys and hottie girls, Santa Monica wants OUT! All brilliant Celery founders and unfounders are invited to blow this pop shop and head for the hills — that is the Noodle Shop in Harvard Square at 2100 hours — that is like NOW!"

He cranked up "Le Freak C'est Chic!" to top volume.

A few people started doing disco combined with Gangnam-style moves.

Marshall even had a disco ball that worked sometimes, but in the first week, it fell down and hit him in the head when one of the most important VCs was visiting. One of those things this class of Celery will not forget.

"Like the French angle, c'est chic, n'est-ce pas?" He whispers to me, "What's with J-C anyway? He's been playing the lonely boy all of a sudden, notice?" Marshall winked at me.

"Seems like."

"I'll send everyone the address and then we should rally the troops and get outta here. Think we'll get the MortalWarriors out of here to party?

"Good luck, the G.I. Joes look pretty serious tonight," I said.

"They figure they can out-work and out compete all of us, but does the green camo face paint really make a difference?" Marshall said, turning back to the left where they had check out their startup HQ. They even had set up a tent in the office, where they disappeared to hold meetings or take naps.

As soon as the email went out, you could see some people just ignored it, others stood and stretched, and of course it brought the Russians, the Israelis and the Romanians running down the hall. They were never shy about hanging with the women of Celery and the prospect of picking up more "American Geerls" out on the studenty streets of Cambridge.

Barb, her team of Bing, Bong, and Lincoln, together with Sonya, Alex, three Russians and four Israelis were ready to go. I tried to look over casually at Jean-Claude to see if we had gotten him interested. He looked in the zone, typing code, glued to his screen, not aware of anything disco, food, party, or real world.

"Um, Monica, my darling," Marshall whispered urgently in his velvety quiet voice. He was trying to tell me I was not casually looking at JC, but essentially staring and some new person had turned the corner and was heading for us. "Check it out."

Some older guy.

Some MIT professor type.

Some handsome older professorial type guy who happened to be Franz Flanders — my advisor at Caltech who was now at MIT.

"Professors Flanders!" I blurt, stepping up to shake his hand, "What brings you to Celery?"

"Monica, good to see you! Maybe you can help me, I'm looking for the CEO of a startup," he was scrolling through his phone trying to find the name.

That narrows it down, I think. He was always a bit absentminded in a classic professorial manner.

In typical Celery style, we were instantly mobbed by all the teams to shake hands with Flanders. The Russians, the Israelis and then others started introducing themselves to Dr. Flanders, saying how they'd heard he was working on this, and what did he think about that? It was a little nerd swarm. He gave up looking at his phone and chatted with the crowd.

"I can see you're in good company," he said grinning at me. We invited him to join us in the Square, but he said he was busy. We all started getting coats and scarves. The Russians were good at bundling up rather fashionably in cashmere scarves.

"So who were you looking for? There are only ten companies here."

"Wait, let me look it up. Here it is – BeSpoken4."

"Jean-Claude, alors!" Marshall said with a thick phony French accent.

Sonya piped up, "I call him Jean-Cloud."

Flanders laughed.

I pointed him out. I was actually blushing. I could feel it.

"He's over there, I'll take you over," Sonya said and saved me the trouble, but I followed along.

They walked down the hall toward his work area. J-C had headphones on and never looked up.

Sonya tapped him on the shoulder.

"Ah, oui, Professor Flandres," he pronounced the word "Flanders" the way none of us could.

They shook hands. Sonya and I headed back to the big group.

"Let's get out of here," she said.

We headed out. I glanced back and saw Flanders glued to the big monitor as Jean-Claude showed him … something. I wasn't sure what he was showing him. Wished I could have stayed to watch.

"Girl … " Marshall said forcefully and broke my trance, "we have to leave baguette boy behind, let's go."

I gave him a shove. Baguette boy.

"Shut. Up. Marshall."

The T was pretty empty when we all piled into the car, only heading two stops away, for Harvard Square. I was still thinking about my Cloud Boy when the train started to move, leaving a few people on the platform.

Then suddenly, I saw Flanders and Jean-Claude together rushing through the turnstile heading in the same direction, trying to catch our train but missing it. I don't think Jean-Claude saw me as the train left, or if he did he was very good at looking completely uninterested.

Maybe they were going to join us, the thought flashed through my mind. A girl can wish.

At Harvard, our merry group hurried down the ramp, up the stairs, chasing one another, seeing who could mount the stairs fastest, never using the escalators. Of course the Israelis made it to the top first. It was a swirly snow outside and Slava took his black cashmere scarf and wrapped it around my face in a sexy way, his arms encircling me like a hug. "Stay warm and dry, Monica" he said in a friendly way.

We headed toward the Noodle Shop, past the Coop, past the Curious George store, down JFK Boulevard into a wintry night. It was a very romantic scene, except the guy I liked wasn't there.

Dinner was long and energetic and delish. They seated us at a large, square table and we got talking about Agile programming and Lean Startups, both of which were all the rage. My programmers seemed to have the Chinese guys from EverGrow all keyed up as they argued about the pros and cons of iOS versus Android. They wanted to leave to drink beer in a bar we all liked. The guys were almost beginning to shout when the waitress came over to give us the check.

Marshall told them to just cool it. "Your boys are wound up tonight, tight as you," he said to me, up close and personal.

"What's that supposed to mean?"

"Girl, I know you wanted your French boy here and then Flanders messed that up," he said.

"Flanders, yeah. You know he nearly flunked me out of Iterative Systems 203," I said.

"Flunked, oh yeah, let me use Google Translate … 'flunked' for a blonde girl who graduated from Caltech summa cum laude that means … B+, right?" Marshall teased.

He already knew me so well, I gave him a punch on the arm. "You're so smart."

"No, YOU are actually," Marshall said plunking down some money and handing the bill to the Indians, "Okay Math Majors, it's all here in black and white, put your money where your mouths were."

We paid the check and headed down toward the Square to our bar of choice.

There was a main room and then an upstairs pub room that was warm and happy, full of students of all ages and nationalities. It was a good place to watch the snow pile up outside on the street, the traffic all red brake lights, windshield wipers and occasional honking. There was a big glass window that looked out on the red bricky buildings and on the side alleys leading into Harvard Square. I saw students bundled up in scarves and hats and hoodies, many without real winter coats, freezing as the snow tried to unwrap their unsuccessful attempts to keep warm.

I felt happy mostly with a little nagging wish that Jean-Claude had come with us, but full, warm and one beer into the evening, it was getting to be mostly okay. I didn't feel like bundling up right away to leave.

"Here comes your Russian," Marshall whispered, noticing Slava changing seats. "You know he's got a thing for you," he said.

"No he doesn't," I protested, but it was a lie. I knew he did like me. The problem was, I only had big sister feelings for him and not much else.

"Yeah right." He tossed it off, knowing there was no point arguing. He got up and let Slava take his place, next to me.

I knew Slava liked me because I had actually heard him talking with his friend in Russian about me. I didn't tell anyone I knew Russian. With all the Russian programmers in the startup community, it was good to keep that kind of thing to yourself. I spoke French, a bunch of Russian, some Spanish and a tiny bit of Mandarin Chinese.

"Moneeeka," Slava said seriously, "I need some help with the pitch, with the technical part. Can I give you my pitch?"

"Sure," I said.

He delivered the pitch for his company. His Russian accent wasn't helping with the pronunciation of certain words. We worked on those words.

"Who's going back to Celery?" one of the Chinese programmers asked. We all got up and started layering the coats, scarves, gloves and anything else that could keep us warm and dry.

Most of the programmers were heading back to the office for a long night of work, but a few of us, with Marshall in the lead, wanted to swing by a pub on Church Street.

Slava walked with me as we headed to the pub, crossing in front of a restaurant called Nirvana. It was supposed to be Tibetan or something.

"This is NOT what Tibet looks like and not what nirvana is," Sanjay said loudly, in his heavy accent. "This is like Disneyland Indian. Foolish, very foolish."

We all laughed and as I turned to look into the front window of the restaurant, I saw him. Yep. Him. Jean-Claude.

He was there at a table with Flanders, the professor's wife Julia and some blonde girl just about my age. Hell, she looked just like me. I felt a rush of blood to my face.

Jean-Claude looked up, as if he knew I was looking at him. It was like the first time I met him. Like we had some connection. He looked right at me, and smiled in a very sexy way. I turned away.

He's out with a girl who looks like me, and he's smiling at me that way? I hate him.

Chapter 12

Crimson Snow Globe

A burst of windy snow blew right into my face like a slap, causing me to stumble. Just keep walking, I thought to myself.

Marshall had seen it all, J-C in the window of the restaurant with the blonde, my slight stumble.

Slava saw nothing, as he was looking the other way, but then I took Slava's arm for support and headed toward the pub quickly.

"Slava, I know a song in Russian, I'll sing it for you," I said.

He looked thrilled.

I sang Podmoscovney Veshera —Moscow Nights.

Marshall came over to check on me. "And you know Russian? Monica you are one weird chick," he said, letting me drag Slava ahead.

Slava looked like he had won the lottery.

"Gavareet Po-Russiky?" Do you speak Russian?

I admitted it. "Yes, I took six years of Russian in high school and then a few at Caltech."

"Why didn't you tell me?" Slava asked.

"I don't like to boast," I said.

I was singing just to keep me from going back to Nirvana and slapping J-C for that look, or to keep me from crying, or keep crazy Slava from trying to make the moves on me or God forbid kiss me. We made it to the pub and Marshall was trying to calm me down, while Slava went to buy me a drink. He got straight vodka for them, some new vanilla-infused vodka for me.

"I can't believe we saw him, just saw him there," I said to Marshall as Slava settled back in, too close to me.

I drank the vodka right down. There was nothing good about a snowy night in Boston, with the possibility of the wrong guy kissing you, while wondering if the guy you want to be is kissing is cuddling some effing Norwegian princess.

"Norwegian? You don't know if she's Norwegian!" Marshall replied, breaking my trance.

"Hey, did I just say that *out loud*?" I must be in bad shape.

"No, I was embedded in your brain," Marshall started laughing. "All you said, was 'Norwegian princess.' That's all."

"I'm losing it."

"And as for Jean-Claude, you don't know anything about who he's with and it's not your problem, admit it."

"He's married, I know that," I said.

"Good girl. Keep thinking that."

"I'm drunk," I said.

"And that married thing. You've seen how well that works, right?" Marshall said. "God knows why *we* are fighting for it."

Slava leaned closer. "You look very beautiful tonight."

"No, I look tired. Did you get anything done this week with all the meetings? I never get any time to code. I hate it."

"You need more," Slava said and went back to order more vodka.

When he came back with another round, I knew this night was getting silly.

Marshall and I tried to knock it back our shots like the Russians. I started coughing.

"Christ, man, you really ARE Russian," Marshall said to Slava, gasping after the first drink. "This is not one of those user-friendly vodkas."

"Da," Slava said and made a face that suggested Marshall scram and leave me alone with him, which is NOT what I wanted.

"Marshall, try this, it's vanilla vodka," I said, sharing the vodka Slava had bought me.

"Oh shit, this is reminiscent of the light fresh flavor of battery acid," he said. "You can do a quick pivot Monica, if your NightLight technology doesn't work. Sell this stuff to run mobile devices."

"It's BrightLight not night light," I growled.

Slava wasn't looking too happy with our twosome turning into a threesome. The door opened and a bunch of cute girls came in, one in a white sheepskin coat with matching big white fur hat.

"Slava, check her out, now there's a real Russian princess!" Marshall sounded thrilled. He went over to talk to the ladies. Slava and I drank more and practiced his pitch again. He knew enough to back off from the romancing.

Nights in pubs in Cambridge. The talk was pretty damned educated, very funny most nights, but I wasn't in the mood, distracted and cranky, feeling a need to keep turning and looking at who was coming in the door, hoping it was J-C.

"You're good to go with that pitch," I said. "Just try to remember why you felt passionate about the idea in the first place."

"Passionate yes," said Slava, smiling a little and looking straight at me. "Maybe we're all a little bit crazy, to be passionate about stupid lines of code on a screen."

"Slava! I can't believe you said that! Don't let Suzy hear you!"

Marshall, per usual, had gotten all the girls including the Russian princess excited and drunk and now dragged them over to play with us. I was getting tired.

"You'll love this, the Russian princess IS actually Russian," he whispered in my ear.

"No way!"

"Way hey!" Marshall high-fived my hand and missed it, whacking the brass bar hard. "Ouch! Shit man!"

We made hellos and howareyou, whoareyou noises for another fifteen minutes. Slava and the princess were chatting in Russian and he was getting all debonair and sexy with her.

"You'll owe me for this, I'm taking Slava off your ass," Marshall assured me.

"Excuse me, Professor Plum?" His last name was Plum and he really had been a professor.

"I'll walk you home, let's get outta here, Miss Moneeeeka," he said with a phony Russian accent.

Marsh was good. He was a good friend too and I was glad he knew it was time to drag me home and make me take the best medicine — a long winter's nap. The program had every intention and ability to burn us out and if we didn't keep things in balance, we were going to fall off the edge. Marshall had told me just that on the first day when they wanted to introduce us to twenty-five different mentors, scattering endless meetings across our calendar over the first few days. He'd whispered to me in the meeting that I should try three not thirty and he was spot on.

The snow was really pounding as we walked between Harvard and Porter Squares. It was great to have a friend who lived a few blocks past where I lived near the Porter T stop. We trudged along rather quietly. The storm was like watching a crazy polar bear circus, people slipping and sliding along the boulevards before you.

"I think the Russian princess was slightly cross-eyed, did you notice?" I said.

"Yes!" Marshall said excitedly. "Yes, that totally turned me on!"

"You are so crazy," I said, and we were at my door.

He gave me an all-business brotherly hug, making the world seem reasonable for a little while longer.

My apartment felt so empty when I entered it. The snow made the city quiet and far from home for a girl from California. The big front window was a gorgeous illuminated square of silver white streetlight and swirling furry white snow. It looked like some wide landscape painting someone had hung on the wall, as if this were a museum. I got into my pj's quickly and into bed, still thinking of what it might be like to be in J-C's bed tonight. It was strange to want someone I didn't know at all. Never spoken more than a few words to.

Would I ever get close enough to even ask him the thousands of questions I wanted to ask him? I looked over at the pillow and it took my breath away to imagine his face right there, up close next to me. It would probably never happen.

I was cold under a pile of blankets, so I spun my feet around like I was riding a bike. It took a while for the bed to warm up. It was strange to ache for someone tonight here alone in my bed in a snowstorm, someone who didn't live very far from me, someone I hadn't even known a month before and now I wanted to know everything about.

Chapter 13

Café Latte Later

In the morning, there was more snow, lots of it and I was glad I had warm boots. Because so many of the teams had come to Cambridge from all over the world — hot places for instance — I knew a lot of them would be having a helluva time with this weather, since they didn't have the boots, the coats, the hats, the gloves. They never thought of anything but showing up to write code in skinny jeans and tees. Some didn't even own a coat, I figured, but just managed with hoodies.

It was cold and sobering, a day to get back to reality, no boys, no beer, no vodka, no Russians, just fretting over the presentation I had to give that evening. Still, I was thinking about what to wear, as if this monkey house of geeks ever noticed any thing any of us girls were wearing. But the alums were coming over and that meant we had to give it our all.

I was thinking of what version of my presentation to use. I had thrown together about ten different PowerPoints and they were getting mixed up in my mind, what worked best, which one didn't work so well. Again, with the alums visiting, you had to up your game.

Marshall had shown me his presentation and it was really, really good. It didn't seem fair. He had been a CEO of a startup before, so I guess it made sense. He was an Olympic swimmer in our group and I was busy sitting on the edge of the pool blowing up my water wings, hoping not to drown.

He had offered to help, but that felt a bit like cheating. I wanted to do it all myself, as little coaching as possible, like taking the SATs the first time with no prep just to give yourself a kind of baseline, to see how bad you were. Doing it myself was a great and ambitious plan, but in the end I finally broke down and begged him to look at my presentation. We'd planned to meet for coffee at 9:30.

By 9:15, I was at the coffee shop across the street from Celery waiting in line for coffee. I was looking for Marshall, when Jean-Claude walks in with his team.

Christ. I really didn't want to see him, but luckily he was busy with his guys talking about something. They were in an animated discussion, nothing easy to break into. I could kind of watch them without them noticing me. Well, until his short guy programmer Gaston waved hi, that is.

I waved hi back to Gaston just as J-C was turning to see what was going on. I turned away quickly, not giving him the time of day.

I had decided it was all cold-shoulder all the time for J-C from now on. He was going to have to make a really big effort if he wanted to get near me after seeing him with my doppelgänger blonde girl the night before.

I wanted to get away from them all fast and of course, there was no such luck as the line for coffee and pastry was long and slow. Marshall was nowhere to be found.

I ordered my coffee, took the little tag with my number on it, to wait for it.

In my head I was messing with his name, just like some idiot schoolgirl who writes J-C J-C J-C J-C J-C all over her notebook with big hearts in a pink pen. Jesus Christ, I thought, you're hopeless, girl! And I thought, yeah J-C = Jesus Christ. Yep.

Sonya came in the back door, which had funny sleigh bells hanging off it. We were in the middle of Cambridge, very much in city mode, but the bells sounded like we were in an old Vermont country store. Outside, the snow hit hard in long straight white lines, as if to demonstrate its resolve and determination to bury us.

"Jesus, he's SO looking at you," she whispered, looking over at J-C and his team.

"Why did you say "Jesus"? I was just thinking about Jesus," I blurted to her. "And I'm not looking at him. He was out with Flanders and some blonde who looked just like me last night at Nirvana. I swear."

"You better pray to Jesus, girl!" She was giggly like a kid now and I was worried I'd catch her giggles.

"I think Cloud Boy is a good nickname," I said.

"And J-C and Jesu Christy Boy, Cloudster, yes, many variations on that theme, I know, I know." Sonya was right on my wavelength.

The girl behind the counter called my number, "33!"

'That's me," I said, pushing toward the coffee she was holding out for me.

I never saw him.

Sonya swears, J-C wasn't watching either.

Hmmph.

I reach for MY coffee.

J-C reaches for MY coffee, but seems to think it's HIS coffee.

We collide.

I manage to send it flying all over his sweater.

"Oh my God," I say.

"Excusez moi!" he says.

Contact.

This is the part where you have to slow down the video to super slow. I want to see my hand manage to brush his chest, as I reach for the coffee. Sonya and I have now gone over the scene a few hundred times to figure out the motivation of the perp.

He had to have pressed himself between my hand and the coffee. He put his chest — and it's a really handsome, strong, good-looking chest — in an expensive French ski sweater, right in alignment with my hand, so I not only managed to spill the coffee down his front, but end up with my hand … really, Sonya swears by this … really, my hand was right on his heart.

These Frenchmen. How do they do it?

Here's this random young man I have no business even talking to. He's too young and he's married. I'm still married. Great. As of the night before, I didn't want to ever speak to him again, and here I am this morning with my hand on his heart, after baptizing his torso in hot coffee.

And even the rush to movement. I'm moving fast, he's moving faster, I'm backing into him essentially, which is why I didn't quite see him, then we are both stopped dead in our tracks and coffee is splashing him and I'm completely staring up into his face, with my hand on his heart like we're dancing. What eyes.

"Oh my God, are you okay?"

"Pas de problem, ça va, ça va," he's saying, trying to keep from grinning ear to ear.

He's looking into my face like nothing in the world could be better than taking a coffee shower with me. In fact, he laughs a little and that we could be standing in a shower together darts through my mind — and I think he was thinking the same thing — and then I'm laughing too, because I'm looking at his big brown eyes.

Brown eyes, dark chocolate melting gaze, black coffee, I am suddenly flushed with heat. His heat, my heat, I look at Sonya.

Sonya is grinning like she's watching the funniest scene, but then pulls herself together, hands me a bunch of napkins.

I notice my hand is still on his chest, as does she and she motions for me to take the napkins and take my hands off him.

"Oh, here, sorry," I start wiping him dry, but of course this means following the spill down his chest toward his belt and that's just not a good idea.

I'm getting fidgety and girly and nutty as I say, "Really, I'm so sorry, excuse me, Jean-Claude," I pronounce his name in a pretty French way, like I have something delicious in my mouth.

His eyes flash and he grins at this.

It's written all over his face.

He likes me saying his name.

He is fast on his feet, he knows what to say after I say his name.

"Well, Monica, I will tell you, it's really" he says, rather slowly, giving me a drop dead look deep into my eyes, "it's okay, as long as you're not flirting with me."

"Not to worry," I say.

His co-founder, François, waltzes over also grinning and mumbles, "Quel accident! Qu'est-ce que c'est dommage," with a slight sneer.

I'm back to reality. "Really, if you need something to wear, I have a Celery sweatshirt in my cube back at the office." The coffee lady is there with a mop and bucket to clean up the floor.

François hands him the right coffee, "Voleur," he says, calling J-C a thief, "c'était à elle. Oui, ce lui-la, c'est à toi. Tu l'as fait exprès."

The coffee girl has made a new drink for me. Sonya saves me, taking it off the counter. "Here, take this one, we'll see you all later," she says and practically drags me off, in the direction of the door.

We walk.

They stand there.

Sonya is giving me a penetrating look and repeating under her breath, "Do NOT, I repeat, do NOT look back at Frances Romance."

"Thank you, thank you, thank you," I say to her.

We are at the door.

There's a crowd coming in, so she steps back and I step back and some how Jean-Claude is right there.

I mean right there.

Right behind me. And he doesn't step back. He steps forward, so he is right up against my behind. He takes my arm in a sexy way and pulls me closer to him.

Most guys just don't do what he does.

He pulls me toward him and kind of gives me a hug. It's a full embrace, but so fast. I am blushing and I could faint, but then we all move again. It's crowded. I don't even think Sonya saw what happened and she's right next to us.

Then the crowd has passed and he kind of guides me through the door with a hand on my arm, like we're dancing and he's taking the lead, out to the street, into the snow. Then he steps back and turns away, turning toward his co-founder, and says something funny and casual to him in French. I don't catch it and they go off in another direction — all like he didn't do what he just did.

And in that moment when he pulled me to him, I couldn't help imagining how nicely we'd fit together in bed. And I smelled him and he smelled so like HIM. A little sexy sweat, a little eau de cologne, a little café au lait, bittersweet.

I look at Sonya whose eyes are as big as saucers. She doesn't know what happened, but she sees in my face that it must have been serious. Something delicious. I feel like I'm twelve years old, not thirty-two.

I am not breathing at all well.

Marshall calls, giving me an excuse to break away and answer the phone.

"You got it bad and that ain't good," he says.

"What?"

"Look up, over by the T sign," Marshall says. He's standing twenty feet away. "I just witnessed that little 'entreprise' with Frenchie. Coffee, tea or me?"

"Don't. Don't say a word. And where the hell have you been, if you weren't late, none of this would have happened."

"Right," he said, hanging up.

Chapter 14

Lunch at Calamity

Sonya was a good partner in crime, not that we've committed any crimes yet. Really, we just loved to talk and she was truly gifted at gossip. She valued it. She knew it made the world go round and should not be treated dismissively.

Now that we were on the East Coast, The Girl Exploratory Theory and Identity Team (GET IT) had to have a high security headquarters location, a lair, where its two founding members (Sonya and I) could discuss celebrity gossip, as well as more local romantic targets and plan surveillance. We chose the girls' shower room for this.

By the way, she's bi. Not super annoying in-your-face bisexual or cranky or political or show-offy bi, more like cuddly stuffed animal bi. She falls into bed with guys and girls in a slightly random fashion any evening, actually any morning, noon or night, since she's just sort of earthy and sexy and always has been.

She and I had an understanding that I'd never been into that type of thing, I'm too boy crazy, so she knew not to try hitting on me. I need her coding and surveillance skills and good old plain-vanilla Girl Scout friendship more than I need her getting sexy with me. We're building a company here; we can't be spending time in bed messing about. But we love to gossip.

The shower room was one thing we didn't need to build. It was there. Runners and fitness freaks needed a shower room, of course, but also it was a tradition in accelerators to have a shower room in case your coders spent the whole night working, and at dawn, they needed to get cleaned up and throw on a new tee shirt. The guys' shower room was constantly busy. The girls' shower room never was. So we've taken it over, as GET IT headquarters.

Sonya and I had already figured out that the shower room was the safest place to hang out and tell secrets and gossip because you could lock the door. It was much safer than the ladies room. In there, you never knew who might be listening to you, like the wife of one of the important mentors or who knows who. The shower room is about the size of two big offices, the front room being lined in metal lockers like any gym, with a big open tile floor, a stack of nice clean fluffy white towels and a bin for used towels. The inner room has a sink, two big shower stalls and a big mirror.

Sometimes the only way I can relax is put towels down on the floor in the locker room area and stretch out on my back, as if we were laying out our yoga mats for a class. Sonya and I shared our earbuds and listened to music together, lying there on towels like we're at the beach. It's actually kind of cozy.

The day after the coffee event we were checking in with one another. I need serious help on the subject of Cloud.

"Towels!" I said.

She did the honors, laying them out, as well as rolling some into pillows, one for each of us.

"Music!" she said. I handed her the left ear bud and she slipped it in her ear.

I zipped through the playlist. Rhianna came up. There are things about Rhianna, the singer, that I find pretty darn weird really. Like the way she does these kinds of dark, BDSM, beat-me-up-I-love-it kind of music videos. Other times she just the girliest girl ever. And her song about a guy making you feel like you're the only thing he cares about, since most guys totally don't know how to do this, is brilliant. Very simple and speaks to a serious need, like a good new product from a startup. It should be that simple and that desirable.

Yes, it's what any self-respecting female wants, for a guy to make her feel like she's the only girl in the room, at least tonight.

I stopped the song and we talked about Cloud and what to do next. She outlined the game plan and the obvious choices — advance, retreat, confuse the enemy with some of both.

The third choice was intriguing: create confusion. We crank the music up again.

She is good, my girl Rhianna, at stating the obvious and simple. We play the song again. Going out with a guy who has his eye on every other girl in the room is for the birds. This is the problem with going out with a guy who's better looking than you. It never works.

You can love her smarts, Ms. Rhianna, but you're always left saying, "Why the hell was she going out with someone like Chris Brown?"

And then we were listening to her singing with Eminem and he just nails it with his hot/cold description of falling for someone and how you forget to breathe when you're around that object of desire.

My mind's wandering. This is the way Jean-Cloud can make me feel. St. Cloud is a suburb of Paris. In French, it sounds like San Clue, rhymes with "glue." There is a pretty park in Saint-Cloud, I would like to walk there with him. George Brassens sings about it, "au Bois de Saint- Cloud, il y a des petites fleurs."

Sonya stopped the music.

"I feel like this about someone," she said shyly, "but I don't think she feels it back."

"Want me to guess?"

"You'll never guess. She seems like, you know, a total guys' girl."

It is easy to guess then.

"Wait, not your darling Russian roommate?"

"Yep, I kind of like her," she was blushing.

"Irina!" I said slowly, "Wow, girl you are interesting. I can't figure out which way she goes at all. She seems like she's just always being pushed around by all the men she knows. You might be just the thing she needs."

"Think?"

"Never know until you try," I said, trying to sound supportive, but actually worried my friend will take a hard fall over this one.

I put my earbuds back in.

"Listen to this," she said. It's FreezePop, their song Dopplegänger.

"I was out with a friend, trying to put the past to bed," Sonya sang along.

"I love this one," I said.

"I saw you ... with a girl who's looking really familiar ... " she sings.

"Crap, its like him in the restaurant ... "

"She looks like me, she looks just like me," Sonya knew the right medicine.

"Exactly."

"Wait, I know what to do! I need to talk to Suzy." I sat up, suddenly knowing where to go with all this stuff.

I jumped up and rudely yanked the earbud out of Sonya's ear.

"Hey!" She said.

"Oh my God, sorry!"

"Now what?"

"Get up, come on," I said, pulling the towels together and tossing them in the laundry bin.

Sonya and I ran out of the shower room and down the hall to our desks. We grabbed pens, notebooks, phones. I had a great idea to share with Suzy. I turned the corner and nearly run smack into Jean-Claude and his team. They start making guy noises and stupid faces at Sonya and me. It flips my switch. I'm Warrior Work Princess suddenly. Not softheaded at all. I am job maker first, heart breaker second.

Did I mention we are in a COMPETITION? I mean this is mano à womano and I have no intention of letting some guy just win without a fight, or worse, letting him get under my skin and ending up all moony over him when I'm supposed to be building a company. That's what I came to Celery for. To make this idea into a company that knocks everyone's socks off, especially Nick Belden's socks, not that my nearly-ex wears socks much. He's mostly all flip flops all the time.

I went over to Suzy's secretary, Roan, to book an appointment.

"I need to do lunch with her," I told Roan.

"Getting a lunch with Suzy is always a challenge, Monica," he explained to me seriously, like delivering malignant cancer results.

Roan was a very interesting, redheaded Japanese guy who used to work at the MIT Innovation Lab and was just as crazy as the lab was. Roan was very modern, very gay. He was another Celery hot shot and a "he knows everyone worth knowing" person. Soaking wet, he must have weighed barely 90 pounds and wore the skinniest skinny jeans in black and actual Hermés scarves and of course, amazing shoes, everything from espadrilles to combat boots. Sometimes Celery seemed like a wax museum of the most amazing people. Could they be real? Yes, they were. And they didn't stand in the corner silently. They were alive and funny and inspiration and made you want to keep at it.

"Roan, if anyone can get me on her calendar, you can. Tell her it's all about feeling this is a hostile environment for a woman CEO," I said seriously.

Marshall walks by. "It's the Clic-Clac à Pois, isn't it? The equestrian theme is still all there, just understated, doncha think?"

They were talking Hermés scarves.

Roan just about whinnied and neighed like a pony, when Marsh hit him with that obscure design critique.

"You are so right! Don't you love it?" Roan squeaked.

"Yes, but the Indian ones in 2010 were even better," I said.

"I … HAVE … TWO … OF … THEM!" Roan is now completely excited. I've seen him wearing them, so I know he loves them, just like I do.

"You little bitch!" I said and we hugged one another.

"I'll try to get you in her book," Roan gave us a bunch of fluttery eyelashes, looking at his boss' online calendar, which meant it really might happen. "Let me check with her."

I walked back with Marshall. "Thanks."

"Thank YOU," he said.

Later, I was working with my developers and noticing that Jean-Claude had either moved his desk or switched desks to a place where he could look right at me. It's a little obvious. Sonya thought it was hilarious and did a phony French accent all morning to annoy me. The large monitor we used for team meetings was set up in that direction, so I was forced to look right at him.

I wondered how many Celery people knew about the coffee incident. It seemed like a lot of other teams were looking at me, or maybe I was just paranoid.

If you actually want to have people looking at you in an accelerator, there's one foolproof method. Have the program directors come over to your cube —instead of you going to see them. They don't do it often. But as if my day couldn't get crazier, Suzy came hurrying toward me and interrupted our meeting.

I know all the other teams were watching. It's like a weird family with a mom who singles you out as her favorite. All the other kids get jealous.

"Monica, lunch works today if it works for you," Suzy said.

"Yes, that would be great, thank you, Suzy," I say, somewhat stunned. Today?

"12:30?"

"Yes, 12:30, that's great."

"Ask Roan what restaurant he booked, I don't even remember where, some place in in the square."

Like anyone doesn't know Suzy's favorite place to eat in Kendall Square? It was Calamity, a place designed to look part caveman with several big roaring fireplaces and part futuristic spaceship, shiny metal surfaces and odd silver tubes. It was becoming a real "see and been seen" type of place for Internetty types, a joint I never liked. I thought I'd left the coolness game behind in Silicon Valley, but now Kendall Square was beginning to suffer from the same disease.

Still, like Roan said, getting a moment alone with Suzy was tough and it kind of blew all the other CEOs' minds when they saw you walking out with her, which is just what I wanted them to see when she and I threw on our coats, hats, scarves, gloves, then yanked our boots on and headed out. She always looked amazing and model-gorgeous. She was wearing an amazing coat, big fluffy puff of charcoal fur, but it was actually furry faux fur. She looked ready for a high-class Iditarod up Fifth Avenue. The coat and hat were all grey and soft, the boots are crimson, with straps of black leather crisscrossing and holding them on as if she'd tied them on in a snowdrift. She was a wild woman crossing the Taiga.

I flashed on my mom visiting me at Caltech once dressed in fur on an eighty-degree day, looking so out of it. I felt that flush of shame to have been mean to her, because she was only trying to look cool, but blowing it. She and I had a tough time when I was in college. She was on her third marriage to a dentist in Laguna Hills, a guy I didn't like at all, but he was kind to her and even kind to me, helping me with college bills when he really didn't have to.

We got to the restaurant on time, we had a reservation, but they still made us wait ten minutes. I guess this is what exclusive restaurants do. Three people drifted by and then went all goofy to see Suzy. She's very popular, but does she get it? It's all about her having access to people with money, not really about her personally. When she steps down from this gig, will she be shocked that they weren't so crazy about her after all, but more about the connections she had thanks to the job.

After we're seated, I wanted to ask her about my pitch. And about Jean-Claude a little if I can slip the subject in. Instead, she launched right into another topic.

She wants me to ask Nick Belden — oh yeah, that guy I'm hating on and unhappily married to — to speak at Celery when he comes to Boston for something he's doing at Harvard next month.

"You know we're not *exactly* getting along," I said.

"Yes, I saw that stuff in *Gawker*," she said, "but I thought maybe it was just not true."

"Unfortunately, *Gawker* gets it right most of the time. It just never seems possible that some of the stupid people they cover actually did the stupid things they did, but Nick did," I say.

"I like the Nick, the other Nick. Nick Denton," she says about the founder of *Gawker* and the other sites.

"Yes, he's no fool."

"So do you think you could ask Nick, your husband?"

Even his name makes me wince. "I'm not sure it would help you if I asked. Let me think about it. I can tell you how to get him, best time, best mode. He might do it for you, but only if he knows I won't be there that day."

The waitress brought over the menus. They had a big comic book graphic with the word, "Calamity!" written across the front and a spy guy in a fedora in profile.

Yeah, calamity is what I'd call Nick coming to Boston.

"So what did you want to discuss?" she asks me.

"Oh nothing much," I say. She's thrown me off my game mentioning Nick.

"Well, you can help me with something I'm doing. I'm writing about the challenges female entrepreneurs face for a thing in the *Sunday New York Times Magazine*. What are your top three? Oh hell, look who's over there."

I look over. Yep, it's Jean-Claude having lunch with some Belgian VC. I think his name is Fred, but I can never remember the guy's last name. They get up and head over our way to say hello.

"Fred!" she says. "How are you?"

"Calamitous, to be sure," says Fred.

"Salut, Suzy, salut Madame," J-C says. "Monica, come with me I want to show you something," he takes me by the hand, over to the hallway by the kitchen, out of their line of sight.

"Fred told me he needs to talk to Suzy alone," he said, smiling. "He asked me to take him over there and then go away. No flirting. Wanna hear my pitch?"

"No, but go ahead," I said with an exhausted breath. "Hey, what's Fred's last name?"

"I don't remember," he said.

"Great, thanks."

"Here, you sit here. And I'll stand up there, like pitch night." We were on a fairly empty hallway where there was a black leather bench, ten feet down from the restrooms, out of the line of fire, where the waiters were rushing by with trays.

"My name is Jean-Claude Longrée. My company is BeSpoken4. I've built a worldwide network to unable people to buy and sell haute couture fabrics – silk, wool, leather." He spoke very, very fast, messing it up on purpose to make me laugh.

"Unable?" I said.

"Enable, shit!"

He repeated it with the correction, but still at a ridiculous speed, flailing his arms around a bit.

"Slow down, you're going at a helluva rate," I said.

"It sounds better fast," he said.

"No, it just sounds too fast. And your arms are doing this." I waved my arms around like an octopus.

He burst out laughing, "No one could look as funny as you look right now."

I swing at him and give him a quick, "shut up!"

He did his pitch again slowly, much better this time, with a little less movement.

Men are always looking at women's bodies. Do they know we're always looking at theirs too? He had a great body, very fluid but muscular, like a dancer. Did he understand that making me sit on that low bench meant I was eye level to his belt buckle? Was he doing it on purpose? I didn't want to be looking at him from that angle. I mean, I did like looking at him that way, but not in a public.

I stood up, as he finished his pitch and walked right into Fred.

"Bravo!" Fred started clapping for Jean-Claude's pitch.

"Fred, this is Monica," J-C said.

He shook my hand. Great, I *still* didn't know his last name. I pulled my card out of my jacket pocket, hoping he'd give me his in return. He didn't.

"Oh, you're Monica Belden," he said emphasizing Belden. "I know Nick. Isn't he here next week?" My card said "Monica Kroy" actually.

"Yes, he's speaking at Harvard."

"He is?" J-C blurts out. It's clear he's surprised, and not in a good way.

"Yes," I say calmly, like, hey, not to worry, kid.

"I've got a ticket already," Fred said. "Listen J-C, we need to finish up with what we were talking about. Monica, will you excuse us?"

"Certainly," I said, and headed back to Suzy.

"Nice to meet you," said Fred. Apparently I was destined to never learn his last name.

It seemed like there were often amazing people you met at Celery who everyone knew so well, or everyone pretended to know so well, that they flaunted the fact they were on a first-name basis. This resulted in us new kids feeling like idiots half the time when we had to admit we didn't actually know their names.

As for being on a chummy first-name basis, everyone seemed to know Nick. And everyone knew Nick would be here in Cambridge next week. Great. I was hoping I could avoid seeing him.

I sat back down with Suzy who was on her phone.

She hung up quickly. She was good about that.

The menus at Calamity were transparent plastic sheets stuck onto the screens of Etch-a-Sketch toy boxes. We sat there holding red and grey kiddy toys, reading the most adult menu ever.

"What's the fascination with kale?" she asked me looking over the menu. "It must be some Mark Bittman thing."

Chapter 15

Lawyers

Lawyers. Oh, lawyers! It's not that I can't stand them, I know they are necessary, but they are so the opposite of entrepreneurs. We're constantly thinking of amazing things, optimistic outcomes where new ideas change the world and put money in everyone's pocket. They, on the other hand, are forced to look at worst-case scenarios, imagining failures and exit strategies of businesses and marriages. And then orchestrate the unpleasant but fair removal of money from some pockets and transfer to others. So they can't help but consider doom and gloom. They're paid to face the ugly cold truth.

My lawyer called to tell me Nick wanted to meet downtown at his lawyer's office near Post Office Square. Even the going downtown part was annoying. I tried to spend most of my time on the Cambridge side of the river.

She told me to dress nicely, like a flight attendant basically, and then to head downtown to meet her before we met them.

"Is it about the cheating clause?" I asked Mary, as we sat at a table in a Starbucks on Franklin Street.

"No. They want to dilute your shares in his company," she said.

"*His* company, yeah, right, that I founded with him and I came up with the idea for it and I hired all the key developers."

"In the meeting, you won't like it, but you have to let me talk for you. I'll ask for more than you deserve and they will get all hot and bothered."

"You know what Mary, I don't even care," I said.

"You DO care, because it's an aggressive, semi-abusive step on his part to try to cheat you out of something that is rightfully yours, but getting him on record being such a jerk helps define his character if we go to trial. And it is serious money. They've been approached by Oracle to be purchased," she said.

"I know, I've been hearing about that," I said.

"Yep, so here's the thing, are you going to be okay with seeing him, letting me do the talking and not talking yourself?" Mary asked, leaning forward.

"I can be cool. Feel free. I'd rather put my hands around his throat, but I'll resist," I said.

"If it gets out of hand, I'm gonna show the other lawyer the cheating video," she said.

"Whoa! You ARE going in with the big guns." I sat up in my chair. "I like this."

"He doesn't think we have anything like that," she said. "I want him to see how serious we are."

"I'll hand you my phone, just say the word," I told her.

Downtown, we arrived before them and sat in the waiting area admiring the carpets. The offices were so fancy, the mahogany so weighty, the silence so exclusive, the carpets so plush, the legal secretaries looked like little movie stars. It was all going so well, until we got into the conference room and heard what they were proposing.

And the part about being quiet and cool and letting my lawyer talk? Well, after the offer they made, I jumped up and yelled, "ARE YOU KIDDING?"

Mary just turned to me slowly, with a chilly stare like she's a marble statue, as if to say, "stop talking NOW."

I sat down. She didn't have to say a another word.

"Listen you, it's more than you deserve," Nick blurts.

Nick's lawyer is glaring at him.

"What did I tell you?" the lawyer says to him.

"I don't care if you told me to shut up or not, she can't talk to me like that."

Things started to calm down, but I could see this was just the evil hors d'oeuvre to a poisonous three-course meal Nick planned to serve up.

The meeting continued and Mary was squeezing my hand under the table when I got ready to interrupt and complain again. We began to discuss the company.

"And I'm afraid we're only going to be able to give you 10,000 shares after you recruited your technical team to Boston to work for you, devaluing the original company."

I let out a semi-grunt, laughing at their version of the story. I scribble, "TELL THEM / NOT TRUE," I show my lawyer. I have calmed down.

"My client is not agreeing to that offer. It's a lot less than seems fair," she said, "And she did not solicit the three members of the technical team. They left of their own accord, once they heard that your client had cheated on her."

"That has not been proven or substantiated. We both know it would be considered hearsay in court," his lawyer said smugly.

"Really? What about this?" My lawyer shows them the video on my phone.

"WHAT THE HELL!" Nick says, jumps up and grabs my phone from her and smashes it against the wall, nearly hitting me in the head with it. My lawyer again grips my hand like we've just won the lottery.

His lawyer looks ready to kill him, "Nick, sit down!"

My lawyer is perfectly quiet and relaxed."Of course we have back-up of the video and it's in a safe place, as well as available on YouTube in a private account, which we could easily reset and then release it to the public. I think you might want to think about that."

"You fucking bitch," he says, looking at me like he wants to hit me.

I was only surprised he'd taken so long to use the F-word. Not like him at all.

My lawyer delivers the classic line, as we stood to leave, "We'll see you gentlemen in court."

I scoop up the remains of my iPhone. I'd been thinking about switching to Android. Nick has always pushed me to embrace new technology.

The two of them sat there looking flummoxed, as we closed the glass door on the conference room. Then I saw Nick jump up, stand there hulking over his lawyer, red in the face, yelling at him. His lawyer stands, pushes Nick down in the chair and points his finger in Nick's face, as he yells back at him.

"Punch and Judy," I said, nodding that way.

"You didn't tell me he had such a temper. That was a lucky break for us," Mary said at the elevator.

As we get into the elevator I heard Nick yelling at his lawyer. "She can't get away with this."

Actually I can and I will.

PART THREE

Chapter 16

Risa

The guys always got nervous when there was an event for female CEOs only. And of course, they had to make fun of it and act like it was unimportant, but even *they* knew our meeting with Risa Levinson was going to be phenomenal, and they were truly pissed off they couldn't attend. Everyone knew what an amazing entrepreneur Risa was, how spectacularly rich she was and about her amazing half-naked photo on *Fortune* magazine the week her company went public. Clad in only scuba gear and a bikini, she did look like a Bond girl. But the guys claimed it was more about getting to meet her brilliant husband who invested in just about all the Boston startups that hit it big and they wanted to be on that list.

So it really got under their skin when the guys heard all the girls at Celery were invited to her Back Bay townhouse for a day-long event and they were not. In fact, they began protesting and telling Suzy and Walt they should be allowed to attend, since they all needed to meet Brad

Levinson. But that wasn't happening and on one fairly sunny warm morning in March, when the daffodils were doing their best to push out of the ground and get the concept of spring launched, we "ladies" headed downtown to Risa's place in Back Bay off Beacon Street.

I'd tried to calm things down with J-C the night before, but he just seemed to ignore me. I told him that we couldn't go any further, it was a bad for both of us, and that we should both be focusing on our work.

These were apparently the magic words. He was texting me non-stop trying to change my mind.

"So we should get together and talk about your wife and my divorce?" I emailed him back, trying to stop the cascade of text messages.

"It's not what you think, I'm not in love with her," he replied.

"Heard that one before."

"Really, let's talk."

"Good. Bye." was my reply as I headed to Back Bay.

The Levinsons' place took up a big two-townhouse-wide plot of land, had a garden in a center courtyard, a bird bath fountain in blue mosaic, Italian windows and terraces on the inner court going up four stories and on top, a glass penthouse that looked out on the Charles River, with an amazing view of MIT, no surprise there. They faced Mecca, the holy place called the Massachusetts Institute of Technology that made them famous, that rocketed them into the entrepreneurial cosmos. She'd met her husband at MIT's Sloan School of Business, while she was an undergrad in engineering at MIT. Then she did an MBA at Stanford. The two were a lethal combo and their first company – her idea and her prototype – was sold to Google making them millionaires before she was 30.

I'd heard things about her – that she was absolutely fearless and had so much chutzpah, had walked out of meetings with Sergei Brin and Larry Page when she didn't get her way. She had quite the reputation. When Brin got married, two large private jets left SFO for the wedding in the Caribbean and Risa and Brad were on the first plane with the happy couple.

So it was so much fun to arrive with the other girls, ready to hear what the Queen of Startupland had to say, ready to be inspired at a time when all of us were getting pretty exhausted and a bit downhearted about how things would turn out for our companies with Demo Day looming closer and closer.

We were all dressed up, even the geekiest of us were in pretty fancy outfits. This was a big deal, so when Risa appeared at the door in yoga pants and a workout top, it was jarring.

"Oh yes, the Celery girl geeks," she said as her assistant showed her a listing on her clipboard. She welcomed us like we were something on her calendar she'd almost forgotten about, took us up in an elevator to the top floor, sat us in a large living room with a stunning view of the river — its brighter blue color a little more springtime-ish and well matched to the cheery lime-green leather sectional couch that could seat about 25 people. She disappeared into another room, leaving us with her assistant or houseboy or whatever he was, to take our coffee and tea orders. She left us there for easily a half hour, so we picked up things to read from the coffee table made of two bright green, blue and yellow surf boards and pretended to relax.

She returned in another outfit, some sort of white priestess gown, with tall white suede high-heeled boots, her hair in a taller white turban that looked like it was made of foam rubber. Drama queen for sure with a touch of sci-fi movie. Irina had met her match for outrageous outfits.

"Da!" Irina whispered to me and Sonya.

"I have an hour to tell you some things no one else will tell you and after that I have a day set up with about five other speakers I trust and like, and then they can help you each with your particular companies. I've assigned each of you to one of these advisors for a breakout session after lunch.

"By the way, please turn off anything you have with you, phones, iPads, iPhones, anything that can beep or burp or make any noise to interrupt us. And all of this is off the record, no quotes and no tweets and no blog posts and no sharing anything online about this. I've told Suzy if I see anything go public, I'll ask her to make sure you don't stay in the program.

"And, please, no questions while I talk for the next hour. I hate being interrupted. I'm sure I'll answer most of your questions anyway."

After this little speech, she'd just about worked us over to the point where we were all silenced.

Hmm, bully, I thought to myself. She must have gotten pushed around a lot in business by a lot of guys to end up with this thick a skin. She was like a little schoolyard bully girl, but a very pretty one.

Risa was weirdly human and like a fun best girlfriend you grew up with, but also super powerful, successful and arrogant. She started talking about growing up with three older brothers — as if to answer my bully question right off. She went on to talk about how she was always following them around and always expected to be one of the guys.

"I got to this coed boarding school when I was fourteen and I was used to being taken seriously. And I realized if I stood up like a young man and talked authoritatively about something, instead of being hailed like my brothers for their insightful opinions, it went the opposite way. It made people not like me at all. I saw that the popular girls never answered first in class and were always wasting time with their hair and makeup, and they made a point of acting more stupid than the boys. It was shocking to me. I had learned to argue with my brothers and my dad. They took me seriously and I expected no less of the world.

"So at school, I figured out that if you came on like a competent young man with confidence and credibility, most guys didn't like you and many girls didn't either. I realized they think you're either a lesbian or a bitch or both if you stand up, show confidence and speak your mind. And they just can't deal with a sexy, funny, smart woman who can hold her own."

There was a video screen behind her – almost the size of one whole wall – very big. She hit the remote and showed us two videos.

It was the "You can't handle the truth" movie clip with Jack Nicholson screaming at Tom Cruise.

"They can't handle it. So we have to be a little … sideways," she said, and turned sideways theatrically and stopped to see if we were listening.

"We need to be a bit sideways in our approach, slightly oblique, unexpected, come from an unusual angle. Powerful women are an instant target. A man hates losing out to a man, but he really hates losing to a woman. And as for guys taking orders from a woman, it's even worse. It's just very difficult still for many men."

She recounted a few more anecdotes about being "sideways," then her assistant pointed at his watch. "Let's take a break. Half an hour. Yes, you can turn your phones back on."

I'd managed to replace my iPhone with an Android in a record two days time.

I had a text from J-C. "At Commonwealth and Exeter. Pls cum talk 2 me." I had to remember to tell him that wasn't the right abbreviation for "come" in polite text.

I checked the time of the message. It had been sent five minutes before.

I texted him back. "Not a good idea."

"Please," he instantly replied.

Oh hell. I decided to give him a break and headed downstairs. I texted back, "5 minutes." The only other girls going outside were the smokers.

I walked through the courtyard and quickly turned right at the main gate and ran right into him.

A different him.

My soon-to-be-ex Nick Belden.

"What are you doing here?" I was stunned. "Did you come over to smash up my new phone?"

"Hi Honey. You know, we really just need to talk," he said sounding all sweet, but taking my elbow forcefully.

"I don't want to talk." I pulled my arm away, but he yanked it back, "Sounds like your lawyer told you to make nice with me."

"You need to come home," he said as if it made all the sense in the world.

"Home? I am home," I said.

I could see Jean-Claude beyond him, walking toward us.

"Let go of me," I said to Nick.

Jean-Claude rushed up. "Are you alright, Miss?"

Nick looked at him, "She's fine."

"I asked her, not you," Jean-Claude said.

"I'm better, now," I said.

"I was just leaving," Nick said in his usual surly tone, dropping my arm like I was a leper. He stormed off in the other direction.

I turned and walked back into the Levinsons' courtyard.

Jean-Claude followed me.

"Thank you," I whispered to him.

"My pleasure, Madam," he said, trying to be near me, but I backed away. "Can we talk? Just, deux minutes?"

The others were going in, I could see.

"I have to go," I said.

"Tu me manques," he said.

It was that inside out way the French had of saying, "I miss you."

"I really have to go," I said.

"Please give me another chance," he said.

Those eyes of his. They were just too much to look away from.

"Coffee later, just that, okay? I know you like coffee," he said.

"Okay, I'll text you," I left.

He watched me walk back inside. I turned at the last minute to look at him. He smiled back and gave me a thumbs-up.

Upstairs, I told Sonya what had happened.

"Nick?! Here?!"

"He's in town for some speaking gig."

"All we need," she said, "I'll tell the team to be sure not to talk to him."

"Ranji might try to knock his block off. You know Ranji's really good at karate."

"Duh, yeah!"

"I'm going to head into the ladies room before we start," I told her.

In the safety of the bathroom, I leaned against the wall to read a text from Jean-Claude.

"Madame. Happy to serve as your knight, any time. Count on me."

He was the strangest combo of cutting-edge modern and medieval. I smiled.

Risa was back at it. We settled in for the rest of her talk. She was talking about high school.

High school, ugh. God, she was telling me exactly what I'd gone through. She was spot on, describing my life then. It was a nightmare.

"So we're about, say, 15 or 16," Risa started. "We girls go through that time of suddenly seeing our adult sizes. That is, the form you will take for the rest of your life, and it's a shocker. The little dweeb guy from your history class in middle school is suddenly a giant in high school, but he's still the idiot you knew when he was younger. But now he's tall and male, you see others taking him seriously. And you notice if you're pretty, men are treating you like something good to eat. If you're not, they are ignoring you. Great being a girl, isn't it?"

She was telling some hard truths. It was so right on and jibed with everything we'd gone through. We clapped and cheered through parts of this speech.

"In high school you stop fooling yourself and you realize you're going to be a short curvy female the rest of your life, who men only take seriously in terms of your sexual identity and shape. It's like your brain stops being important to them. This is bad AND good. That means they never expect us to outmaneuver them and never know what hit them when we do. Our bodies have already betrayed us by the time we're about 16. They make us physically vulnerable to men, by their smaller size and men's obvious strength and larger body mass. And our hormones make us vulnerable to men. We are drawn to them and want to engage with them on that level. We want to mate. But all that works to keep us from being respected by them. They write us off, so we have to write ourselves back in.

"And that's just what happens in startup land. Any guy who walks into the room to pitch an idea is all about being a guy with a brain and any woman who walks in, if she's pretty, is taken seriously as a potential sexual conquest, but dismissed in terms of her intelligence. Or she is not sexy and she comes in and is tolerated since some men might have sisters or mothers who look like her and realize she may have good ideas, but they are instantly disappointed that she is not sexy. Because men's hormones from 15 to 50 are all about 'cherchez la femme' and they can't really turn that off. And the older males are even worse. They look at us like someone to bed, despite the fact that they are married or even if they are not, they have no right to even think of touching most 18-year-old girls — it's disgusting.

"And as a woman, you start to see many ways men cut women out of the game. You begin to understand the games going on all around you.

"So by the time you're about 25 and have some experience, you go in to pitch and see a guy is judged by his brain and his ideas, while you will always be judged by your cute outfit and curvy body.

We all groaned in agreement.

"It's not that they don't take you seriously because of your lack of experience or your idea isn't good or whatever. They simply can't take you seriously, because you're a woman and really — no matter how you look — you *are* beautiful. I want you to take that with you today, even if you take nothing else. You are beautiful and I want you to know that. And I don't mean, isn't being a female wonderful, but more the fact that you shouldn't ever let anyone else define your beauty.

"So here is the sad secret. They do take you seriously under one set of circumstances. They take you seriously if you're connected to another man. You want to talk 'valuation' when it comes to your companies — there's another kind of valuation we need to think about first. I know you don't want to hear it. You don't want to believe it's true. And I know all our smart lesbian sisters will hate this news, but if you want to have the alpha males take you seriously, you need to connect with some man that has high value.

"They will take you seriously if you're with a man. He's told the tribe you matter, setting your valuation in advance, because he wants you. Which is why they took me seriously, because I was with one of the most powerful guys in Silicon Valley.

"So they say you need more than one founder, or maybe two, or fewer than three, but what they don't say is that you should really start by being a man, not a woman, and then getting another male co-founder. So I say, be the most beautiful woman you can be and get a male co-founder. He can be the person who speaks because other men can hear him and they can't hear you as a woman.

"You could say just about anything about your startup and no man will hear you if you're a woman because he's busy thinking, 'I wonder if I could get her into bed?' And if you were thinking about sex all the time, how on earth could you be interested in someone's excellent elevator pitch? Who cares about startups when it comes to sex? Sex always wins."

"Think about it. Even Hillary Clinton, with all her experience as Secretary of State and all the years in the White House with her husband, making her ridiculously qualified, everyone still talks about her hair and what she's wearing! It's absurd.

"And notice all the bullshit that has been said by male VCs about why they don't like to invest in married founders. Truth is, it's all about the fact that it's harder for VCs to manipulate or cheat a young male founder if his wife is privy to everything going on. They don't want you in the mix. You're too smart.

"They flip the switch in high school. They change the rules. You learn about sex. You learn about rape and you learn men are in charge because of their physical superiority. And every elevator pitch you make for the rest of your life has to be part seduction, to make the men listening think you might sleep with them, and part self-effacing manipulation to take your good idea and let a man, your co-founder, say it for you. You slip it into the conversation without a fuss, wait five minutes and then let the men in the room think it was their idea, because only their ideas are brilliant. A brilliant woman is too much trouble.

"So my advice is go to Silicon Valley and take the shittiest job with the best startup you can and find a guy you can work with — might be another intern sitting three feet from you, might be the CEO of that startup. Get a co-founder who can help put you on the radar."

I raised my hand. I was hearing my heart beat in my throat. I was getting sweaty.

"I did that and he stole my idea and he's pushing me out of 'our' company," I said.

"Are you Monica Kroy?" she said.

"Yes," I said, surprised she remembered.

"Kind of a special case, let's talk after this," she said, and seemed to sweep my question under the carpet.

"What happened to Monica can happen to anyone, but do I know who Monica is. Notice? Did you know her name when you met her? You should have. Does she prove my theory? Does she get noticed? YES!"

This was her brilliant advice? Hmmm. Was it still so bad out there that all of us women founders were still in the trenches, trying to get noticed?

"Let me put it differently. Is it hard to get noticed? Yes, very difficult and as we sit here two geeks at a coffee shop near MIT are planning one more startup company and another bunch are at the Starbucks in Harvard Square and more out at Babson and some down at Mass Challenge. In fact, their class is ten times bigger than yours, so there is a lot of competition out there. It isn't easy to ever get noticed, but I'll teach you how."

She was dragging us from downhearted to totally depressed. I thought her little pep talk might have a happy ending, but wasn't optimistic.

"Any questions? It's time for lunch."

Whoa, was all I could think. I know we ate some lunch, but my head was elsewhere. I emailed my lawyer to tell her Belden had shown up. I went over to talk to Risa one on one.

"What do you think about all the green initiatives? Are there any that you think are really innovative?"

"There's one in Colorado out of Boulder that's mind-blowing, and one in Amsterdam you should check out," she said. "I'll ask my assistant to send you stuff."

"Thanks," I said and actually blushed.

"You're on the right track though. I think renewable energy and environmental startups will go from nice-to-have to desperate-to-have soon enough, I'd say in three years. If I were launching something now, I'd only work in that area. Oh, there's also a guy at Harvard you should go see. He's an Israeli, you should meet him. I'll email you about it."

Three other women came over to talk to her. We were sharing the day with some of the Rock Health women, an accelerator for biotech and medical startups. I was intrigued by what they were doing, but the testing for anything pharmaceutical or medical meant clinical trials, which took forever. As an entrepreneur who liked to move fast, I could never sign up for that. They had to be pretty persistent to outlast all the objections and regulatory issues – years and years of them.

I got a text from J-C as I walked over to get some lunch from the buffet table. He wanted to meet me after the meeting for dinner. I texted back, "Not sure when I'll B done."

He was quickly back, "Coffee doesn't work. Dinner? 7:30 my house."

"Should work," I texted back.

"Dinner matters," he said. "And 2 neighbors will be there."

I did owe him.

"OK, I O U for saving me."

"Pas de problem, Madame."

After lunch, the afternoon was focused on business, a long discussion of which VCs were willing to work with women, how to approach them and the "black list" she called it, of VCs to avoid. There were breakout sessions in a few rooms of her big house. She wanted to recommend each of us to a certain investor after we'd given her a briefing on our companies. We lined up on a bench outside her office and then went into her office one by one to give her our pitch.

When I came in, she pushed back from the desk, walked over to the far side of the room and looked out the window at the courtyard below. And then she said, "I saw him downstairs. You need a restraining order. He's really a bastard."

I flushed hot to hear her. I couldn't think of what to say.

"You know, right? Did he ever tell you?" she looked me dead straight in the eye.

I didn't know what she was talking about.

"I dated Nick. It was a long time ago," she said.

Wow.

"No, I didn't know," I said.

"Very few people know," she said. "It ended badly. I don't like him."

"Same here."

"So I have an idea for you. First I'll help you any way I can to get away from him and even do him a little damage. Second, I want you to get in to see as many VCs as possible, as soon as possible. I want you in there ahead of the rest of the Celery teams, because he will be trying to block you I'll bet."

"I'm ready to go," I said, though I really didn't feel at all ready and it was scary. Still, I'd gone to all the pitch meetings with Nick on Sand Hill Road and many others by the time I was 25, so it wasn't new to me.

"Let's start with the golden oldies, then the newer shops. You can practice on the Route 128 crew first. Take your developers — they're guys, right?"

"Yes, Ranji, Puff and Sanjay," I said.

"That's perfect. I'm going to call Metcalfe at Polaris for you. He'll put you through your paces and even though he growls like an angry bear, he's a sweetheart. I'll set you up with as many appointments as we can this week. And let's get something in the press about you, on the tech blogs."

"Sounds good." I was thinking about what the heck I should wear.

"You're thinking about what to wear," she said.

"HOW did you know that?"

"Hey, I'm a girl too, right?"

"I know what I'd wear in California, but this is different."

"I'll take care of it, I'll have one of my assistants take you shopping."

"You REALLY don't like Nick, do you?"

"He owes me and he definitely owes you," she said.

"Thank you," I said.

"Does Mr. Perfect still snore?" she said with a snicker.

"Yep. Like a lawn mower. " I smiled. "The noisy kind."

Chapter 17

Dinner Matters

I gave Sonya the dirt on the meeting with Risa when I came out. Getting to the good stuff first.

"We're pitching all over the place and her assistant is taking me shopping," I told her.

"Way to go!" Sonya said.

"Yes, she said it just like that. She's stepping up to help all the teams led by women," I said. Especially the ones led by people Nick wanted to destroy.

"That sounds crazy, but it was nice of her."

It was growing dark, even cold and a bit wet. We hurried back to the Charles Street /MGH platform to wait for the next T car with the well-dressed Back Bay residents and many medical people dressed in blue scrubs who worked at Mass General Hospital and all the other hospitals in the area.

Sonya and I parted at the Kendall Station. She had to go back to work and I was headed to Jean-Claude's for dinner, but I didn't tell her that. I didn't want her to know what a bad job of avoiding him I was doing. It was embarrassing; to tell him it was over the day before and now show up at his house for dinner. Was I ever this goofy in love with Nick?

The train rumbled out of the station. I was thinking of how I first noticed Jean-Claude's odd habit of vanishing at the end of the day. Whatever we were doing at the Celery offices — meeting with all the CEOs or the teams, or listening to a lecture or seminar by some famous mentor of ours — at about 7 o'clock, Jean-Claude would invariably get up and leave. We didn't know why he did this or whether it was a privilege or accommodation that the directors had extended to him for some reason (religious? dietary?), but he seemed to have permission to just leave.

I really missed him I noticed one evening in the first few weeks of the program when he just disappeared at 7. Then I found out what he was up to. He was going home to cook dinner.

Dinner? No entrepreneurs bothered with an actual dinner. A burrito or a slice of pizza was the usual. And less than nobody actually *cooked* dinner. It was just one more wild thing about the Wild Boy of Aveyron. He cooked and ate dinner at 8:00 most nights, even when all the other programmers wanted to spend the whole evening coding. This was very un-American and very un-entrepreneurial.

We figured he must have an important secret meeting with some VC or finance guys, but it wasn't that at all. He was just going home, to go to the market, shop for fresh food and cook.

The Broadway Market near his place off Prospect in Harvard Square had the fresh things he liked and good

French bread too. That's where we found ourselves at the end of the day I'd spent in Back Bay at Risa's townhouse.

"Your brain can't work all night, the small wheels start burning up. No lubrication. Very bad. Ce n'est pas bon. Dinner matters," he explained.

"You must think this country is really crazy," I said.

"C'est un pays des sauvages," he said.

"Thanks, I get it, we're a nation of savages," I said.

"I have … invitées, so I can't just abandon them. They are … mes invitées … my guests. Actually just four of us tonight," he explained as if it made all the sense in the world.

At the market, he poked at the fruits, smelled all the vegetables, sent me to find a good loaf of bread and talked to the butcher about the lamb chops.

"They loaned me some of their best pans – like a risotto pan which I love," he said.

"Who they?"

"My neighbors, the ones I invited tonight."

"I always thought you left early to visit mysterious millionaires and then worked all night," I told him.

"Some nights I work; mostly I don't. I get better ideas when I eat well and when I sleep well and when I …" he looked up at me.

His eyebrow raised in a seductive way.

The French had no trouble communicating essential truths.

"Don't you?" is all he said.

"No, I'm an American. We work like crazy idiots all the time," I said.

"I'm afraid you think you are machines," he said.

"Maybe," I said.

"You work like silver robots," he said.

"Row boats?" I said.

"You know." He spelled it, "R-o-b-o-t-s."

"Robots, right, thanks," I said in my robotic voice, "wel-come-to-the-land-of-the-free-home-of-the-brave! Have-a-good-day."

He leaned over and poked me in the ribs.

"Hey, Mister," I jumped. "Let's not forget the meat." The butcher had wrapped it up and put it on the end of the counter. I pointed at it.

"Thank you sir!" he called after the butcher, as we picked it up.

We headed down the next aisle.

"More work doesn't mean you get more ideas or better ideas. It means you get tired and may miss the best ideas," he explained. "We need cheese."

The cheese counter was on the other side of the store. We found some excellent cheese. He showed me the French ones and explained that for some of the types, like Camembert, they only sent the bad ones to the U.S. because the really good ones were unpasteurized.

"It's about the AOC, you know, appellation d'origine controlee, tu sais," he explained.

"Whatever you say," I said.

He found a local one from Vermont and after unwrapping it and smelling it, decided it would do well enough. It was a little stinky.

Tonight his guests were a sexy Spaniard named Raoul, who played the mandolin and his wife Seema, a painter. They lived down the hall. They were already at his place waiting for us, since he'd given them keys to his apartment. He was strumming his mandolin, stretched out on cushions in the front room. He was another startup guy. She told me she was studying at the Harvard School of Design.

We sat in his living room, playing and singing while Jean-Claude made dinner in the kitchen. We drank dark red wine they had brought, very strong Spanish wine. They sang some folk songs I knew and we made good harmony together.

I went in to help Jean-Claude with the dinner prep and talk shop about Celery. After a while, Seema wandered in.

"Jean-Claude, why didn't you bring Monica sooner? She has a good voice and can sing with us. Do you want to sing with us on Saturday at Passim's?" she asked me.

"Wow, thanks, but I'm busy that evening."

"It's ready. Shall we start?" J-C said.

We sat in his front room as he served up lamb chops, cous cous, salad and wine.

"When do you have good ideas?" Jean-Claude asked them.

Raoul was an entrepreneur. He had started something like the Spanish Twitter. He was about 30 and very rich J-C told me.

"In the shower or making love," Raoul said.

We laughed. His wife gave him a rather ambiguous look, as if she were saying, "Making love with whom?"

"No, really, do you think working all the time helps?" J-C said, "Because Monica and I were talking about it, how Americans work like robots."

"The best ideas," Raoul said, "come about when you are playful, not workful."

"So why does everyone work so hard in these startup accelerators?" J-C asked.

"I think they feel guilty if someone has given them money. That they need to look busy, like they deserve it, like the investors are getting something for their money," Seema said. "But it's a factory worker mentality. It makes no sense."

"Where do good ideas come from?" J-C continued, then started filling our glasses.

"In vino veritas!" Seema toasted. We clinked glasses.

"Think about good ideas lately," Raoul said, "All the big companies in the last 10 years – Facebook, Twitter, Instagram – they are all one thing."

"Simple ways to connect?" I said.

"Just that first word," he said. "They are very simple. Like a hit tune, it's usually a simple song with simple lyrics. I Want to Hold Your Hand."

"It's hard to be simple," I said.

"Yes. But they are also about connecting people," J-C said, "and some are more social, some started as a way to … you know, chercher la femme. They are about love."

"Not so." Seema didn't like this.

"Mais oui. You know FB started that way, Zuckerberg said so. And Twitter's important now for world leaders, but at the beginning it was just trying to see if there was a pretty girl you liked in the area you were in and what she was doing," Jean-Claude protested.

"I call those b2g apps, boy-to-girl apps," I said.

"Yes," Raoul smiled provocatively at me. "For dating and mating."

It seemed oddly flirtatious, right in front of Seema, but she wasn't watching.

"Best platform there is," J-C said. "It's nature, most of us are here to find a mate and then make children."

"You are such a caveman, Jean-Claude, really!" Seema said with a tone of disappointment.

"Perhaps," J-C grinned, obviously liking the idea of being a cave dweller.

"You know about Chanel and how she started," Seema said.

"Chapeaux," J-C said, like everyone knew this.

"Yes, she made hats, but she was always trying to create something classic and simple, stripped down," Seema said.

Raoul was playing with his tablet. "Edison failed about 200 times before inventing the light bulb. The problem is, the only people who really get the 'failure' thing are artists. They are completely used to tossing sketches out, and writers too, with their balled up, crumpled paper. They know how to throw away ideas, and it's really acceptable for them. It would be strange if they didn't throw away bad ideas on the way to good ideas, but hardware and software folks still feel like the stuff is sacred and to scrap it all and start over seems crazy."

"Maybe because it was so expensive before," J-C said. "It was when you think of it like in the '80s and '90s before you could run everything out of the cloud."

"The mighty cloud!" Seema said dramatically.

"Yes," I said.

I went into the kitchen to get more water. I was getting too drunk too fast on that Spanish wine. I was running the water and turned to notice Seema entering the kitchen. She came right over to me.

"You have a beautiful voice," she said, stroking my face.

She certainly was friendly.

"Ah, thanks," I said.

And then she came right up close and kissed me.

A real kiss on the lips.

I was really surprised, caught off guard. Then she smiled, touched my hair and went back into the living room.

Whoa. I was not expecting that and I couldn't even figure out why I hadn't resisted. I drank a full glass of water, as if it were an antidote.

When I went back into the dining room, she was seated closer to me, but reaching across the table, stroking J-C's cheek.

This was certainly getting confusing.

"It really doesn't matter," she was saying.

I wanted to ask "what doesn't matter," but felt shy.

"Do you think it matters, Monica?" Raoul asked me.

"What?"

"Do you think it matters," J-C said, "if you sleep with some of the people on your team? I mean in a startup."

"Well," I said, taking a minute to take this all in. "I think it matters or might matter a lot to the other people on the team you DON'T sleep with. That kind of thing always has a way of becoming public."

Raoul had his theories. "But Monica, think of it this way. You need a team that completely trusts one another. You need loyalty. And the team should be small enough that there are no secrets or hidden agendas."

"Are you making a case for sleeping with every one on the team? That's an interesting version of team bonding," I said. "I'd vote no on that."

"As for secrets, darling," Seema began, "even between us, there are secrets and there are only two of us."

"Secrets?" he said, arching his eyebrow at his wife.

"Oh yes, deep dark secrets, like what I bought for dessert," she said. She went over to the desk where J-C's computer was sitting. She pulled a cake out of a white bakery box.

"Red velvet cake!" Jean-Claude was excited.

"I love that," I said.

"Monica, didn't you work for your lover at your last startup?" Raoul asked bluntly.

My favorite subject! Great. Was this Nick Belden Day?

"My lover? No, I mean, yes, but he wasn't my lover, he was my husband. And at first, I wasn't working for him, my husband and I were co-founders."

"You started your company after getting married?" Seema asked.

She was looking at me in a sexy way. It was undeniable. She was coming on to me. It made me really uncomfortable.

"We started it when we were dating, then we got married after about two years," I said.

I told them the very abbreviated story of my husband, how I was worried he was trying to cheat me out of my shares. Raoul was very savvy about this type of thing and I wondered what hell he'd been through, or put others through when selling his company.

"What a tale!" Seema said.

"Didn't the Zynga guy try that?" Raoul said.

"Take the programmers' options?" I asked.

"Something like it," J-C said. "Stupid fucking idiot. The guys who built the thing, those are the guys you should treat like royalty, instead of kicking them in the head? C'est fou, quoi!"

"It happens," Raoul said.

"Let me get the cheese plate," J-C said, getting up, "Monica help me."

"Sure," I said getting up.

In the kitchen, J-C told me his neighbors wanted to sleep with both of us.

"What?" I said.

He started laughing.

"I'm kidding," he said.

"Don't mess with me," I said. "His wife just kissed me!" I whispered.

"She did?" he said looking surprised.

"Yes, when I came in here for some water, she layed one on me. A real kiss. What's her deal?"

"She may like zee girls," he put on his phony French accent.

"She freaked me out a bit," I said.

He started to smile.

"Come here," he said, "I'm sorry this is a crazy night for you." He gave me a hug, a surprisingly brotherly hug. It wasn't exactly how I was feeling about him, but in that moment, it was exactly right.

"I have to go actually, after the cheese course," I said, pulling away.

"Busy girl," he said, not looking at me directly. I got the feeling he wanted me to stay, but wouldn't admit it.

"Yes, true. I already took too much time away from the factory," I said.

"All work, no play makes Monica a dull robot," he warned.

"You don't think I'm going to let you win this competition, do you?"

"I already have won," he said, like it was obvious.

"You sir, have thrown down the gauntlet," I said.

"Well, Madame, I guess we'll see about that on Demo Day," he said.

"We'll see long before then!" I taunted.

Back in the room, we finished up the dinner. I offered to clear, but he told me not to bother. Over on the desk in the corner of the room, I saw his computer's screensaver with the Celery logo in green and silver and the red velvet cake next to it.

"No time for cake?" Seema asked.

"Sorry, not tonight." I loved that kind of cake, but Seema seemed a little dangerous to me.

We said our goodbyes and I left the three of them to finish the wine, as I headed home to Porter Square. It occurred to me that maybe the three of them were sleeping together or had before. An unsettling thought. And to leave his house after being kissed, by the wrong person, that was even more confusing. I knew one thing though. I didn't want to be with the three of them. I wanted to be with the Frenchman.

It was so cold out, I pulled my scarf up around my head, nearly covering my face. That helped, but remembering what he looked like, how he smiled, what he said during dinner, replaying it again and again warmed me up even more. My whole body wanted him.

As I approached the T station, I walked right into a deep puddle of slush, getting my boots drenched, since I wasn't watching where I was going, but thinking of him instead. It had looked about an inch deep, but was more than three inches, very wet and very messy. When I finally got home and took off my boots, my socks were soaked and my feet were bright red.

I drew a hot bath, whipped up lots of bubbles with a new bath gel I'd splurged on at Sephora and lay there, thinking of him. The thought of sleeping with him on a cold night like this one gave rise to a terrible longing. I was seeing him again, as he had been at dinner, close and attentive, leaning over to serve me more wine. Wishing he'd leaned further over to kiss me. I was remembering something true and funny he had said about startups at dinner. Thinking of where I wanted him to touch me. Thinking of where I would touch him.

After my bath, I made my way to the bedroom, dried off quickly and slipped into the sheets. It wasn't easy to fall asleep at first and just as I was about to, even after my body did that funny jolt when you feel as if you're catching yourself from falling down a flight of stairs, a text noise woke me and I reached for my phone, knocking over a plastic tumbler of water on my nightstand. No major damage. Luckily it was almost empty.

The text was from Jean-Claude and said a simple "beaux rêves" and goodness knows I needed sweet dreams. I texted back "U 2" and put the phone on a dry place on the nightstand.

I did dream, first finding myself on a path in Harvard Yard, on a warm summer night, looking up at a building where the gothic carving of the words "In Vino Veritas" were engraved, then looking down to see I was naked and finding this funny but fine. After this I was running down a street to get back to J-C's apartment, banging hard on the door to get in. Seema opened the door and took me by the hand to the kitchen where Jean-Claude was.

The refrigerator door had all the schedules and welcome stuff from Celery on it and pictures of the mentors and a big picture of Nick Belden. Then it all changed and the door of the refrigerator was as big as an actual door and he opened it to show me a courtyard and a path and wanted me to go with him, but behind me Raoul took my other hand and pulled me back in the room with Seema.

They were in the kitchen. She was naked and he was kissing her and pushed me toward her, but I ran back to the door, trying to follow Jean-Claude.

But he was gone.

Then Raoul took hold of me and was making love to me, his face too close. Suddenly he was invisible but still I could feel his hands stroking me. I tried to step away from where he seemed to be, but he was wherever I moved. Even when I stepped far back, he was then behind me touching me in a very seductive way. I felt like it was impossible to resist climaxing. I pulled away and tried to open the doors and cupboards looking for Jean-Claude. Then I saw Raoul's hands reach for me again and looked up, but it wasn't Raoul, it was Jean-Claude. He was full of calmness, without saying anything, making me feel safe and wonderful. Giving me permission to cascade over the edge.

I woke from the dream with a rush of wetness between my legs and my heart pounding between my ears and in my toes and in my throat and everywhere else a heart could strangely travel.

Chapter 18

Beach

The week started early Monday morning at the fanciest place in Boston, Arlington at Newbury Street. Risa and her assistant met me at the Taj Hotel for breakfast and rolled out the battle plan. They had decided I was the perfect Chanel girl and dropped a ridiculous amount of money on me at that chic boutique. Sonya was running our Monday team meeting, letting the developers know they'd be heading out to meet VCs with me, while I was trying on Chanel classic pumps. In the afternoon, I worked with Risa on my pitch and the assistants took the rest of my team shopping.

We hit the biggies on Tuesday and Thursday, meeting with Polaris, Charles River, and GrandBanks. By Friday, it looked like three firms were ready to go in together on a first round of financing. Risa called me with the good news.

"They all have partner meetings on Monday, so you'll need to go back in to close the deals," she explained.

"Yikes," I said.

"Don't worry about it. You'll be fine," she told me.

The next week I had three more second meetings on Monday, and three new ones with Matrix, General Catalyst and Spark. Someone had leaked the story to *TechCrunch* and there was a piece about us and who we were talking to. It said we were close to a deal with the first bunch of VCs I'd visited. This made it touchy with the second bunch. It was like someone publishing the names of guys you'd slept with – it wasn't clear what it did for your reputation.

Risa didn't like the leak and called me a few minutes before the Monday partners' meeting at Polaris. "You didn't say anything to the press did you?"

"Not a thing," I said. "And nobody on my team did either."

"That means one of firms did, which is interesting," she said.

"I'm going in now" I had to hang up.

Ranji was waiting for me in the lobby of the Polaris building. He looked great.

"You'll kill them," he assured me.

"Or they'll kill us," I said. "Whatever happens, we have two more meetings today."

One of the pretty assistants who are all pretty, but pretty damned smart first and foremost, took us into Bob Metcalfe's office first. Bob wasn't only a little terrifying in temperament, but also an engineer who really knew his stuff. I'd been scared when I met him the week before, but now I was meeting him and six other partners. True terror.

We waited in his office before meeting the crowd in the conference room next door when they were ready. It's rare to meet someone who looks younger and thinner than their picture, but Bob did.

"Are you running the Boston Marathon next month?" I asked him, as he looked almost gaunt.

"No, no, I'm not a runner. I like to walk and bike," he said.

"Very reasonable," I said.

"But a bunch of our guys are running. Check out the blog."

He showed me a blog post about the guys at Polaris who were running the 116th Boston Marathon. They'd been practicing in the snowy streets for months.

We chatted about other runners at Celery who planned to run this year in the 2012 race. The walls of his office showed off other amazing things he had done and I tried hard not to be totally intimidated.

"We have a startup team of vets called MortalWarriors, who are all running this year," Ranji told him.

Bob asked after the directors of Celery. He was old friends with Walt, from their MIT days. His assistant poked her head in to say they were ready for us in the partners' meeting.

We headed in, shaking hands with all the Bills and Johns and Steves. They looked like buff prep school guys in very expensive, well-ironed blue shirts and khaki pants. VCs always gave me the feeling, "we're rich, brilliant and muscular, and you're totally wasting our time."

The meeting started with a thud. The shortest guy said bluntly, "Why would anyone want to buy this?" as an opener. I explained the problem we were solving, the "pain points" as they called them and managed to satisfy their first volley.

"I want to address the Hillary issue," the next one said. He was bearded, a little grey around the temples.

"Excuse me?"

"We know you were the wife of a very successful entrepreneur, but being the wife of a big dog is not the same as being Big Dog."

This is a thinly veiled version of, "Why should some girl be CEO?"

Ranji let out a slight grunt, giving voice to how I felt about this idiotic question. I didn't have time to show my displeasure, but launched into the truth.

I explained how I basically handed Nick Belden the idea for the first company and coded it myself. I wasn't some geek trophy wife, spending my days puzzling over couch color swatches or picking out lighting fixtures for the mansion in Los Altos all those years.

As a woman, it was always tricky to avoid sounding like you had a big head. It's fine to have a big head if you're man, but not if you're woman entrepreneur.

They shot a few more questions at me and Bob got up to say why my company deserved some funding. They asked us to step out of the room.

Ranji said, "Jesus Christ, that sure was fun."

I snorted quietly.

"You did a good job," he said.

"I guess we'll find out how good."

Then they signaled for us to come back in.

"We don't like to waste time. We voted and we're going to have to pass on this." Bob said, shooting an annoyed look at the one with the beard, like he was the dissenting vote. It was strange. After Bob's optimism, I thought it might happen, but we didn't have time to linger, so we thanked them and headed over to Charles River Ventures to attend their partners' meeting as well.

After the first meeting, it seemed to go even better at Charles River and Ranji answered some technical questions very well.

Again, we did *not* get a thumbs-up. They passed.

I called Risa after this.

"I wish I could tell you what's going wrong. I don't get it. They were so into us last week."

"It may be the press you got in *TechCrunch*. They all like to work in stealth mode as long as possible. They don't like to be outed," she speculated.

We rallied and headed to the next meeting. Again, things were going well from what I could tell and Ranji agreed, but we continued to get the thumbs-down.

It had started to rain, making it an even more depressing day. And then, as Boston weather likes to do, the rain became snow and then icy little pellets of sleet. I wanted to yell at the sky, "You're ruining my very expensive Chanel pitching duds, so just stop it!"

At the last meeting of the day, one of the VCs brought his Magic 8-Ball to the meeting and they were all joking that the ball always told the truth and provided the best investment advice.

We did our pitch, the best of the day in fact, because by now we just didn't care. Ranji explained some technical considerations to the group expertly. I was proud of him.

They asked us to wait outside the glass conference room.

Ranji and I watched as they shook the 8-ball and all leaned over carefully to read it and motioned for us to come back in.

"The 8-ball says, 'Concentrate and ask again!' "

They shook it again.

The youngest partner showed it to me, "Very doubtful."

The senior partner said seriously, "Sorry, we'll have to pass."

Ranji knew enough to say a polite good-bye, thank you and drag me out of there before I punched one of them in the face.

"Just walk, walk, yes, keep walking," he whispered to me and practically pushed me all the way down the hall.

"That was the STUPIDEST thing I've ever seen," I pulled out my phone.

"No tweeting it. Please, restrain yourself."

"Oh. My. God!" I said loudly.

"Just walk, just walk," he chanted.

We left the premises and I called Risa's office to tell her about this last run-around.

Risa was trying hard to keep up with what was going wrong. But none of the important partners would even return her calls, which she said was seriously strange.

By mid-week the weather snapped into warm again and Risa ordered us to take the day off. It was very good advice. It was March, but actually warm for Boston, nearly 50 degrees, hardly beach weather, but I wanted to see the ocean. I asked Sonya to go with me down to Woods Hole, on the edge of the Cape, to keep me out of trouble. The guys stayed back in town to do a code review. They'd done a new mock-up of our app, and were hoping to complete a working prototype.

There are days when your usual optimistic, upbeat, cocky, entrepreneurial attitude just abandons you by the side of the road. Your little car of dreams can't go one more mile or meter further. Sputter, sputter, sputter, dead. You just are out of gas. You have to take a rest from the non-stop pushing, pitching, dreaming, hoping of it all. You need to get away, relax, rest and then come back to it.

Everything you loved about your product you hate. Everything you thought was inspired seems pointless. Every problem you've been trying to solve, doesn't seem worth solving. You are in a dangerous spot. You need to just step away.

That's how we ended up on a bus to Woods Hole. I had never been there, but an old boyfriend worked at the Marine Biology Lab and lived in Falmouth and was always inviting me there the summer after we broke up. It sounded great, but he sounded sad and wanted to get back together and I wasn't going to step into a mess again. I would have only been a bigger heartbreak for him, so I never went.

It was cloudy and cool, not very nice but as soon as the bus pulled out of the station, the sun broke through and I decided to call that a blessing for our road trip, a thumbs-up sign from on high.

Of course, the real funk I had fallen into was about Jean-Claude, and Sonya knew it and knew not to bring it up, at least at first.

It was spring and there was suddenly no snow and some sun and even some flowers blooming.

"I can't believe how long it takes to get around to spring here compared to California," I said. "It's like a joke. How do people live here?"

"I know, it's pretty crazy," she said, paging through a big glossy fashion magazine.

Reading *Vogue* and *Elle* and eating red Australian licorice as we headed to Cape Cod on a half-empty bus, already put me in a better mood. It was a "to hell with everything and everyone" kind of day, which was fine for me.

We were good with one another when we were talking and good without talking too. I had earbuds in for the second half of the trip, listening to love songs from the '80s. You know you're in love when you can listen to really schlocky sticky music and get all mushy. Some of the songs actually brought tears to my eyes. Yes, I Wanna Know What Love Is. Who doesn't want to know?

The bus reached the last stop all too soon and we shuffled out and down the stairs to explore Woods Hole. The first thing you see at the bus stop is the ferry for Martha's Vineyard.

"Hey, wanna take the boat over?" Sonya asked me.

It did sound like fun.

"Actually … I don't think so, because of getting back and all, it might make us pretty late and the water looks churned up."

"Hey Chica, what happened to my risk taker?"

"Don't ask why, but today has to be about comfort, no adventure for me. We're always trying new things, risking this or that. Well, today, just forget about risk today. Today I want meatloaf."

"Meatloaf?"

"You know, comfort food. I need a rest from 'pushing the envelope' as they love to say. And no out-of-the-box thinking today for me. I'm thinking no envelope, no box or if we find a box, I'm crawling into it."

"Wow," Sonya said. "I don't usually hear you sounding like this."

"Don't tell anybody."

Something about Woods Hole reminded me of the old sea shanty-type town where Popeye lived in the crazy *Popeye* movie. I loved that movie. It had all the right sun-bleached wooden shacks with ropes and harpoons hanging everywhere and dried fish skeletons and buoys. But with all the research labs at the Marine Biology Lab and Woods Hole Oceanographic Institution and other facilities there, it looked like MIT mixed up with Gilligan's Island.

I started singing the opening theme to Gilligan's Island.

"A three-hour tour, a three-hour tour … " I sang ominously.

"Hell, girl, do you know every TV show theme?"

"Come listen to my story, 'bout a man named Jed, poor mountaineer barely kept his family fed …"

"I sure don't know that one."

"Beverly, Hills that is, swimming pools, movie stars," I sang. Wish I had a banjo.

We walked past the tourist shops, and restaurants and ice cream stands, most not open yet. The town only started to boom after Memorial Day.

We came to a restaurant called The Fishmonger.

"This work for you?" I said pointing at the menu.

"Looks good and best of all, it's open!" It was so early in the year and most places were closed.

They didn't have meatloaf, but we got the next best thing – seaside comfort food. We ordered fish and chips, both of us, and beer. It was funny to drink beer, when it was just us girls. Seemed like the beer thing was always about Celery parties and the other geek guys around us who were busy drinking beer non-stop.

"I can't mess with him," I said.

That's the thing about girlfriends, you can say a statement like that and they know exactly who the "him" is — in this case Jean-Claude; and they know what "mess with" means — it meant get involved with him while I was doing the Celery program. Girlfriends know whether you really wanted to talk about it or you were just making an announcement, drawing a line in the sand, mostly for yourself — in this case, I didn't want to talk about it. Sonya got all this.

"Until you destroy Nick."

"Exactly."

Toward the end of lunch, after the waiter went off to get our check, a guy came over to our table and introduced himself. Tall, Ivy-league attired, nearly a crew cut, in full red Nantucket summer slacks, white Lacoste polo shirt, navy blazer, gold buttons. Classic.

"I'm John Alexander from Alexandria Ventures. Aren't you Monica Belden?" he asked.

"Yes, hello John," I said, shaking hands. "This is Sonja Hernandez, my CIO."

"I'm sorry it didn't work out last week, I had to go to California," he explained. He had cancelled at the last minute.

John was the lead venture capital guy from a firm I'd been dying to meet, the top of the top firms. I was surprised he even recognized us.

"I don't know if you know what's been going on, but I was at a party for a new startup out there and I heard your ex has been trash-talking you to all the VCs."

So THIS was the reason all deals were falling apart.

"Really?" I said.

"Yep, and that he placed the piece about you in *TechCrunch*. One of the editors at the party was telling me it was unusual for someone like Nick to call them up out of the blue," he explained.

"I didn't know that," I said. Risa was really going to be on fire about this.

"Listen, I'm heading to Martha's Vineyard today, but I'll be in the office Friday. Why don't you come see me and give me your pitch?"

"That would be great," I said. "We'll be there."

"Here," he said handing me his card. "Call my assistant and ask her to find you a half hour."

"Thank you so much." I did sound like a big baby.

"Have a good time on the Vineyard," Sonya said.

He looked at his watch. "Next ferry is leaving in ten minutes. Call Jacqueline, she'll set it up."

He was gone and I looked at Sonya.

"Ask me if I'm surprised about Nick," I said.

She said some scary nasty swear words in Spanish.

I called Risa.

She was just as angry as I was about Nick sabotaging our deals.

"I'm thrilled you'll get to see John, he's a great guy and his shop is so hot right now," she said.

Take a day at the beach and you never know what will happen. Things can change.

We spent that day walking the town streets, visiting shops, then going to the beach, getting sandy, but not swimming, since it was still too cold. We felt like kids on vacation. Even if it was only one day, we needed it. I slept the whole way back on the bus, which was great because I had been staying up late too many nights in a row. We got back to town in time for the pitch-night dinner.

Chapter 19

After Midnight

I went into the main conference room to look over our pitch before the meeting got going. Jean-Claude breezed right in and sat next to me, first saying a friendly "salut" and giving me the standard unsexy two-cheek kisses of greeting. Still, for me, there was nothing unsexy about him. He was like a drug walking in, a drug I thought I had kicked. Didn't he know we wasn't supposed to be there tempting me? I pretended to be fascinated by my PowerPoint slides and a few minutes after he'd settled in, Sonya ran in and begged me to go work with her on something about our pitch she said was all messed up, so I excused myself and went back to our desks with her. I was glad for the excuse to avoid him. I just couldn't sit next to him without wanting him. It was too hard. We slipped back into the conference room just as the meeting was starting.

Suzy came in grinny and happy-looking, striding along next to the tall, way too handsome Aussie team leader, Chris. They shared a laugh over something. Then she got up in front of the crowd, she did a Dr. Jekyll flip from smiley to grim, letting her inner bitch awaken and give us hell.

"Welcome to Get Real Week," she said. "I have to say I'm not at all happy with where you're all at after this many weeks into the program. I need you to get real about what you're doing and how you're showing your ideas to the world. Most of you have a bad idea, bad software and aren't even a quarter of the way done coding a real prototype. We're past half way through the program. Honestly. Your stuff sucks."

This will be fun, I thought. Still, after a week of real pitching to real investors, this couldn't be that tough.

"And tonight, I'm sure you CEOs are ready to pitch, but I want to pick someone else on your team to present. By this point, everyone on your team should know the value proposition of your startup down cold. Anyone on your team should be able to pitch. Brightlight, you're up first, bring your team up here Monica."

My team was exhausted from working all night for a few nights. I was hoping to hell Suzy wouldn't pick one of my developers.

We stood in line and Suzy walked up and down, as if she were a drill sergeant checking to see if our shoes were shined and our uniforms in perfect shape.

"Sonya, do the pitch," Suzy said. "The rest of you sit down."

Thank goodness she and I had the quiet day at Woods Hole and some sleep on the bus home. Sonya pulled it off quite well, I thought, but when she was done, Suzy fired question after question about the product and what it did on different platforms, who would buy it, what it cost. Sonya was sweating her way through that, but handling all the rough stuff.

When she finally sat down, we all took a deep breath. She'd saved our team, but the rest of the room was getting very tense.

Jean-Claude's group went next and his lead engineer was really nervous. It wasn't good. He struggled through the pitch and then they gave the floor to the Russians, but he wasn't going to get away that easily. Suzy interrupted Slava and gave J-C's team a stern critique.

The Russians had even more trouble, and more troublesome comments from Suzy. Team after team, the funeral procession marched along. Suzy used every team's mistakes to lash out at all of us, reminding us of things we had done wrong. We were never so happy to see the food arrive for the dinner break.

At dinner, each team sat together, just helping the presenters nurse their wounds on the teams that had already presented, or trying to pump up the teams who hadn't gone yet. Marshall was really sweating it, since his team was the least prepared.

Keeping away from Jean-Claude was easier because of all the team bonding going on, but it didn't mean I didn't want him. I missed him. I wanted to talk to him. I wanted to kiss him. But that was not going to happen, I chided myself. I looked over once to try to steal a casual peek at him, only to find him staring at me in a sexy way. I looked back to my team and asked a question, just to avoid his look.

We piled back into the conference room and Marshall's team was up. Suzy picked Sheba, the manicurist and I just about prayed she'd pull it out some how.

Sheba got up, cleared her throat and began. She was right on it. She delivered the elevator pitch seriously and authoritatively. I saw Marshall's shoulders go from tense to relieved in just a few moments. Sheba knew she was hitting it out of the ballpark and got a little looser and funny. It was awesome. When it was done, Suzy started the Q&A and Marshall asked if the other teammates could help Sheba out, which they did. I don't know how many others knew this team was nothing but an experiment, but I looked at Marshall with big eyes to say, "Amazing!"

The whole evening was unpleasant and long but then, even though most of us were tired as hell and just wanted to leave, Suzy sent us back at our desks to fix the problems that had come up.

Suzy was patrolling the halls, like we were bad kids at school in detention as we got back to work with our teams to get a new version done, or test the current version, or publish a new release. Most teams left at midnight, but my team and J-C's team at the other end of the hallway were there until 2 a.m. I was glad I'd slept earlier on the way back from Woods Hole.

Finally, I sent my team home and was alone at my desk. J-C sent his team home right after this and we were the only ones left. He walked over to my desk and I was never happier to see him.

"Stupid macho bullshit startup robot stuff," he spit out.

I laughed.

"You're right. It was like we were body builders and we had to press 800 pounds before we could go home."

"Totally stupid," he said.

"Wasn't Sheba great?" I asked.

"Yes, very good."

There was an awkward silence between us, a rare thing. I looked at my screen.

"Ça va?" he asked.

"Good enough, but tired." I got up to get ready to go, pulled my coat on.

"No, I mean. Are WE… okay?" he asked.

"Sure, just tired," I said not looking at him. "Just tired" was the great girl lie. It should set off fire alarms in any smart guy's head. It really meant, everything is wrong with us, pal, but I'm going to let *you* figure that out.

Mostly, I was trying very hard not to look at him. Again, any smart man should know this meant big trouble. He let out a breath, indicating he wasn't sure what to say.

"It's just us here, I think. I mean, no one's left," he said looking around.

"Yes?"

"You're knowing how the locking up works?" His English wasn't good this late in the day, especially on a day like this. He got a little sloppy and said really cute things.

"Are we really the last ones?" I was surprised.

"Yes, all alone, just us," he left his tone ambiguous, it could be suggestive or it might be simply factual.

"I think we just pull the main door closed behind us," I said.

"I'll go with you," he said. "Give me … une minute." He used an app on his phone to call an Ubercab.

It was so hard not to want to follow him anywhere and curl up next to him in any bed we found, but I had to avoid that. Still, at nearly 3 in the morning, I wasn't going to argue about taking a cab with him, since it wasn't safe to leave the building alone.

He went back to his desk to get his stuff.

He saw something on his monitor and registered a little jolt.

He beckoned me to come over and then made the "shhhh" sign by putting his finger to his lips.

He pointed to his monitor, which was reflecting the offices behind him, the little lights in the windows and at the end of the hallway, in the screen you could see Suzy and Chris the Aussie in a very steamy embrace. They couldn't see us from where we were.

He raised an eyebrow.

I made a face back at him, like, no big surprise, and shrugged. Having a Hugh Jackman look-alike hanging around the office was nothing easy to resist. And he was a really nice guy.

He made a "let's go" gesture with his thumb like, we'd better get out of here.

We packed up quietly and headed out.

Riding the elevator, we didn't say anything.

When we went outside, there was a fancy black Ubercab he'd called.

He opened the door to the cab, let me in and then said good night quickly, with another French social kiss, one on each cheek. He did not get in the cab with me, but told the driver my address, closed the door and left. I saw him walk off in the other direction, as if he had an important appointment somewhere in Boston at 3:30 a.m. The cab pulled away from the curb, did a U-turn and we headed away from him on the lonely street.

Chapter 20

Bettina Across the Universe

The girls were all in the conference room, waiting to meet Bettina Hein, the CEO of Pixability. I had heard nothing but great stuff about her and couldn't wait to hear what she had to say. She'd started a company, sold it and this was her second software company that helped companies be successful on YouTube. In fact, she was the author of *Video Marketing for Dummies*. How the heck any CEO had time to write a book was hard to imagine.

It was one of those lousy early spring days – cold and grey and icy even though it was almost April. Thanks to our "evening" ending at 3:30 a.m. and the bad weather, I was nearly late for the 10 a.m. meeting. I couldn't wait to hear Bettina speak when they announced she was coming a few weeks before and now I could barely get there on time.

Irina in her geek glamour girl Russian finery, a black and silver velvet vamp dress with a slanted hemline, slinked in. Slava, her CIO waddled behind, arguing with her in Russian like an unhappy bear. He was definitely not in a good mood. She let him have it about something, serving him a blast of Slavic syllables that made him leave the area.

"I told him this was GIRLS ONLY and he better get out of here fast," she said. "It is, isn't it?"

"Yes!" Barb, the CEO of Evergreen said with a grin.

"Yes!" I said. "But maybe you said something else to annoy him?"

"Well, he's been getting a little lazy and blaming me for some things he should be doing. And I think he's having wooden head, I mean, you know, a hangover."

We all smirked. Thanks to last night's fire drill and extreme team pitch night, we were all in a sorry state.

Johanna, our Israeli CEO came dashing down the hall. Same story: A guy from her team was following her, asking her something and then another guy from her team and then another.

"God, they're like my kids," Barb said. "Mommy, Mommy, where are my shoes? They can't manage a minute without us."

All of us went to the door, pulled Johanna away from her carnivorous team and stood with arms crossed. "No guys!" we told them, and they looked a little dejected, but turned and left us alone.

"Hey, I'm liking this day more and more," I said.

Suzy came down the hall alone, in a rush, and turned toward the elevators. It was just 10, when our meeting was supposed to start.

Three other guys came down the hall – the programmers from the MortalWarriors team together with the cute kids from Marshall's team. Sheba and Gloria joined us.

You could watch the hallway all day and never be bored. Exit stage right, entrance stage left, Greek chorus marching in tragically after late-night drinking and before-morning coffee.

Suzy came back with Bettina in tow, and ducked her head in. "Give us ten minutes, okay ladies?"

Bettina has the simple chic elegance of a European; I think she's German or Swiss, but never remember. She's got this cute long straight hair girl geek way about her, but she's serious business too. She's uniquely regal, but also approachable.

More guys came back from the other direction. It was like a silent movie now with cops running one way and then the other.

"Where are they all going?" Irina asked. "They are crazy today."

"We should put it on YouTube — put a secret Celery Hall Cam up and film people running up and down the hallway here, speed it up, post a week's worth," I said.

"The guys are just trying to interrupt Suzy, so they can meet Bettina," Irina said.

Johanna asked me, "Who is Bettina exactly? I know Suzy sent her bio around, but I didn't get a chance to read it."

"Who is Bettina?" Irina said. "Amazing woman. Just amazing!"

"Big, big, big, high-profile Woman CEO dear," I explained. "Hey, someone Wikipedia her," I say.

Barb had been messing with the projector and the screen, so she searched for Bettina Hein's Wikipedia page.

She wasn't on Wikipedia.

"You are kidding me?" I said. "She's not on Wikipedia?! Another MIA Wikipedia woman. You know this is getting ridiculous."

"I saw another blog post about it," Barb said. "Everyone knows it's going on — that men write Wikipedia entries for all their male friends — really unimportant guys are on there and so many prominent women are not. It's just ridiculous. I didn't give money to them this year for that reason and I *know* Jimmie Wales. I told him personally."

"Me too. I mean, I didn't give them money this year because it really got to me. Where does he live? I thought he lived here in Boston?" I added.

"No, D.C."

"Here's her bio from her company website," Johanna said.

We approached the screen to read every detail.

Five women standing before the big screen, looking up at it like it was a big mountain to climb.

"Oh. My. God. I want to be her!" Irina said, standing there reading it in her black velvet snake dress and over-the-knee leather boots.

I realized we were getting so used to Irina's amazing outfits, we were starting not to notice them. Or we were all just very tired.

"She already sold a company … how old is she?" Barb said.

"Thirty-eight, I think," I said.

"And she's written a book too," Barb said.

"And listen to this, 'Bettina holds a Masters of Science degree from MIT, where she was a Sloan Fellow, a law degree from the University of Constance and a degree in business administration from the University of St. Gallen.' No slouch!"

"And she's a mom," Barb reminded us.

We're all standing there looking at the screen and then I turn and I see Bettina standing in the back of the room watching us, with a sly grin.

"Good morning," Bettina says. "So do you want to read about me, or see me live, in action?"

We started laughing. We sat. She set up her computer in front, then found a link to a YouTube video of her speaking at a conference.

"Let's start with this video. We'll be talking about video today quite a lot."

It was a video of Bettina talking about entrepreneurs and what makes them succeed. Why one makes it and another doesn't. I'd seen it a number of times. It was so right on and so helpful.

After it's over she talked about her experiences from school, then her first company, then selling that one, then starting this one.

"So ladies, I think if you watched that YouTube lecture I did, you'd come away with a few things I consider vitally important. What was your takeaway?" she said.

"Your English is perfect and I'm jealous," Irina said.

"I lived here as a kid," Bettina explained. "What was your entrepreneurial takeaway?"

Barb said, "Have guts. Try everything."

"Exactly," Bettina said. "In fact, there were three things I mentioned. You need three things to make this journey as an entrepreneur, male or female. You need naïveté — so you don't realize how hard it is in the beginning. If you weren't naïve, you wouldn't even try it. Secondly, you need chutzpah, the audacity to put yourself out there, to push your agenda. And you need perseverance. Like Rome, no company is built in a day. In fact, it takes day after day after day, so you must be okay with slogging along, building a company like any other. It means getting up every day and just plain going to work. It's not always exciting.

"So I want to throw out a challenge to you this week. It's about being bold. I call it the Chutzpah Challenge. I want you to think of something way outside your comfort zone, something you really have never done and would like to try, and do it and make a video of what you did and post it on YouTube."

"Only business-related?" I asked.

"No, it can be anything – it's wide open," she said. "Write down five things you have never done and would like to do. Please no scary sports challenges like skydiving. Keep it on the ground."

We spent about ten minutes noodling through this and wrote down our personal five things.

"Let's break into a few groups, and talk about what you all wrote," Bettina said. This took a good half hour and talking about the things people dared to do was pretty amazing.

After this, we got up to pitch all five of the challenges we'd written down.

"Okay, you start Irina. Come up and tell us what you wrote," Bettina said.

This was worse than pitch day. We'd written pretty personal stuff.

After we each presented our five ideas, Bettina picked one of the five and suggested we focus on it.

Irina had a funny list. Out of her five, Bettina picked, "Meet the president of Harvard," as her challenge.

I went next.

As I walked to the front, I looked over to see more guys hanging out in the hallway watching what we were doing. Jean-Claude's team was there, but he was not. I wondered where he'd gone.

I like to sing. I had "Sing in the Subway" on my list, except in Boston it was called the T. I had a friend who had been a subway singer in NYC and I always thought she was insanely courageous. I decided to sing until I made $100.

"Sing in the T and video it for me," Bettina said, giving me my assignment.

Barb said, "All I dare to do is have a kid-free weekend to myself." She said she could make up some long complicated story to tell her husband so he would buy into taking the kids away.

Not having kids, the rest of us didn't seem to get this, but Bettina understood.

"Don't make up any stories, Barb. I'll give you one. Tell him you're working with me for the weekend and you need him to take over."

"By the way, I know you can use your phones for video, but let's just use these to keep it consistent." Bettina gave us tiny video cams and a cheat sheet on making a video. We picked partners to work with as we pursued our challenge. Irina and I were a team. Suzy came in to grab Bettina for lunch.

"See you all next week," Bettina said, "And remember to be fearless."

I went back to my team's area and told them a little about the meeting with her. I wouldn't tell them about the challenge I picked yet. Sonya and I went to lunch and I told her my singing in the T plan.

"So when are you going?" she said.

"I know we're busy and I don't have time to do it at all," I said, "but I'd love to just get it done. Everything video I've ever done takes ten times as long as you think it will."

"After last night, I think we're doing a good day's work if we can just keep our eyes open today," Sonya said, as we walked back to the office.

"And Irina has to film it so I have to check on her schedule too," I said.

Sonya settled back into her desk to work. I headed down the hall to find Irina.

Irina told me Suzy had cancelled an afternoon event with a mentor – he was stuck in California so we had a free hour.

"Now," she said, grabbing the camera.

We ran down the hall to my team.

"Singing in the T. Let's go. Hey, we need a hat … " I started looking around. None of mine were in the office. Puff had a perfect pork pie hat in black wool on top of his cubicle. He was coding and had his headphones on. I waved my hand in front of him.

"Can I borrow this?" I asked my great programming genius.

"Yes, and can I ask why?" he inquired.

"Going to sing in the T and pass the hat," I said.

"That sounds unproductive," he said. "May I go with you?"

"Wait, because you're feeling unproductive?"

"No, mostly because I like to sing," Puff said. "You know I've got some history in the Bollywood films."

"What? Why didn't you ever tell me that?" Sonya blurted.

"I like to have a mysterious past," Puff said, grabbing his coat.

We started down the hall.

"Where to?" Ranji said as he saw us heading out.

"Kendall T," I said.

"Why?" Ranji was often monosyllabic, not that he wasn't totally fluent in English. He just never wasted words.

"Bettina Hein gave us a challenge to do something we've never done. I've never been a subway singer and now I have to do it until I make $100."

"Come with us, Sanjay. I know you can sing," Puff said.

"You were both in the movies?" Sonya asked, her eyes wide.

"No, but we were both drunk at the first Hacker Ruby on Rails thing and we walked across the Mass Ave bridge singing most of *My Fair Lady*," Puff explained.

"I Feel Pretty … tired," Sanjay started to sing, then stopped.

"Good Lord!" I said.

We all thought he was quiet and shy and never said much and certainly didn't think he could sing. And he could really sing.

"Sheesh, you have a great voice," Sonya said.

"I'll go, that is, if it's all right with you, boss lady," Sanjay said.

"More than okay! I need you!"

In the hallway, by the elevators, we told a few more people what we were doing. I hadn't expected to get much company, but I was wrong about that.

By the time we were down in the Kendall Subway, there were ten of us; six singing and the rest watching. A few stragglers went to the soup trucks to get the engineers' favorite lunch – a big bowl of Thai soup served up by cute Thai ladies in the long food vans that parked along Carleton Street near the Kendall T.

We started off with the Beatles; most people knew some Beatles songs. The Celery people who weren't singing were trying to charm the money out of the pockets of passers-by.

Not surprisingly Irina got the first gentleman who walked by to hand her some cash, even though she was our cameraperson.

And the guy spoke Russian – looked like a professor. They chatted in Russian and she did girly smiles and laughs as they talked about whatever the hell they talked about.

She put ten dollars in the hat after he headed down the platform.

"Score!" I said. "Great job Irina!"

Of course this got the rest of them going – the guys that is – since they didn't like Irina outdoing them.

A bunch of VCs we knew came by and left us less than $2.50.

"And they just gave Scvngr $250 million!" Sonya mentioned.

"You've been reading your blogs I see!"

"Si, Señora," Sonya said.

"Lousy two dollars and thirty cents and they even made a request – anything from *Les Misérables*," I said.

Again Puff amazed us and launched into *I Dreamed A Dream*, heading toward them on the platform, with a damned fine imitation of Susan Boyle.

The first hour got us to about $55 but after a bit, the crowds thinned out and I was going to have to come up with something new to make my hundred bucks in any reasonable amount of time.

Puff and Sonya were my only pals left. They were sitting on a wooden bench counting the money.

"You guys should go back," I said. "I'll be fine. This was MY challenge anyway."

We talked a bit, they wished me luck and then they went back to the office.

From the other end of the platform, I saw Marshall walking my way.

"Girl? What the hell are you doing here?" he said.

"Guy? What the hell are you doing here?" I said.

Irina got a good shot of Marshall right up close.

"When you're alone … " he spoke the words very slowly and seriously, "And life is making you lonely, you can always go … DOWNTOWN." He pointed to the downtown direction sign on the wall.

"Nice song," Irina said.

"No, I'm really going downtown, I mean," he said.

"Wait, before you go, let's sing that, we can get some cash, I'm sure," I said.

We launched into a Dionne Warwick version. We managed to get another ten bucks from a mom with twins in a stroller. I felt bad. She probably needed it more than we did.

The train came and Marshall had to jump on it. He was gone quickly.

I was in a Dionne Warwick mood at that point, so I tried to remember the words to *Do You Know The Way To San Jose*? I remembered Nick and I used to sing it when we were stuck in traffic heading south on the 101 for meetings in San Jose.

I finished that and started singing, "The moment I wake up, before I put on my makeup."

"I say a little prayer for you," Roan chimed in, coming from the other entrance.

"Roan!" I said. "Good to see you!"

Irina caught him vogue-ing for the camera, the subway platform his new runway.

"I so adore Dionne Warwick, I'm combing my hair now and wondering what dress to wear now …" he was so sleek in his Russian Navy Officer coat and big Russian hat, dancing to the song and pretending to try on a new pretty dress.

The train pulled into the station.

"Oh hell, I have to go," he said, and gave me a movie kiss and was off.

He got into the front of the train and while J-C and his team got out of the last car of that same train. Busy day at the Kendall T.

They all looked at me, J-C's main guy François smirked, leaned over and said something in his ear. J-C headed toward me, but the rest of the team just waved and headed the other direction with François leading them in a quick race for the stairs.

"Alors, qu'est-ce que tu fais?" J-C asked me.

"Singing for money," I said.

I felt a little shy and silly, didn't expect to, but I did.

"Hello, comrade" he said to Irina. She nodded.

Jean-Claude said, "Let me count the money."

He bent down and counted my money in the hat.

"Sixty-five dollars. How much do you need?"

"I need a hundred bucks," I said.

Some people were coming in from the far end of the station.

"Let's hear you," he said, stepping back, crossing his arms. "Sing and I'll get these guys to give you twenty dollars."

I started in on, *Somewhere Over The Rainbow*, the ukulele version.

As they passed, Jean-Claude said, "Wow, I'm so sorry to hear about your mother passing away," then he bent down and put $20 in the hat.

The other guys shelled out $5.00 each.

After they left, he gave me a thumbs-up.

"That wasn't really very nice of you," I said. "And my mom is alive and well in L.A. by the way."

"It helped you, didn't it?"

Three women passed by, well-dressed carrying small blue bags from Tiffany's.

"I can't BELIEVE someone stole $15 right out of your hat," he just about shouted at me. They kept going, like they couldn't care less.

"Damn," he said. "I was thinking that would work. Let me sing with you."

"Sing what?" I asked.

"We must know a song we can sing together," he said, scrunching up his face trying to guess one.

"Beatles?" I said.

"Hmmm, maybe … "

"Yesterday?"

"Too sad," he said correctly.

The platform was empty now.

He started to sing.

"Words inside a paper cup … ba, bum, ba, bum, ba, bum, bum, bum," he couldn't remember the words.

"*Across the Universe!*" I loved that song.

"I don't know the words," he said.

"I do, wait," I pulled paper out of my purse and scribbled them down for him.

I couldn't remember all of them but it was enough.

Irina said, "This is good. Maybe we can just post it on YouTube and raise the money that way. Is that cheating?"

"I'm sure Bettina would be fine with that," I said, "but it takes a few days to set up a real account if you want people to pay you."

We sang and if you love to sing you know one thing about hearing a new friend sing with you — it's a treat if they have a good voice and you can blend yours with theirs. He had a great bass voice à la my favorite — Elvis. One more sexy thing about him. And I didn't really want to stop.

We sang along, "nothing's gonna change my world, nothing's gonna change my world."

Irina was filming and giving us a thumbs-up periodically which I figured would make the video a shaky mess.

Slava came down the platform looking for Irina.

"Okay, okay, okay," she said.

"You didn't even see my text?" he looked angry.

"Okay," she packed up and headed out. "I come with you now. Stop making that face."

They were gone, and I sat on the bench, but Jean-Claude stood by the hat and launched into a song in French. It was Piaf, "Je ne regrette rien."

More coins clinked into the hat.

"I don't know if it counts, if I don't sing with you."

"No matter," I said.

He sang another song but not one person gave him a dime.

"I guess they didn't like that one," he said.

"The hat's too full now, they don't think you need it."

And after a while, he said, "You don't have to finish today, do you?"

"No, I have a week," I said.

"Good. Let's go somewhere," he said.

I wanted to go with him so much, but I had sworn off him. It was so hard to resist.

"I should go back and meet with my team," I said like lead.

"Just take a little time," he said.

"Don't you remember what I told you? I really can't see you. I can't see anyone until this divorce stuff is over. No one should see us out together."

"Do you love that guy?"

"No, mostly I hate him now," I said.

"So let's go then, you'll have time to work later, I promise," he said, as if it were no big thing.

He picked up the hat, straightened the money and put the bills in my hand. He put the change in my other hand. Then he put the hat on his head, looking even cuter now, took my hand and we walked up the stairs of the subway together.

I was just flushed with heat to have him hold my hand. How did he turn me into a 13-year-old school girl again and again? It was crazy.

It was evening by now and he said, "I know a nice restaurant on the other side of the river."

"It's freezing though," I said.

"But the wind is not like before, not as bad," he was right. The wind had died down a little.

"Still … " I said.

"And there's a poem written on the bridge. I want to show you to it," he said.

"Really?" I wasn't in the mood to correct his gaffe — show you to it.

"Yes. I'll show you, I mean, I'll show IT to you," he said.

"Okay, okay," I caved. I wasn't much good at resisting him. He could probably talk me into almost anything.

"I understand we can't be together. I'm not a big bad wolf. I won't eat you for dinner. I'm a civilized modern man," he said. "That's all. Trust me."

I couldn't think of the right thing to say, so I said nothing.

And he put his arm around me and we started across the Longfellow Bridge.

Now the buildings of Boston were lit with little pearly lights against the darkening sky. The river looked a little scary. We walked across the bridge spanning the Charles River, no sharks there, but you would not want to fall in on a cold night. Jean-Claude showed me the long line of poetry painted on the bridge walkway. It was the text of Longfellow's poem. Some was covered in snow.

My French friend read the words below our feet, "He said to his friend, 'If the British march, by land or sea from the town to-night, Hang a lantern aloft in the belfry-arch of the North Church tower as a signal light.' "

"This is great," I said.

"You know this, right? They teach you this in school. One if by land, two if by sea," he recited it. "We learn 'Gallia est divisa in tres partes' in our history class." We made it across the bridge and he led me down Charles Street to the prettiest part of town, Beacon Hill where all the red brick townhouses from the 1800s stood tall. It was too cold for sightseeing, but I asked him if he'd seen Louisburg Square. He had. He asked me whether I'd seen this new French restaurant called Chartreuse, off Chestnut Street, and I told him I had not.

On the way, we stopped at a wine bar on Charles Street called Bin 26 where everyone seemed to know his name. Then we followed it with dinner at the new place. He was keeping me at arms' length in a gentlemanly fashion. He was talking about the startup scene in Europe, about friends in Paris and how Berlin was getting to be an excellent place to find office space, lots of developers from Eastern Europe were flooding the place. Also about Trento, Italy where there were amazing things going on. He might go to a program there after Celery was done. I didn't want him to go so far away.

After dinner we were out on the street again, waiting for a cab.

"Remind me, again, why we can't fall in love?" he said. He was playing with my hair and it looked like he was getting ready to kiss me. We were a little drunk. I wanted him to just do it.

"I … don't ask me that. I can't do it but … I can't even remember why," I said finally trying to be serious, but it only made him laugh.

"Well, try to remember and get back to me about it later, Madame," he said in a business-like manner, but he was brushing my hair back from my face, and bending low to kiss me.

It was just a perfect kiss, but didn't last nearly long enough. I looked up into his eyes, surely I could find more kisses where that one came from.

"Because we're married too," I remembered.

"I told you, didn't I? I did that for a friend to keep her in the country when we were all working on a startup. I did it to stop all the visa problems."

My heart was just knocking around inside me, making noise.

He must have read it in my expression.

He wrapped his hands around my waist, pulled me tight against him and started really kissing me. That other had been a lackluster warm-up drill compared to this one.

"Oh, honey," I said, breaking free.

"You like?"

"I like, but I'm a little drunk," I whispered to him.

"That's okay. A little drunk is okay," he kissed me again.

We walked past the Liberty Hotel.

"Hey, let's go in," he said. It was great. They'd taken the original city jail and converted it into a luxury hotel. I showed him the bars on the windows they had saved and restored. We took a cozy banquette table in a far corner of the bar. He ordered some oysters and they brought us bread and butter which I gobbled, so I wouldn't be so silly drunk. We couldn't have been sitting closer.

"You know what's happening?" he looked at me seriously.

"I think I know," I said looking at him with a sexy grin.

"I didn't think you'd like me," he said.

"What? You can't say that! Guys should never say that," I told him.

"Well, it's true, so I *can* say it, to you," he said.

"I thought you'd think I was too old or too fat or too American," I said.

"You are," he said and then grabbed me. "NOT! You are perfect to me. And you are perfect for me."

"And you are flirting," I said.

"Yes, correct. I am, Madame."

We talked about nothing and then a bit about Celery, and then he launched into an actual discussion of Agile Programming, which he found frustrating because people always confused a unit of two with two days or two weeks and it wasn't supposed to be strictly interpreted that way, according to him. "Agile has no perspective on time. The people judging it don't know merde, don't know shit, should not be making the assessment because they are marketing managers or other stupid cons."

Not your typical romance, but hey, we were code monkey CEOs after all. I argued against his point, saying it was useful and precise enough to get the team all thinking in the same direction and that was valuable enough from my point of view. He was so stubborn. It was making me laugh.

"Did you really think I didn't like you?" I asked him.

"I wondered," he said.

"I like you too much, that's why I had to be away from you."

"I like you too much too, but it makes me want to be *with* you, not away from you."

We talked and talked and drank a little more and ate more than that.

He pulled up his Ubercab App when we started to get tired. A cab came too quickly. There was the question in the air, where we would go, would we stay together tonight? The driver never had to ask where to take a person who called for a cab, as that information was part of the request when they used the app.

"I have to be un-French tonight and be more American than you," he said.

"You mean … you're going back to work?"

He nodded and made a sad face. "I told my team I'd meet with them."

"I thought maybe … "

"I hope so too, but not tonight."

When we pulled up to my apartment, he asked the driver to wait and walked me up the three flights of stairs to my door. We kissed on the landing. Then he headed back downstairs to go to work at Celery.

I dashed inside and ran to the front window to watch him leave. I wished he hadn't gone. I felt so mixed up, with just about every emotion fighting it out inside me. I wanted him, that was for sure, but I was also afraid of the whole thing. I even felt a little jealous of his team taking him away from me.

And then I felt something terrible. I didn't know I could feel that way.

I felt really competitive.

He's going back to work.

And I should be too!

I pulled my laptop out of my bag and checked in with the team to see what they were doing while I was away. There was a pile of messages and everyone on my team was online.

There was one from Sonya in caps, "HELLO GIRLFRIEND, 8000 HITS SINCE 6PM?"

I didn't know what she was talking about. I clicked the link to a YouTube video of … yep, me singing with J-C. Irina had edited it and posted it. Well, we did look good together. We looked happy. Okay. Shit. Admit it.

We looked like two people in love.

There were tons of comments.

One comment said, "Romance starting up at the Celery?"

Of course it was by some idiot called "ANON-doncha know" instead of the usual chicken shit "anon."

This wasn't going to make my lawyer happy, but it was too late now. I had to decide to keep it up or take it down. I listened to the audio. We weren't bad as we sang *Across the Universe*. I've always loved that song.

As for nothing changing my world, it was just about the opposite. Startups were all about changing the world. It was time for work.

I rounded up the team online for a hangout on Google+, to see where we were, to see what more we could do in an evening. Puff had something up his sleeve, something big. We worked until 3 a.m. then went to bed, very excited about our next big thing.

Chapter 21

Alexandria Pitch Meeting

The meeting at Alexandria was the next day over on Newbury Street. We got there early and were waiting in the lobby. Puff had been working all night on the prototype, which he showed me. It worked! It was great! And it made our concept so much easier to understand! Now we could show them the real thing, instead of a slide deck full of dreams and some silly elevator pitch.

They had a young associate meet us at the lobby. Her name was Veronica Belancourt. I'd read her bio on their website, which was enough to make me shake in my shoes. She'd gone to Groton, Harvard, Harvard Business School, and much more importantly, between Harvard and HBS, she and a friend started a company that was sold to Viacom for a few million bucks.

She was one of these brainiac girls who was also really pretty. Everyone in town knew Alexandria was the one venture capital firm that was all about brains and female leadership. It was also known as a firm where they stuck to a 50/50 split of male/female partners, something mostly unheard of in the venture world. I'd been Googling them and reading their website for days. It had been founded by a married couple, two young hotshots from Silicon Valley with top cred, John and Doerte Alexander who'd met at Kleiner, Perkins in Menlo Park. She went by "Dot," short for Dorothy, not dot com as Sonya had inquired when we discussed them. They had four daughters now.

Veronica took us down the long hallways that looked more like a museum than an office, pausing in front of a display about the Great Library at Alexandria.

"One of the Seven Wonders of the Ancient World," she explained.

"Yes, I've read about it," I said.

"It did get burned down, but it's not clear when exactly or by whom."

I always like a good "whom" in the morning.

The place was aggressively brainy, and they wanted anyone who entered their hallowed halls to know that.

She checked in with the receptionist and handed us badges.

"We're in Hypatia," Veronica mentioned. "The conference rooms are named after the scholars who studied at the Great Library, which was part of the large group of buildings that made up the Museum of Alexandria."

"Hypatia was a mathematician, wasn't she?"

"Yes, exactly, one of the most famous women mathematicians," Veronica added.

We walked down another hallway with amazing views of the city around us. The rooms we passed were Eratosthenes, Hipparchus and Erasistratus. I had to wonder how the receptionists managed with a mouthful of Greek names like those. Naming conference rooms had become a bit of a fetish these days. Often as not they were just named after sports teams at the suburban VCs or one we visited had names of stadiums: Lambeau, Wrigley, Fenway. One firm founded by MIT geeks I'd seen in Kendall Square had rooms also named after mathematicians: Fibonacci, Grothendieck, Gödel. I remembered them telling me there were no rooms named after women because there were no important female mathematicians. Wrong!

We set up our computers in the Hypatia conference room, and Veronica had another assistant come in to take our drink orders: water, water and water for all.

John Alexander came right in, instead of making us wait, which was more typical in the big firms. He was familiar and pleasant, not haughty and impatient. Most of these guys knew how to put on airs, constantly reminding you how important they were. He apologized that his wife was busy this morning and wouldn't attend our meeting. I was sorry we would not meet Dot Alexander in person.

It wasn't like the other pitch meetings. It was friendly and fun.

Puff showed the prototype. John Alexander asked three questions. Then he asked Veronica if she had questions. She had two good questions and he complimented her on them.

Then I did a one-slide intro to the team — who we were, where we'd gone to school and worked. John asked me if there were any concerns with the intellectual property being claimed by my former company. Would my lying, cheating, bastard of a husband say he had any rights to BrightLight?

Key question.

"Since I was a founder and never signed any IP agreement, as well as the fact that this application is nothing like what we were doing at the other company, I'm pretty sure it's clean. But let me get my lawyer to confirm that for you."

"Sounds good," he said, not seeming too concerned. At the end of the meeting, one of John's predictions proved false.

Out in the hallway there was a woman in a stylish black suit and heels pushing a stroller filled with a baby, accompanied by three little girl cuties in pink dresses who came running, yelling "Daddy!" The girls must have been 6, 4, and maybe 3? Or did they have twins?

So here was the other founder, after all. My VC crush and hero, Dot Alexander.

She came in with all the familiarity of a volleyball coach, shaking hands, saying a pleasant, "Great to meet you," to Puff and me.

The girls were jumping all over their dad and Dot came over to sit next to me to watch my demo. We took her through the prototype and then my slides.

"Nice and short," she said. "I like that best of all."

"So what's the deal?" she said to her husband.

"Priscilla just spilled grape juice all over me," he said.

"Easy to fix. What about the IP?" she asked.

"Sounds clean but she says she'll have her lawyer get back to us."

"So then, we're in with Monica or what?" she pushed.

"Unless you see a reason to say no, I'm a yes," he said.

"I like it," Dot said."Let's do it."

"It's a deal," he said standing to shake my hand. "Girls!" his daughters were hanging all over him. We shook hands quickly.

"Mommy, make Daddy eat lunch with us at that place, with the pink drinks," the smallest one said.

"Thank you, I'm so excited," I said, shaking Dot's hand now.

Puff jumped up. "Thank you, thank you very much," he said, shaking John's hand and then Dot's.

Veronica said, "I'll walk you out and get our next meeting on the calendar."

We pulled our stuff together as the whole family headed back down the hallway. The girls were singing a song by Taylor Swift. Their mom was steering the baby carriage. Their dad had a big purple stain on his nicely pressed white shirt. A perfect family if you asked me.

Chapter 22

Surfing the Web

Not only was the apartment Sonya and I found for her a great place, but it was the closest apartment to Celery, so once Sonya talked Irina into being her roommate, they started hosting a lot of parties there. One night after another pitch-a-thon at the office, Irina threw a white party.

Everyone had to wear white (we were sick of seeing the guys in dirty tees and infrequently washed blue jeans) and this created a cool look as we lounged around the mostly white furniture in the apartment. We ordered white pizza and, of course, drank White Russians. Jean-Claude had some amazing white clothing in his closet, no surprise, but he and his team could only stay a short time, since they were too busy kicking their prototype in the ass, getting ready for the last month. I acted like it was just fine. He did give me an amazing ten minutes alone, as we went into the far bedroom to hang up his coat. He was really good at pressing me up against the wall and nearly going the whole way, but I made him stop when it came to messing up our clothes enough that everyone would know what we'd been doing.

Of course, it wasn't really okay with me that he had to leave early, but Sonya talked me off that ledge by reminding me any girl with the least bit of self-respect should be fine letting an almost boyfriend disappear now and then. Some days I didn't know what he wanted or what I wanted, but I knew he took the Celery program seriously and so did I, so I could deal with it. And, she noted, I was the one who had cooled it off with him to begin with anyway.

Her apartment was one of those pretty things you just luck into and don't want to ask why; you just grab your good luck and run with it. It was large with a great view of Harvard Square. Irina and Sonya each had their own room and between the rooms there was a massive living room, with a super modern, cool futon fold-out bed thing that looked like a piece of origami, in white canvas. It was cute and couchy one minute and then unfolded into a large, perfectly comfortable king-size bed. And she had another futon couch on the other side of the living room as well — also white.

Slava played bartender, doing the drink of the day, but also serving up his favorite clear and white vodkas — plain vodka, vanilla vodka, coconut vodka, more plain, more vanilla, more coconut — and soon enough, we were all having trouble standing. Then the guys decided they needed to take off to a bar in the South End where someone had spotted Matt Damon and Ben Affleck and tweeted it, so we girls let them go. We were too tired to go anywhere, whether it was three blocks, much less 30 minutes away. That was just not our idea of fun.

Once the guys were gone, it was just Sonya, Irina and me, so we started cleaning up a little, but then realized we still felt like partying. As if we needed anymore, Irina brought out a bottle of the really good vodka, no silly flavors, just the real stuff and then put on these old CDs of '50s dance music and soon we were singing surfer tunes and dancing to all sorts of bikini beach music.

We danced and danced and it was after midnight when we stopped and realized we were still in our daytime white clothes, so Irina dug through a suitcase and found us something along the lines of white pj's. She gave me this rather amazing white silk nightshirt to wear. It was sexy as heck, but then what wasn't, when it came to the Russian princess' wardrobe.

Sonya found sheets and blankets for us and put a pile on the chair for later. I was flopped out on the couch as they went off to change. Irina returned inhilarious 1950s baby doll pyjamas in rather sheer white dotted swiss, with a deep cut décolletage revealing her wonderful cleavage. Of course, they came with matching lacy panties. She bounced around to another surfer hit. She wore white marabou high-heeled satin mules. The girl followed one fashion icon: Barbie.

I was very tired and very drunk and I'm not into girls, but I couldn't stop looking at her amazingly perfect breasts, which were now busy doing a few inspiring bounces as Irina pranced around the room showing off a famous 1960's dance, the Pony. With one last bounce, both pretty tits had escaped the neckline of her nighty, now stood at full attention, nipples nicely perky for all to see.

"They're REAL!" I blurted out.

She bent over laughing, looking at her bare breasts and yanked her nighty up to cover them primly, "Oh yes, darling!"

I was still looking, so she laughed again, then flipped the bottom of her nighty up, just to flash me and stood there shaking them proudly. "And you should see my mama's!"

"I'm sorry, I didn't mean to sound like an asshole, like one of the guys, but I didn't think they were real."

"No big deal, dance with me," she pulled me up and now was doing some wiggly dance to the Beach Boys. "Pretend we are surfing on a surfboard and there are sharks," she said and pointed to the carpet and screamed, "Ahh! Sharks! Quick, jump on my board." I stepped behind her and we surfed away, getting a few more miles from the beach.

"What the hell are you two doing?" Sonya came in sporting a very tight white stretchy tee, showing off her rack as well. I was outclassed by these ladies in the boobs department, for sure. On bottom, Sonya was waltzing around in a set of snug white boy short panties, styled like boy's underwear but very girly, presenting the cute curves of her butt in amazing ways, since the panties didn't do much of a job of covering anything.

"Sharks!" I yelled. "Get on our board!"

Irina grabbed Sonya, who might be a good six inches shorter than her and placed her in front of our surfboard threesome.

"Bend your knees," I yelled. "I went to surfer school in San Diego. You gotta bend your knees or we're dead."

"I'm gonna fall," Sonya yelled.

"Shark!" Irina yelled and grabbed Sonya around the waist. I saw Irina bend down to either whisper in Sonya's ear or kiss her. Sonya rubbed her butt up against Irina's front.

"I'm gone," I said, and dived into the futon. I lay on the plain futon, just about wiped out for the day.

The song switched to another surfer song and I watched the other girls get into a frisky frug, tossing their arms up and down. Irina did a pretty excellent monkey and Sonya was now reviving the pony, more bouncing around.

You do some crazy stuff when you're drunk, but at this point I was fighting a battle between silly drunk and solidly snoring, any minute.

"Monica, come on, play with us," they said.

I got up. I was game.

My phone beeped. Goddamned guy. I looked at it.

"Alors?" Jean-Claude texted. Amazing timing.

Isn't it always that way? These guys always want a piece of us girls, just when we're really having fun. He must have picked up my vibe. He would have liked seeing me in a silky, sexy, satin nightshirt dancing the night away with my curvaceous pals.

I tossed the phone on the couch and started dancing. We were moving into the '70s and they were going all ABBA now. We were off our surfboard and on the disco dance floor with "The Winner Takes It All", singing and dancing along until the neighbors started banging on the wall between songs.

"Uh oh!" I fell back onto the futon. Irina turned the music down and dimmed the lights to change the mood.

She found some Barry White, giving the whole evening a more quiet, sexy feeling.

Irina did a really fine Barry White sexy singer guy imitation using a pink hairbrush as her microphone.

That's about the time I must have slipped off to sleep for a little while. I woke later, because I had my hand curled under me in an uncomfortable way and it was all pins and needles. I shifted around and looked toward the room. Now the lights were off and there were candles lit on the table and Sonya and Irina were dancing to Billie Holiday. I could see them without even lifting my head. There was a blanket over me. I didn't remember how it got there.

Since Irina was taller, Sonya had her head against Irina's chest pressing against her breasts. The music was slow and they were grinding slowly against one another. I could see Sonya was reaching one hand down, petting the front of Irina's panties with two fingers and the Russian was making purring sounds and small moans. They stopped dancing when the song ended, and didn't start up again when a new song began. The classic music reminded me of an old sexy word, "petting." That's what they were doing, just not in the back of an old Chevy, but it was definitely petting. Sonya was fluttering her fingers against the front of Irina's panties. She also bent her head lower and took Irina's nipple in her mouth, sucking hard, making a slurping noise.

Irina let out an "Ahh," of pleasure.

I'd never seen Sonya in this type of action, but I knew one thing about doing business with her. Never underestimate her. I'm sure she was only warming up.

Now she went down on her knees and started licking Irina between the legs. Irina was swaying and speaking Russian as her lover pressed her harder. She might just fall over, in her high-heeled marabou slippers, if they weren't careful, I thought.

Sonya's hands went up to Irina's breasts, eased them out of the top of her nighty and took a hold of her nipples. She tweaked and twisted them as she licked her lover.

Irina grabbed Sonya's head and pressed her harder against her pussy. She was gasping, now repeating something in Russian that sounded very hot, but I couldn't translate.

Sonya suddenly stopped and stood up, took Irina by the hand and took her over to the other futon. She made her sit back. She lifted one of Irina's legs with big sexy marabou slipper and all, hooked it over her shoulder, and then the other, opening her partner wide, getting close up to Irina's pretty lace panties. Irina was moaning and her heels were slightly digging into Sonya's back. Sonya licked her way down to the high-heeled slipper and took it off, flinging it to the far side of the room. Then she repeated the process with the other leg, slow licking toward the foot, jettisoning the other slipper as well. Now the seduction was getting faster, more aggressive.

Suddenly Sonya went down, buried her head between Irina's legs and started licking her through the mesh panties. Irina grabbed Sonya's hair and pulled her partner back, so she could take her panties off.

Irina was shaved clean and fresh.

"Yes," Sonya said looking at her.

Irina had thrown her head back, covering it with a pillow, as if she didn't dare watch. Sonya pressed her partner wider open, relishing the lovely pink parts.

"Very beautiful," Sonya said. "Keep your legs spread open like that for me."

"Oh, Sonya," she was trembling.

Sonya took a finger and ran it slowly up the wet part of Irina's wide openness, then circled her finger around on her clit.

She put her finger in her mouth, taking a quick taste.

She swiped more wetness from her lover's pussy, then pushed the pillow from her face and slipped her finger into Irina's mouth. "Taste it before I suck you. You're salty sweet."

Irina sucked Sonya's finger, tasting her own flavor.

Sonya lowered her head and slowly sucked her lover's sweet spot as Irina let her head flop back. Sonya crept one hand up, searching again for Irina's bosoms, grazing the flat of her hand across one hard nipple, then the other, which both poked up with excitement.

This put her right over and Irina grabbed Sonya's head as she came hard, in a furious jolt. Sonya wrapped her arms around Irina, just to let her know she was safe, she was held, and she could come back to Earth whenever she wanted.

While they were busy, I turned away, pulled my blanket over my head, feigned sleep, feeling a bit guilty having been the lucky voyeuse. Yes, voyeur, voyeuse, entrepreneur, entrepreneuse, bravo, brava; you rarely heard the female version of certain words, did you?

I could tell a hangover was already chasing me and would likely win out in the morning, but now, I was wet from watching them and wondering where my boy J-C was, wishing he was doing the same things to me. I'm sure he would be very good at it and not miss a trick.

PART FOUR

Chapter 23

Mountains

The Xtreme team was getting extremely itchy being stuck indoors, in the office, day in and day out, not even being able to test their software, or so they said. They probably just wanted to bust out like the rest of us and do something fun. So they organized a trip to Mount Washington for any of us who wanted to catch the end of the winter camping and ice climbing season in the White Mountains. It was late spring, cold, rainy, windy. I didn't even want to cross the street for coffee and a scone at Cosi.

"As if," Marshall said, reading the email about heading north to someplace called Tuckerman's Ravine.

"Not your thing, I figured," I said, biting my tongue to not laugh out loud, thinking of Marshall in the mountains.

"Hardly," he said. "Do you think you can go climbing in an expensive Italian suit and Gucci loafers?"

"That's just what you wear, expensive Italian suits. I was trying to think of the right term, the right thing to call those," I said.

"There's actually one word," he opened the side of his jacket to show me a label that read, "Armani."

I went back to the daily emails.

"Do you think I should go?" I asked him.

"You? You're kidding, right?" he said.

"Well, I used to do a lot of that stuff out West. Have you been to Yosemite?"

"Nope," Marshall said.

"Check it out. Suzy's paying for the mountain trip. You can stay at a place called Highland Lodge, it's not some tent. And they have 'the L.L.Bean equipment room' with all the gear and clothes you need," I told him.

"All the equipment I need? What, to read a novel and finish my PowerPoint? I think I have that already, right here, down on Earth. Doesn't Suzy know all these North Face-wearing geeks don't know anything about facing north, or facing the North Face or actually climbing anything? Sounds like a waste of time."

He had a point. I shouldn't go for a few reasons. Unfortunately, there was one reason I was tempted.

"Wait, is your French amigo going?" He caught on fast.

I nodded yes.

"Busted."

Irina walked by. "We're going, Russians love mountains," she said.

"And Siberia," Marshall said.

She whacked him with her scarf.

Yes, Jean-Claude was going. I'd heard the day before. For a guy in love with fashion and big cities, he actually knew his way around the mountains. In the usual J-C manner, had found some guys at EMS in Harvard Square to loan him all the gear. He came into the office wearing a harness and all sorts of ropes and those shiny metal carabiners hanging off him. Everything was in bright orange and bright blue, like a stylist had put him together.

"You make everything look runway," I said.

"We do have some Alps in France, vous savez, Madame," he said, "Look at this Petzl Gri-Gri. C'est superbe!"

"It sounds like something to eat," I said.

"You should go," he was slowly looping a bright orange rope around me.

"Get that thing off of me!" I threw the rope back over my head.

The bright orange harness on his hips and with grey leg holsters circling each thigh was truly hot.

"My code's a mess, I needed the time to work," I said.

"Work work work, very American," he said. "I thought you were a California surfer chick girl," he said.

"I'm a Demo-Day-is-in-six-weeks-freaking-out chick girl," I explained. "Va t'en!"

He went away as I asked, but I couldn't resist stealing a peek at him, sauntering down the hall with an ice axe hanging off one hip.

There were lots of invitations to events at the Celery program, so you had to get good at turning things down politely and consistently, in order to get your work done. You just had to, so no one had a problem with you saying no. I remember thinking at the end of high school how glad I was to be done with homework, then in college realizing homework just gets harder and even then, after finishing college, realizing most jobs and projects were just more homework, but at least you got paid.

But this time, Suzy personally made a pitch, which was strange to me. She wasn't exactly a big outdoors person. She was also dressed in her REI best, nice hiking pants, cool boots, a suede coat.

"Suede? I don't know about that," I said to my pal Marsh. "She looks very cool but doesn't it rain sometimes in the mountains?"

"She's getting silly about him," Marshall said.

"Him?"

"Mr. Down and Underwear," he said.

I choked on my coffee. Chris Mooney, the Hugh Jackman look-alike was always strolling about the office after exiting the shower room in his underwear, or something called base layers. It might as well have been underwear, considering how well it showed off his extremely gorgeous goods.

"Yes, our resident Aussie movie star," he said. I hadn't told him that Jean-Claude and I had seen the two of them together the other evening.

The trip to Tuckerman's was the same week as the South By Southwest Conference, known as SXSW, the annual Austin conference for geeks, musicians and movie makers.

"It's gotten too big, SXSW, nobody cool is going this year," Roan told us, wandering by one day. SXSW was a good way to get caught up in lots of conference partying and wasting lots of time. It wasn't clear what the upside of attending was when Demo Day was not that far off and our coding time all the more precious.

"Very disciplined of you not to go," Marshall was saying.

"What? Oh yeah," I tuned him back in. "I hear the call of the code, not the call of the mountains. I'm screwed if I don't get this code to jump up and do its thing," I said.

"Yep," Marshall said.

"Did you know the Israelis rented an RV and they are driving to SXSW?"

"Oh my God," Marshall said. "It's a million miles to Texas from here. What were they thinking?"

"They're video blogging it. They left yesterday," I told him.

"I'll have to see that one," Marshall said. "Did you see the tweet about Rich Miner?"

"From Google Ventures?" I said.

"Yep. He said he will pick two Celery companies to work with," Marshall said.

"Whoa. Another good reason to just keep your head down and work," I replied.

The mountaineers left the next day and it meant we had the biggest, emptiest office ever. Happy me.

"Ever get the feeling everything about your code sucks and you want to scrap it all and start from scratch?" I said to Marshall.

"Just about every day, but that's like going on a purging diet and a month-long fast. It sounds like a great way to lose weight, but it's actually harder to just be moderate, work with what you have and improve it bit by bit."

"Are you talking dieting or code base destruction?"

"Both. I mean, don't throw any babies out with any bath water," he said, "Let me look at it."

I left, I couldn't stand watching him read over it, making quizzical faces, wrinkling his forehead about certain things. I went across the street to Cosi. It was empty too. For being bold, independent thinkers, these entrepreneurs were a mob that seemed to move in one big circus all together, all the time.

Jean-Claude wasn't leaving me alone even if he was leaving. He had a unique haiku kind of text style, or SMS as the EU folks called it, where I'd get certain confusing monosyllables in a number of languages at odd times of day. Often I wondered if he had sent me a message intended for someone else.

"N Conway, ice axe smiling," was one I got later that day when Marshall and I were ripping apart my code base and actually getting somewhere.

"What's N Conway?" I asked Marshall.

"And why would I know that?" he look at me like I was wasting his time.

I Googled it. "North Conway. Last big town before they head to Mount Washington I think," I said.

I texted back and Marshall was looking at me.

I guess he caught me making that goofy face girls make when texting their boyfriends.

"Your code really sucks. What have you been doing? Chasing cute French guys instead of nose to the grindstone?"

"Oh, thanks Mr. Judgmental!" I said, I pushed him over and jumped on my code.

"Gotcha, but seriously, let's fix this shit," he said.

Puff, Sanjay and Sonya were also texting me, and all their messages were getting mixed up on my phone.

"Ass seriously frozen," Sanjay alerted me.

I showed it to Marshall

"You should whoop his ass for this line of code alone," he said.

"Sounds terrible up there."

"Glad, glad, glad we didn't go," Marshall said. "Look out the window, snow and sleet, listen to it!"

It was making a light tapping noise hitting the windows, as if asking to come in and join us.

"Tiny Ping-Pong match out there. The game never ends, even when they're all gone," he said. "Look at this line, look what it's doing."

He showed me the resulting mess after he ran a simple test.

"Sharing turkey jerky with a jerk, 90 degrees," Sonya texted me from Austin. She'd had tickets and a room to SXSW she'd bought the year before, so I told her to go ahead and go, even though we needed her here, more than there.

We spent the miserable afternoon in miserable weather, digging in deep, getting both our projects in better shape as the weather worsened. It was a sobering backdrop. We were really close to Demo Day. We had to actually sell this stuff. People had to buy and use our software. I mean, buy it eventually. For now it was all freemium all the time.

Around dinnertime, I started to get updates on the conditions up north from all of my coders and J-C.

"Varykino. Wish u were here Lara," he texted me.

"Who's Lara?" I asked Marshall.

"Oy, were you born yesterday? Dr. Zhivago's bitch girlfriend," he said, annoyed to be distracted as he was looking over his code.

I Googled it. An image of an ice palace appeared with Dr. Zhivago and Lara, his mistress looking very '70s hot in a white fur hat.

"Very cold and icy," Puff explained via text. "Hike off." A brief hike to a place called Elephant Head had been cancelled. The weather was too brutal.

Marshall and I headed home and agreed to pick it up again the next morning.

The texts stopped around 9 pm — early for J-C and the boys. I figured they actually must have made it an early night.

Sonya was ahead of me in time at SXSW, so we chatted a bit by IM, but then I fell asleep mid-instant message.

My phone chirped early in the morning, "Mooney+me going up Huntington Ravine," J-C told me around 6:15 a.m. Didn't know where that was. But he was with Chris the Aussie, so that was good. I was no fan of extreme sports but better to do them with someone who was actually trained in Wilderness Rescue.

Marshall and I had planned to meet at 10 a.m. at the office, but we both ended up there around 7 a.m. There was just so much to fix and test.

At 11 a.m., I got an odd text from J-C: "Sing me a song, keep me safe."

I texted the title *Long and Winding Road* since he was such a Beatles fan, I knew he'd know the song.

Around 12:30, Marshall headed out to get us sandwiches.

"No mayo, no way, mustard only," I told him about my sandwich. The girl always insisted on adding mayonnaise to the grilled chicken wrap.

I had to call Puff since there was something still crashing with a section he had written. I needed to know what he had done with a certain set of lines.

"Hey Puff, what the heck's going on here, you know the section where … ?" I said when he picked up. There was a lot of noise in the background, people talking, a distant siren.

"How did you know?" he cut me off in a very serious voice.

"Know what?" I said.

"About the accident," he said.

I felt my breath get sucked inward suddenly.

"What accident? I was talking about the code," I explained.

"Chris Mooney went up to Mount Washington at dawn in a terrible storm and he's lost. Jean-Claude went after him. And now MortalWarriors are looking for both of them," Puff told me.

"What? Where are they now?"

"Nobody knows," Puff said. "Can't see shit."

"Oh my God," I said.

"Wait, … no." I could hear him asking someone about the status. "No, that was a ranger, but they didn't have any news."

"So is Suzy there?" I asked.

"Yes, she's been right on it, calling the White Mountains Rescue people," he said. "I'll call you back when I know more."

I hung up and noticed that I was shivering.

My hands were shaking.

I tried to text Jean-Claude.

"Pls Be Careful"

I waited. No reply. Ugh. That didn't make me feel better. It could have been a lack of cell coverage on the mountain. It could also mean the worst. But it likely didn't mean anything. I tried to calm myself down into believing that.

Marshall was taking forever and a day to get back with the sandwiches. I had to tell him what was going on.

"That girl did mayo again, I had to have her redo it, nitwit chick," he said, handing me a white paper sack.

"Moonie went up the mountain and got lost in a storm and J-C went after him and now they're both lost and MortalWarriors are searching for both of them," I said.

"Oh shit," Marshall said.

"Puff called me," I said, "Actually, I called him about the code."

"This sucks. Is Suzy there?"

"She called in the local rescue team," I said.

"Thank goodness. She never seems to panic, no matter what," Marshall said, rubbing his hands together. He put his lunch aside and came over to me.

I was banging the keyboard, pulling up anything I could on the weather on Mount Washington. Nothing seemed to tell me anything other than what the first NOAA site had reported. They all used the same data in some other format.

"I wish I were there," I said. Tears were starting to pool in my eyes.

"Come here." He opened his arms, "I am actually capable of giving people hugs," he said, as if this weren't common knowledge.

Marshall just wasn't the huggy type, so this made me even more teary.

He wrapped his arms carefully around me and I let loose crying.

"It's okay. It's gonna be okay. There are people there, guys with those big hats, like Smokey the Bear, forest rangers or whatever they're called, and even guys with helicopters."

"But there are more and more avalanches there. I was just reading something about it," I said sniffling.

"Don't think about that, there's nothing good about that. You can't do anything right now." He un-hugged me. "Sit down, let's think about this. And eat our lunch."

I was starving, he was right. We sat and looked at all the sites we could find about the area, the weather, anything. Too much info. Harrowing details about avalanches and mountain climbers falling into crevasses, more than I wanted to know. After a half hour, I tried to call Puff back but couldn't get him either.

Lunch was done. And there were no more texts. No more anything.

"Now what?" I said.

"Let's code, I know it sounds crazy but it will get your mind off it. See this line. You had a good hunch about it, right before I went to get the food."

"You must be crazy if you think I can code at a time like this. You want me to be adult about this?"

"Try it," he grinned, and knew I was messing with him. "All true geeks know how to hide out between the lines when life gets cray, Ms. Kroy."

He was right. We just dug in for an hour or two, happy for the distraction. It was about 4 p.m. when I finished fixing a part of the code that really needed fixing and still no word from the mountain men. It was getting dark out in Kendall Square, and of course, getting dark wherever they were.

"Great! Jeez, I can't believe this," I said, looking at my screen of no new texts.

"Maybe we should go watch a movie," Marshall said.

"A movie! What, like the one about the guy who loses his arm climbing a mountain?"

"I was thinking a little less reality and a little more Doris Day."

"I'm not in the mood. I'm gonna go home and do laundry or something." I was just at a loss.

"I'll go with you to Porter," he said and we packed up.

Once I got home and Marshall left, it made it easier to think the worst. I wish I would just hear something from any of them. Were they safe? Were they in trouble? Were they in the hospital? Were they ... No. I didn't want to know or even say that word.

I decided to clean my apartment to take my mind off it, but it didn't really help. I stripped the sheets and put on clean ones, then gathered up the other laundry with the sheets and headed down to the laundry room.

Happily, it was empty so I didn't have to wait to get my stuff started.

There were red machines and white machines. A girl who'd lived in the building for a long time told me the red ones didn't work so well. I dumped my stuff into a white machine. I loaded the soap and set the cycles, jammed in the quarters.

I heard a beep, muted. I dug my phone out of my laundry basket.

Puff texts, "On our way home. Your boy saved the day with the warriors."

"How?"

"Caught Aussie as he was about to go over and down," he texted.

"Christ!"

"When u all back?" I asked

"Likely 2-3 hours, maybe > depends on weather."

I ran the washer and both dryers for a few more cycles, finishing my large pile of dirty clothes, sheets, even a bedspread, just to keep busy and sat there testing our app. On a day I couldn't care less about it, of course, it was working really well.

After a while, I took the new white sheets from the dryer and started folding. I climbed back upstairs with the basket and as I reached the mailbox area, saw muddy boot prints across the lobby. The prints led me to the landing and I tore up the stairs to my second floor landing and there he was, Jean-Claude sitting in a pile of gear, leaning against my door, or more like slanting over, half drowsy and half exhausted. He was coated in mud. His orange and blue harness was a shade of brown, covered in muck and dirt. He wore wet clothes, very muddy boots, and a red ski hat pulled down nearly over his eyes. I kneeled down and hugged him.

"Cherie," he muttered and kissed me wonderfully, like he was eating something delicious. "I'm alive!"

"Thank God, but Jean-Claude, you're a mess," I said.

"Perchance," he said with an Aussie accent.

"Let's go inside, but wait, just take the muddy stuff off out here and I'll put it in the washer."

I went inside the door and he stripped everything off, save his boxers. I got him some pj's to put on, men's pj's I had knocking around.

"The shower's there," I pointed to the door.

"Thanks," he said.

He had a beautiful body, my first up-close look. I was glad he hurried into the shower. I couldn't look at him without blushing.

"I'll take these down to wash," I said, leaving with the muddy mess.

I rushed to get the stuff in the washer, but didn't have enough quarters. I ran up and grabbed some from the jar on my dresser, listening to him in the shower. I went back down, added the soap, the quarters and got the whole muddy mess sloshing around and went back upstairs.

When I came in, he was clean and laying back on the bed in the p.j. bottoms. There was a gash on his arm and a large bandage.

"I want to tell you the whole thing, but I'm so tired."

I sat on the edge of the bed.

"Come over on this side, I can't hold you with this arm."

I went to the other side. He threw his arm around me, pulled me to him. We kissed in a sweet way, calmly.

"I'm so glad you're okay," I was close to his face, which was beautiful, and a little wet from the shower.

"I looked at Mooney in his eyes, like I'm looking at you, right before I grabbed him and we both knew he could just fall and die. Just like that. It was terrible."

"What happened then?"

"Then there was so much wind and rain, I just pulled him on me, and held onto him, like a baby. It was like this." He held me tight.

"Sounds terrible."

"The rock was sharp and narrow and I thought we might both fall. Fall all the way down."

"You're safe now."

He held me tighter.

"So we just waited a long time and then the Warriors came. They might even, well, they could have missed us completely. It was difficult to see. They could have caused us to fall, but they didn't."

"They're good at this stuff."

"Yes. I thought of you. I wanted to hold you like this. I'm not flirting with you."

"It's okay to flirt now. It's okay to do anything now. I was so worried about you."

"I said your name and Mooney laughed when he heard it," he was smiling, but looking tired. "So you helped us, see, even though you weren't there."

"I'm glad."

"He told me we had to get off the ledge, so we could go back and kiss the girls we loved."

"Good advice," I said.

He rolled my way and kissed me.

We kissed for a while and then I saw the gash in his other arm.

"You're bleeding. Let me fix it," I said, getting up.

"It hurts. Thank you."

I went into the bathroom and found the first aid kit. I had the right stuff thanks to Sonya pushing me to buy it in the early weeks.

When I went back into the bedroom, he was asleep. The covers were tossed across his lower back, showing off his bare shoulders. They were the most muscular gorgeous shoulders, I loved looking at them.

I bandaged his arm without waking him, not because I was careful but more likely because he was exhausted.

Finally, I pulled his covers up to his neck and kissed the back of his hair, like he was a little kid. I went into the living room to sleep, since I didn't want to risk rolling over, banging into him or hurting his arm. I pulled out the futon bed, made it up for me and messed with my app for a while, making little fixes.

I could finally relax knowing he was safe. I started to fall asleep. My phone timer beeped and woke me reminding me the laundry should be dry by now. I went out quietly, noticing the mud on the stairs for the first time. It was like the bloody trail of a murderer, and so I went back in to get one of those modern mops someone had left behind in the apartment, and took a stab at cleaning up the mess. The little green plastic mop head snapped off as I tried to get the mud swabbed up. I went down on all fours with a rag to finish the job. I threw the whole mess—broken mop, muddy rag—in the trash in the laundry room.

When his clothes were clean and dry, I folded them and brought them back upstairs. Marshall had texted me for an update and I told him all was good. Sonya had heard about it in Austin and she was short and sweet in her inquiry. "WTF?"

I told her the short version and that J-C was in my bed.

"Oh?"

"Dead asleep, not dead! Cray day."

His boots were a muddy mess, sitting on a brown paper shopping bag by my front door. His clean clothes were folded, on a chair in the living room.

So much for our big night sleeping together. We were finally in the same apartment, but in separate rooms. Still it was as romantic and sweet as any time I had ever experienced with him. And we were in one place and safe. I slipped into the futon bed and was out in a very few minutes.

In the morning, he left early, waking me with a kiss to tell me he had to go meet with his team.

Chapter 24

Tell Me A Story

The next few days were intense. He wanted to be with me the next night and I wanted the same, but his investors took him down to New York for more meetings. I was thinking about Jean-Claude all the time and not concentrating on work enough. He told me not to worry about it. I was worried about it.

Suzy noticed and mentioned that I seemed less and less focused on Demo Day, which was coming up fast and I needed to snap out of it. All the Celery teams were getting very tired and tired of getting ready. The big day was closer and closer. Our prototype was getting strong and solid like a little kid you were getting ready to put on the school bus for the first day of kindergarten. It was almost ready to go out there on its own. I had to give it all my attention.

There was a Beer Pong party at the end of the day at Celery, and Jean-Claude asked me if I'd be there, with a look in his eyes that was all about spending the night together. I had promised a woman friend I'd show up at an event she was throwing across the street. He looked really hurt.

"Then I'll come over after it," he offered.

"Do that. It's at NERD across the street," I said. "It's about storytelling."

"The Ant and the Grasshopper?"

"No, not exactly. More like giving your pitch more life."

"I guess I need to make mine better. You still haven't fallen for it."

It was getting silly how much I wanted to spend a quiet, uninterrupted night with him, but I'd RSVP'd weeks ago for Bobbie Carlton's Mass Innovation Nights event and they were always good, and I needed to go.

Bobbie ran a whole slate of cool events and I almost always learned interesting things from her, so even when I didn't care for the subject, it was great to see her. She was smart and no-nonsense about marketing, which was the one part of startups a lot of us nerdy geeks didn't want to fuss with. Engineers weren't much for the warm and fuzzy ways of marketing (a.k.a. bragging) and PR (lying). Let the work speak for you, was what I thought. Thank God for social media, which was a place to hang with other geeks, ask questions, and learn things, It actually helped you market your company in a friction-free fiction-free manner. It let you talk about what you were doing without all the traditional used-car-salesman-type blah blah.

I guess I had a bad taste in my mouth when it came to PR. Maybe it had to do with finding my husband in bed with one of the Valley's hot young PR rock stars. Oh yeah, she was a true innovator all right.

I shot Bobbie an email to say I was coming over and she agreed to catch up with me before the event, if I wanted to come by early. I did. We met at the sixth floor elevators at NERD on Memorial Drive, then she took me downstairs into the big glass auditorium overlooking the Charles River. She was a saucy brunette who always hit the right note of some how looking cool, well dressed, creative, funky but professional all at once. It meant she made everyone from coders in torn tees to VCs in Italian suits all feel like she was their best friend and brilliant confidante.

Say what you want about Microsoft being too corporate or whatever, but the space they built here in Cambridge was gorgeous and really did help foster the amazing entrepreneurial connections happening in Boston. Bobbie had her own business, not affiliated with Microsoft, but used this space to host events for entrepreneurs. It was good to get out of the pressure cooker of Celery sometimes and into a broader cast of characters to hear what the rest of the world was up to. I helped her set up for the event as we talked.

"So what are you seeing?" I asked her. She knew so many people, she spotted trends very early and had a keen eye.

"Of course, Android kicking iOS' butt. Boston getting to be the real 'Hub' for mobile, or maybe always was. And my kids and their friends want off Facebook where they know all the parents are watching them," she said setting out snacks. "How about you with the new Celery class?"

"I just see big differences from California. I think Y Combinator classes and other accelerators out there have more Asian and Indian CEOs. Here we have more coders from Europe, Eastern Europe, Russian. And more women, finally."

"Suzy is taking a lot of heat about that. VCs are claiming reverse discrimination."

"She's good at taking heat." We both agreed to that.

"Can you put these sodas over there?"

"Sure," I said.

Her phone chirped with a new text.

"The speakers are showing up, I have to go upstairs and sign them in. Stay here, I'll bring a few of them down. There's a Brit you'll like."

Brit? I had a super sweet French guy.

"So many Brits, so little time," I said.

The massive room had all glass on two sides looking out on the river and a wide-sweeping staircase in blonde wood that cascaded like a waterfall down to the main floor of the two-level loft space. You entered on top, checked in and descended the dramatic staircase, like royalty announced at a fancy ball.

One of the largest screens I'd ever seen was at the far end of the room, where there was a 50-foot-long butcher-block kitchen island perfect for setting up food and drink. A few dozen people could hang out and lean against it as they. Lining the back of the room, there were three or four shiny metal refrigerators and rows and rows of cabinets with everything you could need for hosting any party. It was a beautiful room for geek meet and greets. Thank you, Bill Gates.

Bobbie introduced me to the speakers. The "Brit" was a classic tall, dark, handsome, nearly movie star good-looking guy. Any woman would want to talk to him. Well, any woman except me. I realized that as I shook his hand. I was thinking about Jean-Claude and not listening to him at all. His name was Spenser Something and he was rather flirty. He was not only sexy, but he had a deliciously great accent. His British sexiness was only making me think of Jean-Claude's French sexiness, which was way sexier. I missed him.

"Sorry?" I realized I'd completely missed what he had asked me.

"What's your take on storytelling?" the Brit repeated.

Up on high I saw Slava and Irina first and then, Jean-Claude in his shades, looking out toward the river where the sun was setting, standing at the top of the stairs. More heat. I felt my heart beat in my throat. All three came down the big stairs but then J-C turned back toward the entry hall, and went back up. Where was he going?

"Once upon a time … that kind?" I was a little dismissive.

"Well, why not start there," Spenser said. "What's it make you feel, when you hear those words?"

"I guess, once upon a time, I don't know. It makes me think, something is going to happen, something strange and unexpected. I want to know more, know what's going to happen next," I said.

"Exactly, so what's your story?" he asked, and gave me an intriguing smile.

Blatant flirt, but it fell flat. If it was a war of the English versus the French, the French were winning. But how could you explain that to a stranger? J-C was in the building now, so everything was different.

"Once upon a time, people had these super useful mobile devices, but they were always running out of power, until a geek girl named Monica invented BrightLight to give them power wherever they went and she saved the day!" I felt a bleep from my phone, a text.

"There you go! But I'm sure you can make it better than that," he said.

"That's all I do anymore – refine my pitch – I'm over at Celery," I explained.

"Impressive," he moved closer to me and I stepped back.

"I wasn't bragging or anything. I meant, we work on our stories a lot at Celery." I was motioning for Irina and Slava to come over. "And these are two other founders from the program."

I introduced the Russians.

"Excuse me," I said, checking the text. Sonya was asking where I was. Then I walked nonchalantly to the other side of the room en route to the ladies room. I went up the stairs and around the balcony, trying to see where J-C had disappeared to, but didn't find him.

They were still talking storytelling when I returned.

The Brit said, "I like Monica's story, have you heard it?"

Slava groaned and laughed a big laugh, "Only about a hundred times!"

"Thanks!" I slugged him.

"No, only meaning that we hear each other pitching all the time. Day. Night. Whenever."

"So here's the trick," the Brit said. "Can you keep it fresh?"

"No," I said.

The Brit rattled off a bunch of good ideas about how to improve my pitch.

I was half listening and half trying to figure out what happened to my friend. The program was starting in ten minutes and I looked up and saw J-C at the top of the stairs again, with some fashionista girl.

She was a pretty, skinny girl with very long blonde hair that went down past her bottom. What was she doing here? J-C had that "coolest guy in the room walking in with the coolest girl" thing down for sure. He was still wearing his black sunglasses, and yes, it was mostly dark out by now.

They approached us and I moved closer to the Brit, which made him smile, and he moved closer to me.

"Another Celery friend, Jean-Claude. He's French, but I don't know the blonde," I whispered into his ear.

Slava introduced J-C to the Brit and they shook hands. I decided to say nothing. The blonde was named Amy. That was much too nice a name for such a creepy-looking girl.

She had eye makeup that looked like black raccoon eyes. She looked heroin skinny and wore a tight black mini dress, black and white striped stockings, odd tall black booties.

She reminded me of someone. Yes, I suddenly remembered. Amy looked like the creepy guy in that old movie, Beetlejuice. Scary. She must be a model.

I wasn't listening again to the other, but watching J-C watching me.

"Il était un fois," J-C said.

"Yes, once upon a time," the Brit said, showing off that he spoke French.

"The designers in haute couture needed the finest fabrics at the best prices and my app let them buy and sell quality materials fast and furiously," J-C said in a rather charming way.

"Your English is awfully good," the Brit said.

"I went to school in England and an English boarding school in Switzerland," he said.

"Oh really? What school was that?" the Brit asked.

"N'importe," J-C said. "One like all the rest."

"Where they spanked the bad boys?" the Brit said.

"Of course, which made us only badder boys," he said with a cynical snicker that was not his usual style. He was looking directly me.

If his face could speak, it said, "What the hell are you doing with that guy?"

The scary blonde purred something into J-C's ear in French. "J'ai soif," she said, a whiney way to say, "I'm thirsty."

Slava picked up on the blonde's request, knowing some French himself, "Here, let me show you what they have to drink." He took her over to the far side of the kitchen.

J-C was being a bit brusque and rude to the Brit. It was almost funny. I forgot how much the English dislike the French and vice versa. Or had I actually succeeded in making J-C a little jealous?

Sonya showed up next, just as the event was starting. She gave me a hug hello and then went over with Irina to pick out some seats a few rows from the front. Irina at the end, then Sonya, then Slava, then the Beetlejuice blonde. J-C and I were still standing with the Brit.

Spenser said, "Excuse me, I have to talk to the moderator for a minute."

J-C came over and whispered, "Sit by me," quietly in my ear. "She's a friend of a friend here on college visits."

"OK," I said. Being jealous was silly and he always knew tons of people so I trusted him.

Jean-Claude went to sit at the end of the row next to the blonde, leaving an open seat next to him on the right. From the other side a group filled in and asked them to move down, so there was no place for me. He looked over at me and put his hands up, like "sorry" he wasn't able to save me a seat.

Spenser the Brit was back and noticed me standing there and said to me, "Just join me in the front, there's an extra chair." then took my arm and led me away from J-C and off to the speakers' area.

I sat there with the Englishman, hoping J-C didn't think I was doing it just to tease him. When Spenser got up to speak, I decided to escape and go back to Celery. So I slipped out the side entrance.

I was halfway down the hall, when I saw Jean-Claude running after me.

"Monica," he called.

"Going down?" There was an elevator right there with someone holding the door for me, so I jumped in it. "My friend … " I said, trying to push the Open Door button, but it closed before J-C got there.

Downstairs, I waited for him.

He didn't show. After five minutes, I decided to just go. On the street the air was refreshing. I was sick of offices and buildings and all of it. I grabbed the T home and when I got there to Porter Station, I never felt happier to just go home for a quiet night. I took a nice long, slow, hot bath, and as I was getting out of the tub, my phone beeped one final text of the evening.

One word only, from J-C.

"Free?"

"Lost your blonde?"

"Done babysitting, yes. Friend's silly daughter looking at colleges. Let me come over, please?"

So this was it, and now it was up to me to say the word.

I texted him three letters.

"Yes."

Chapter 25

Love Seen

I threw the room in order, pulled another pillow out of my closet, put new pillowcases on both of them. The sheets were one day old. It would take too long to put fresh ones on, so I left them as is. Besides, they'd need to be changed soon enough anyway with any luck.

What to wear? Not my robe with nothing underneath. I changed quickly. A long swirly full jersey black skirt, with a tiny black mesh thong under it, together with a tight white camisole, almost a bustier, the way it was low cut and the front showed off some cleavage. Or, to be precise, as the French called it, "décolletage."

I lit some candles on the kitchen table, put the teapot on high and measured out some jasmine tea into the strainer in my pot. The heavy cast iron pot looked a little mysterious in the candlelight. And I loved the way the jasmine tea launched a steamy cloud of flowery perfume into the room. I placed two cups and the teapot on a black lacquer tray. I was getting sleepy looking at the tray, waiting for him, but snapped awake at his urgent knock.

I opened the door. He came in quickly, locked the door behind him, leaned against it, pulled me into his arms, kissed me fast and furious. No words, just straight to the good stuff.

I pulled away. "Good evening, Monsieur," I said, calming things down.

He bowed and waved his arm, "Good evening, Madame."

"You know, in English, it has a specific meaning, the word, 'Madame,' I mean," saying it in a flat American pronunciation, "Tea?"

"What, doesn't it mean a married woman?" He nodded yes to the tea. His eyes were so sexy, his lids a bit lowered and his head raised up in interest.

"Well, it does mean that, but it means something else too," I said.

I was sipping the tea. He downed the cup in one gulp like a shot of whiskey.

He put the cup down, saying no to my offer of more.

"Wait," he hit the side of his head. "Madame. It means, je sais, je sais, like the CEO of a bordello," he said.

I laughed, "Yes, it means, well, the 'madame' of a whore house, as we might say. Yes, the lady who runs the place."

"But you know when I say it to *you*, I mean, a beautiful married lady who is sexy and wonderful and wise."

"Okay," I said. "That works."

He had an irresistible way of looking adult and manly, but also boyish at the same time.

"Does it? I don't think it does. Seems like you keep pushing me away. I want to know why," he asked.

He stood up, took my hand and pulled me to stand in front of him.

"I love to look at you," he said. "I want to look at you all night."

As we were so close together and since I didn't have any heels on, I realized he was fairly tall. We were as close as dancers, our legs were pressed together, one of his between mine, my chest pressed to him. He stroked my neck softly, as if exploring.

"Do you really want to know? You're making it hard for me to talk, Jean-Claude."

"If a customer has objections, you must explore every one of them and address each of them up front." He was quoting stuff we'd learned from one of the marketing mentors' coaching sessions.

"Your English is very good tonight."

"Yes, I really want to know."

He ran his fingers along the straps of my camisole, from shoulder down to the top of my breasts.

"You're too young for me," I said, moving his hands away.

"Not so. And you can let me decide that," he said and bent down to wrap around me and kiss me. It was a truly superior kiss. It was a leave-you-dizzy kiss.

"And," I couldn't think of what I was going to say, "And you're leaving and going back to France," I said.

"Wait. You didn't like my kiss?" he asked, "I'm not going anywhere until you tell me what you thought of that kiss."

"That was a good kiss."

"Good, just good, Cherie?"

"Okay, that was a great kiss."

He tilted his head, looking into my eyes, searching for the truthful reply, making me spit it out.

"Okay, that was a phenomenal kiss."

"Now come here," he said. "No more objections."

He pulled me close again and our bodies pressed against one another.

"Wait, who was the blonde?"

"She's a daughter of a friend of my uncle. She's here looking at universities and I got stuck with her. Who was the Brit and why was he so friendly?'

"Just the speaker, no one important."

"He was handsome," he said, looking at me with a bit of a question.

"Not to me. But she was pretty," I said.

"Not to me. You are beautiful to me."

Good one. There are some things Frenchmen are very good at.

He took my face in his hands, like gathering a bouquet of flowers, brought his lips to mine. He was a very good kisser, not too eager. He kissed me for a while, putting kisses all over me, closing my eyelids with kisses, leaving them in my eyebrows, kissing my hair, kissing my ear.

"Do you like this?" he said.

"I do," I said.

I just looked at him.

He smiled.

"What else do you like?" he was again at the straps of my bustier, close to my breasts.

"I like seeing you here," I said, "in my kitchen."

"I like being here," he said looking around the room. "I like being back here."

"You might like my other rooms too," I said.

"I like your bed, but not yet," he said, not looking directly at me, but looking down at my breasts and letting his hands move across the lacy top of my bustier. He slipped one strap off my shoulder and then the other. He took his time and slowly nuzzled my neck, his whiskers brushing my skin, under my ear, down to my sternum, then holding me tighter and burying his face between my breasts, unlatching the garment in the back.

"Very beautiful," he said, as I stood there in front of him, topless.

"Let me take your shirt off. " I said, "No, don't help me." I went slowly, going button by button.

His body was just perfect and strong, and I was so glad to finally know him this way. Clothes seemed such a bother. His jeans were low slung and the cut of his hips and hard flat ab muscles drew me down lower. They urged me to do away with the belt, the pants, everything. But I held back. I took one finger and ran it around the edge of his pants, along the inside of his belt. He did the same to the waistband of my skirt.

I said, "I've wanted to be with you like this, since the day I spilled coffee all over you."

He laughed. "That was a good day."

He picked me up as he hugged me, holding my bottom, lifting me and pressing me up against his pants. I felt him hard and eager, in no need of encouragement.

"This is a good night," I said.

I wiggled out of his grasp, making him laugh. He grabbed for me and I took his hand.

"I'll give you a tour," I said, leading him down the hall.

"La salle de bain," I said, pointing out the bathroom.

"Yes," he said.

"The extra room, where my computer is," I said.

"Yes," he said.

"The bedroom," I said.

"A wonderful room," he said. "You took me in when I was hurt. Thank you."

"You're welcome. And you're welcome here."

It was dark. We didn't turn on the light. He said nothing, but took my hand and took me to the bed. We stood next to it, in a tight embrace.

The streetlight was illuminating the far corner of the room. We both looked toward the window. The cars going by on the street threw light on the wall, on my dresser, desk, chair, as we stood kissing. He was pressing his mouth hard against me, his body as well. To feel our bodies together, after waiting so long to feel them together this way, was lovely.

"Let me take off your jeans," I said.

"Yes," he said.

"Did you know this might happen tonight?" I asked him.

"I didn't know. I was sad that it probably would not," he said, touching my lips and then putting a finger in my mouth, which I sucked like a baby.

With his other hand, he stroked my breasts.

I put my hand on his jeans, stroking him in return before unzipping him.

He was beautifully hard.

"We should do something about this," I said looking down a bit.

"Yes," he said.

I undressed him slowly, helped him step out of the rest of his clothes. Some guys, long before you get a chance to see them naked, can make you wonder about their size, especially when they act so cocky in the world. Jean-Claude did not disappoint.

Before things got too crazy, I pulled a drawer open next to the bed and offered him a condom, wrapped in bright red foil like candy. He made short work of putting it on.

"Sit on the bed," I said.

He sat and now I stood topless in front of him. My blouse and bra were tossed on the floor, only the skirt remained.

"Shall I take this off?" I offered.

"No."

He ran his hand up my leg, under my skirt and started to stroke me expertly. After a few minutes, I was right in sync with him, very aroused.

"Madame, may I look under your skirt?"

I nodded yes.

He lifted it so slowly, bunching up little bits of it, like a curtain going up on a theatrical performance. He looked up at me and grinned, then he put his head under my skirt, but did not touch me at first.

Waiting for him to touch me was so exciting.

Finally, I felt him lick my leg, a tiny lick just above my knee that made me tremble. The next lick was higher. Then higher. When he was just about to lick between my legs, he moved up fast, managing to take a bite of my thong in his teeth and yanking it off. We were both laughing at this.

Then he stopped, and suddenly pulled me down on the bed and rolled on top, pressing against me, kissing me fast. He took the weight of his upper body on his arms, but our pelvises were grinding as we kissed. I could have kissed him all night like this. He kissed me lighter after a bit, but pressed himself against me harder. Both of us were too ready for the other. We were panting. He grinned. We started laughing.

"This is good," he said.

"Yes. Welcome to my … house," I said, opening up for him and wrapping my legs around him.

"Yes, thank you for letting me in, Madame," he said.

He entered me fast and hard.

"Ahh." It was the sweetest thing. We rocked back and forth and now there was no need to hold back, both of us betraying the long held secret that we were crazy for the other. We made short work of the deed, as if rushing to just get the first time over with, so we could do it again.

"I thought you said you were tired?" He flopped over to the right side of the bed, as we uncoupled.

"I guess you changed my mind."

After the first time, we slowed down and he spent some serious time exploring my body, hardly missing a centimeter, never needing to be invited or coaxed.

"I love this part of you," he said, opening my legs, just stroking me. After a while he leaned down to use his tongue. He pressed closer and closer, opening me wider, as if enjoying a particular delicacy. He stripped me of my skirt at some point, I couldn't remember when and now he went down a little harder, bringing me to climax very quickly. I urged him to climb on top, so he could enter me soon after and take me hard and fast. I had a funny flash of how he looked the first day we met. I was so happy he was here.

After the second time, we were exhausted and snuggled into sleep, until about 4 a.m. I woke to find him wrapped around me from behind, and felt him growing hard again, pressing against my bottom.

He kissed me behind the ear and whispered, "I need more of you."

"Wait," I stretched over and pulled another condom from my drawer.

"We invented them," he nuzzled.

"I don't think so," I insisted.

"You don't think the French invented condoms? Madame, I thought you were familiar with innovation."

"Do you really want to talk about French inventors, or do you want to use this?"

He looked at me sideways, then grinned. That ended that argument.

Now he took his time, making love to me in a languorous, velvety way, leaving me wondering if he'd rearranged my body for good, each limb somehow signaling every other with connected sensuality. He was stroking my left arm making the arch of my right foot tingle, kissing my neck causing my knees to shimmer. He'd reconstructed me like a woman in a Cubist painting, making me forget where my body and his started and ended. We did what people rarely do, but often do in books and movies, crashing into a climax at the very same moment. We rested and then he dove under the sheets, surfacing by my toes.

"Monica, let me tell me you a story. It's a fascinating tale," he imitated the Brit Spenser.

"You are bad! Very, very bad!"

He snaked back around to be head-to-head with me.

"How about this? Is this bad?"

He pulled me close and kissed me hard.

"It's good," I said.

"Once upon a time there was a British idiot," he said.

I started laughing. He was holding me in his arms.

"You're not jealous!" I said.

He rolled away like he was hurt.

"Oh, come on," I said.

"You think I'm jaloux?" he said now back to his French accent. His most hilarious accent of course was his phony American accent.

He jumped out of bed naked, started looking around the room, under the bed. I missed him terribly in a second, but loved him parading around in his birthday suit.

He appeared to be looking for something. A lost sock?

"WHAT are you doing?"

"I'm looking for Spenser," he said, like it was obvious.

"Oh stop it!"

"But, Madame, there's no Spenser here. I can't be jealous, because I'M HERE and he IS NOT!" he said boldly.

"Touché" I said. I was looking right at his cock, which was doing the anti-gravity trick again. I wanted him back in bed right away.

"Look what you did," he said, looking down at his eagerness, "I blame you."

"Get in here," I said.

He took his phone from my nightstand and started texting.

My phone buzzed.

I grabbed my phone.

He had texted: "I'm finding I kind of like you."

I laughed and pulled him into bed on top of me.

"My words went from this bed, up to the stars and back to tell you I love you," he said.

"Whoa. Love me? This says 'kind of like you' I think," I said, showing him the phone.

He texted back a correction, "*kind of love you*"

He was definitely not one of these guys who are terrified to use the verb "love" as if it were radioactive.

I texted him. "Then kiss me."

He did, but did more, sliding inside me bit by bit as we kissed. It was the best ever.

He was good at holding back for a young guy, and we lay together quietly for a bit, wound around and around one another in this new "no clothes allowed" part of our pairing.

"No tattoos," I noticed.

"I hate needles," he admitted.

"I thought you'd have some, maybe a lot of them."

"Not my thing. Do you like them?"

"No, I don't," I admitted.

He slipped his hand very slowly between my legs, then started petting me, into a blush of heat and desire, his other arm around my shoulders and his finger playing with my hair around my ears, licking my ears a little now and then.

"I do have a story for you, dear," he said.

"No pitch please," I said.

"It's nothing like that. Once upon a time in Switzerland."

"Switzerland?"

"Yes, let me tell you my story, you just listen," he said.

He told me how he had been thrown out of an English boarding school and then went to a new school in Switzerland. It was strict. It wasn't a religious school, but the teachers had to wear these black frock coats. He went on to describe a teacher who he esteemed. He said that word, "esteemed," which wasn't far from the word "steamy," I thought to myself.

He had a way with words; he liked to make love to words, just to entertain me. The teacher was a young Russian man, with long, thick straight black hair, nearly shoulder length.

"I would have to share him with you of course. He would think the world of you. He would love you, maybe even more than I do," Jean-Claude explained.

"Did you, I mean, … did you have a crush on him this teacher?" I ventured.

"Not him, I didn't like men like that," he said.

"Didn't or don't?" I inquired.

"Well if you're asking if I'm bi, I'm not. I like women quite a lot, you may have noticed."

"I did."

"I did have a crush on a girl he liked, a girl who worked there," he said. "A teacher?" I asked.

"Just let me tell you my story. I was madly in love with this girl who did the cleaning up in the dining hall after dinner. But I didn't know what to do with her, I was young. I was a virgin. She was older than me, maybe 25 and at first never noticed me or paid me any attention, which really made me sad. I often sat after dinner pretending to study, but I was just there to look at her washing the tables because I was infatuated with her. She had long thick yellow braids like you wear some times. I imagined her undressed with the braids hanging down to her breasts. I liked to imagine her sitting in my room on a chair near my bed tout nu. What's the word?

"Naked."

"Yes, she would have no clothes, just pink wool socks and her braids would hang down in front of her breasts just covering her nipples. This would make me mad that I couldn't talk to her or touch her. She was teasing me and I wanted her, but I was not allowed to touch her. I would pretend not to notice and read my Russian grammar book."

"Russian? I thought this was Switzerland," I was interrupting him for no good reason again.

"It was Switzerland, but I studied Russian in that school. You keep interrupting my story. Maybe you want me to spank you?" He had a good way of arching an eyebrow.

"No, don't do that, just keep talking please," I said.

"I do want to spank you, at work I mean," he explained.

"What?!"

"With the Ping-Pong circles, … those racquets," he held an imaginary one in the air and made a "pfft" noise as he flipped his wrist.

"Paddle," I corrected, "Don't you dare!"

"Then listen to my story, Madame. We're storytelling here, it's serious business," he said.

"She's in a chair next to your bed, with braids, naked."

"Yes, I see you were listening. So I would watch her and I would grow harder and harder just to look at her. I would have to go to her. I would take the braids and brush them over her nipples until they pointed, you understand?" he said, as he was touching me in this way.

"And I would slowly make her part her legs and I would pet her," he continued to show me what he would do to her, by doing it to me.

"You like my story?" he asked.

I nodded yes.

"And I liked to make her purr like a kitty and then she would make louder noises, after I was done petting her fur and I wanted to enter her, with my fingers, like this," he told me all the while doing it to me, but acting as if he were not even touching me.

"One, then two, then three," he showed me as he slipped one, then two, then three fingers inside me in an exquisite manner.

"I like your story very much," I said, trying to hold back from climaxing.

"Well, wait for the rest, there's more to come," he said solemnly. I couldn't even tell if he knew he was making a pun.

"I can hold on," I clamped down on his fingers to show him.

"Nice. I like that. That's the game. You need to hold tight, until I say it's time."

"Time?"

"Time to come. Can you resist until I say?"

"I can try," I said.

"You'll enjoy the dénouement." He looked boldly into my eyes.

"It's pleasure enough, just to hear someone pronounce that word correctly," I said.

"More pleasure than that is awaiting you, Cherie," he said, then pulled the fingers out slowly, all the while rubbing my clit with his thumb.

"Oh hell, I guess so," I pushed his hand away. "More story now."

"Our teacher liked the girl with the braids too. And he asked me to bring her to his room and he would give us both help with our lessons. He said he was the master and I was the student, and said it was important to get the woman ready for the master, and told me how to touch her to get her ready for him, but I was not allowed to enjoy her. He would come in and undress in front of us slowly, but tell me sternly to study my book, not to watch."

"I'm surprised you got any homework done," I said, starting to giggle.

"You are ruining my story! You must listen, Madame!" he said in mock anger.

"I'm sorry, it's a lovely story, I'll listen," I said.

"Sometimes he would take her out of bed, and make her put her hands on the desk and he would enter her from behind," he said.

"I'm not sure what you mean," I said naively.

"Perhaps I need to demonstrate?"

"Yes, I think you better."

"Get up, I'll show you," he said. He placed me in front of the desk, put one of my hands on the right, one on the left far apart, then put his hand between my legs and teased me with little strokes until he'd spread them, farther and farther apart.

"Lift your bottom up a bit, Madame," he said.

He rubbed up against my ass at first, showing off his stiffness, then stealing a bit of wetness to aid in the attack.

"Perfect. You are nice and wet like she was," he whispered behind my ear, licking me in just the right way, not sloppy.

Jean-Claude entered me with a thrust and then he took my hips to move me up and down and I was close to losing it.

"Now you see what I was talking about?" he whispered in my ear.

"Yes."

"You're a good student. Now, you come for me, I think you want to. I want to see you fall apart," he said.

"I'm close," I could hardly talk.

"Me too."

"Let me help you," he said, pushing harder but using his fingers in front, nice and wet, tugging my clit. It was stunning, took no time, was so very intense, "Oh man, oh, oh honey, thank you. Oh, oh, oh." I was riding all the waves he'd started inside me, crashing past him. I let him ride me harder, until he came with an amazing power, crumpling over me when he was done.

We stumbled back into bed. We spooned, his front to my back.

"I don't believe your story, not a bit of it," I said.

He started laughing, "Not even the girl who cleaned up in the dining hall?"

"Not even her," I said.

"I was just trying to take you far away. A story can do that. Did it work?"

"Oh yes," I turned his head to kiss him.

"Good."

"You took us both far away," I was getting tired.

"And now we're back home here," he said. "Let's sleep now." I put my head on his shoulder and he wrapped me in his arms. He was very good at this. Really, he was very good at so many things.

Chapter 26

The Morning After and the Morning After That

The next morning I got a happy-kid-Christmas-morning type jolt when I looked to the left and found my friend was right there, his head close by, on my extra pillow. He was really there. I liked the idea of him there with me. After a minute or two I heard him snoring, not too loudly, and it reminded me of Nick who was a world-class snorer, something I really didn't like. It was funny how Jean-Claude snoring in my bed, on the other hand, was just fine.

Then it got a little louder and then louder and I almost started laughing because it was terrible and then he reached out and grabbed me and started tickling me.

"Fooled you! I was looking at you, looking at me, Madame!"

"You bum!"

The tickling turned into kissing pretty fast. We could have slipped into a morning of more sex, but both of us knew there was an early start at Celery.

"Merde!" he broke away when he saw the clock, "I'm meeting my team in 20 minutes."

"Good luck," I said.

"I have to go. Good bye, kiss me," he jumped up, but leaned over to kiss me one last time.

He dashed across the room, and I watched every gorgeous naked part of him as he fled into the bathroom. His hair was a particular sexy mess this morning.

He was in and out of the shower at record speed, came over to kiss me goodbye and then was gone. I buried my head under his pillow, to steal one last bit of his scent, no doubt some eau de cologne he'd gotten free from one of the designers he knew, worth more than any bottle of perfume I'd ever owned.

I only had about ten minutes more than he did to linger and got to Celery just before we were starting. And I was feeling weirdly shy. To see your lover again the next day, in his clothes, in the office with his team, is paradoxical and almost sexier than the night before. Your body wants to run to him, peel his clothes off and be eyelash close again, but another part of you is just timid and breathless when you recall the things you'd done, the memories of very intimate positions that the two of you are still savoring in your mind. It was tricky trying to reconcile an image of him between your legs driving you mad a few hours before with a sunny office, all of us working together in the conference room. You saw him talking to his team, getting them excited about their work. Then you flash on his encouraging you to let loose in bed, the same voice, a very different venue, a memory of limbs entwined and a landscape of warm welcoming skin. You want to go back there.

And the light of day, it's just too much. Who are all these people around us? This sun, this traffic, these cars, these buildings — make them go away! Get us back to clean linens, our pile of pillows, his lovely collarbone where a girl can slide her finger back and forth, riding his body from shoulder to sternum to rib to hip, like a little private amusement park.

And that first awkward glance, trying to look casual and innocent, but that lightning bolt of knowledge we share, both of us wanting to be sure that lushness of love is still ours and ours alone and wasn't just a complete invention of our overheated brains.

We took our seats in the big room. I saw him on the row ahead of me and when I sat right behind him, he looked back, nodded and was saying so much in one nod. As if he were saying, "Yes, that was real." And the nod signified, "That was wonderful last night and I want more." Shyly, I looked back and my eyes said "That could be arranged." I smile at my feet and I hear and feel him grin back, like a sun radiating heat at long last on a spring day where the morning had been cloudy and confusing, but now the yellow promise of a perfect day washes over you.

You think nobody notices, but how could they miss it? It pulses through your skin, your clothes, your walk, your grin. You are on fire and pretending you're not.

Sonya was sitting next to me, and asked me a question a second time. I never heard the first.

"Sorry?" I asked her. Again, the dumb grin.

"I said, did the prototype work as well as … " then she stopped and looked at me, slantwise, and then Jean-Claude. "Oh crap!"

"What?" I said, grinning, but as if we were talking about software.

"Nothing," she just settled back into her seat. She looked at him and then at me, shook her head to show it was pointless to talk to us. "You'll be useless today right, Chiquita?"

I grinned. She knew.

Yes, it was that great drug, the rush of love and the deep drenching feeling of desire and "who cares?" all rolled into one. It certainly made the world go away, leaving him and me the only two people in it.

I needed a new calendar app that put all my real responsibilities and meetings in a tiny, tiny font, and put "BED" with J-C in big red letters. It was the only way to tell time now. I needed an interface that read "8 hrs 23 minutes 12 seconds" (until I can be in bed again with my lover). That was the only time that counted.

"You are so goofy," Sonya leaned over to tell me.

"Thanks," I grinned.

"You gotta snap out of it!" she warned.

"Okay." Not that I had any intention of doing that.

Roan came in to say Suzy was running late. We'd start in 15.

Jean-Claude made the brilliant suggestion that we go across the street to Cosi and get coffee. He made it sound serious and reasonable, but then winked at me.

I asked Sonya if she wanted any coffee.

"Yeah, get me one and then pour it on him, maybe you guys will wake up and stop grinning."

"Unlikely," I said.

He and I went into the elevator, just him and me and he nearly threw me against the far wall, pressing up against me and started kissing me in the only private no-camera spot he'd shown me that first time. We shared the building with a few floors of Microsoft Cambridge headquarters and the elevator came to a stop, we jumped apart and the doors opened. Three geeky guy engineers got in. They snickered since J-C had my lipstick smeared all over his face.

He was close to my ear, "Je deteste Microsoft!"

I wiped it off.

We rode down with our new friends and finally got to the lobby.

"I want to show you something," he said, and dragged me off to the far elevators where you could access the parking. There were vending machines and next to them, a little cubby space just big enough to slide into and start kissing me again.

A woman, nicely dressed in a grey suit, like a lawyer, came over to buy a soda.

"Shh," he said and pushed me farther into the alcove.

"You've gotta stop," I whispered, but he didn't and we kissed right through the clunk noise when the woman's soda can dropped.

She paid us no mind at first, but then gave me a furtive grin.

"So I guess you had a nice time last night?" I offered when we came up for air.

"Thank you, Madame, I did," he said.

We crossed the street and floated into Cosi. He looked so good to me this morning. Even in front of their case of amazing breads, rolls, pastry, he looked like the best treat available.

The cute perky Asian girl behind the counter asked him, "What would you like?" He looked over at me and winked, as if to say, "I want Monica, over there."

Then he got it together and ordered.

"Café latté please," he said. "Vous, Madame?"

"Same," I said.

We took a booth at the back, away from everyone.

We held hands under the table. He was imitating some of our colleagues pitches which were pretty funny. He was replaying a fight between Irina and Slava. His Russian accent was truly hilarious.

"Wait," I said, seeing something shocking over his shoulder. Suddenly I was barely breathing.

I saw him out of the corner of my eye. It was Dunhill alone, then Nick walked in and shook hands with him. I nearly choked on my coffee and pointed. They couldn't see us from where we were. I felt a rush of anger that snapped me out of my lovey dovey state.

"My ex, with Dunhill," I said.

"Bastard," he jumped up.

"Wait, what are you doing?"

"I'm just going to show him what I think of him."

All I needed. He was playing Knight in Shining Armor for me. I'd told him what Risa found out, that Nick and Dunhill were likely sabotaging our efforts.

A waitress was coming over with a tray of about half a dozen glasses of ice water.

Jean-Claude walked behind her and turned quickly, knocking into her at just the right moment, causing her to spill the cold water all over Nick. Then he just kept going.

Nick was drenched, then he jumped up and started giving the girl hell and yelling "Fuck" within seconds. They never saw J-C, who was at the door by now. I got up and exited the other way, so they never saw me either.

We met on the street out front.

"Your husband is not having a good day, Madame," he smirked.

"But I am!"

"Me too," he took my arm.

Sonya raced across the street. "You left your phone in the conference room. The guy from Alexandria called looking for you. I answered it."

"Wow, did he say anything? Did he say yes?"

"Just wants you to call him."

We headed up in the elevators, all three of us.

"Did they start the meeting?" I asked Sonya.

"Not yet," she said.

Jean-Claude's team was waiting in the hall when the elevator doors opened on our floor.

"Eh, mec! C'est l'heure pour le truc à MIT," his lead programmer said.

"Ah, oui, oui," J-C said. "We have this thing at MIT we can't miss," he told us.

"See you later," I said, and we went back into the conference room, as he left with his team.

The morning meeting went quickly. By mid-morning the office was going full tilt, way too fast for me, or maybe I was just finally feeling tired.

I checked my calls. Risa had called.

I decided to call her first before Alexandria. I got the feeling something was up. It was odd both calls had arrived so close in time.

Risa's assistant told me she was in a meeting, but specifically not to talk to Alexandria until I talked to her. She'd be free in a half hour at the latest, they told me. I decided to go over to Back Bay if she wanted to see me in person. I grabbed the T and was there 20 minutes later.

Her husband was there with some clients and she wanted to get coffee, so we walked over to Starbucks on Newbury Street, two blocks from her place.

"Your ex is trying to get in to see John Alexander, with Dunhill," she said, sitting with me at the table closest to the window.

"Great!"

"I'm fairly sure Alexander doesn't want to work with him," she said, "but he brought them part of the Twitter round and they feel like they owe him. Did you know he's friends with Alexander's wife, Dot?"

"No."

"They knew each other at Exeter."

"He knows everybody it seems like. I saw him this morning."

"Really?"

Her phone started to buzz.

"Sorry." She showed me it was Alexander's main office line.

"Right, yes, this is Risa."

There were a lot of "really?" "yes" and "no's" but I couldn't make out the gist of the conversation.

She put down the phone. "Okay, stranger and stranger. Nick was supposed to see them this morning but he just cancelled at the last minute."

I started laughing.

"What?" she said.

"Well, about two hours ago, my friend Jean-Claude and I saw him at Cosi and had the chance to send a lot of glasses of ice water down his back."

"You have to love that," she grinned.

"Yes, It was great to see. He was furious."

"Still, Nick never gives up that easily. He's not to be trusted. They want to see us again. I'll set something up," she said. "I thought it was already a yes," I said. "Don't worry, they want to help us bring in some more capital, maybe another firm, it's good," she explained.

And so two days later Risa went with me to Alexandria to do our big pitch. She suggested I bring Sonya too. I wanted her to watch Risa in action, but to my surprise, Risa let Sonya and I run the meeting, feeling no need to step up.

"So shall I follow your lead?" I asked Risa.

"No, you're running this. You're ready and it's your baby. You know what BrightLight can do better than anyone." She told me in the lobby as we waited to go in, "You don't need me. But if you do, just pull me in, or kick me under the table."

Sonya looked a little rattled, as we went into their massive conference room with an expansive view of the Boston Common, to find John Alexander, his other partner Gregory Gordon, and their associates Maeve Sanders and Linda Miller Diego dressed expensively, chatting quietly, all waiting for us. That was the good and bad thing about being in love — it gave you a ridiculous amount of confidence and total insouciance, making you not care a fig about the outcome of any meeting. It helped me relax and kick it off with our reason for meeting, our pitch, and then I turned to Sonya to let her speak to the technical side of what we were doing.

She did a great job of what BrightLight could do now, but what we planned in the future for the product. Risa pulled it together at the end, talking about the new companies at Celery and around Boston and why ours was particularly attractive.

They asked us to step outside after this. I always hated this part. It felt like some very polite execution squad deciding on whether to let us live another day or line us up and shoot us. Okay, it was only our idea they might shoot down, but it felt like a heavy decision after months of work.

They only spoke for about ten minutes, which was a good sign and then asked us back into the room.

"Linda, you start," John said.

"We love your team. We love your idea. We think there's more here than you know. It can be bigger," she said.

"Great," Risa said.

"Right," John said. "So Maeve, what's the next step for BrightLight?"

He was letting his associates run the meeting.

"Well, we want to give you the green light, but first we think we need another firm to go in. Do you have anyone else ready to go in?"

"Not yet," I said.

"Good," she said. "John and I can work up a list of folks we like to work with and you can meet with them, see who you like."

"Sounds good," I said.

"One other thing," Greg said.

"Yes?" I turned to him. He was the most senior person in the room. He was so getting my award for sexy grey-haired tremendously fit 60-year-old of the year. I couldn't help it. I love men.

"Can you talk Risa into being on your board?"

Risa laughed. "I think Monica can do that."

"Good," Greg said.

"So we're in business?" John asked. "It sounds good to you Monica?"

"Yes, it sounds very good. I'm excited. Thank you."

"Yes, thank you," Sonya chimed in.

Risa got up, "Thank you all."

John rose and reached over to shake Risa's hand, then mine, then Sonya's.

We were out the door a short time later.

"That was so great!" Sonya crowed.

"They are the best," I said.

"Don't go crazy yet," Risa said. "We still have to find another firm to fall in love with us."

"Oh, don't worry, Monica is good at that," Sonya said.

Chapter 27

Close to Demo Day

I guess we started truly freaking out when we saw the Demo Day party invitations arriving, about two weeks ahead of the big event. I got one, then another, then another, then about fifty. I jumped up from my desk and ran down the hall to find Marshall. He'd been through Demo Day. He'd been a team member of a Celery startup last year. He was the only one who could give me the lowdown.

Then I saw something shocking.

Marshall was playing Ping-Pong in the big room.

Marshall never plays Ping-Pong.

"What the hell are you doing?" I asked him.

"I don't know," he said, dropping the paddle to the ground mid-stroke.

The Ping-Pong ball shot past him.

He was playing against the brilliant Chinese programmer from the Evergrow team, named Bing.

Needless to say, Bing was just killing him.

"Eighteen to three," Bing said.

Marshall picked up his paddle and handed it to me. "Pinch hitter, you finish up."

"Great, this should make it fast," I said, since I stink at Ping-Pong.

It took Bing about two minutes to finish me off.

"Don't go anywhere. I have to ask you about Demo Day!"

Marshall screamed — and he never screams —"Don't say those words!"

Oh hell, this was worse than I thought.

"Game over," Bing said politely.

I handed the paddle to another victim, who wanted to try their luck against the master.

We went to a couch at the far end of the lounge area. Marshall was now pacing the carpet, then stopped dead in front of me.

"Do you get it? I don't think you get it. We are," he said, "the *whole* show."

"I thought you were going to make me feel better. You're freaking me out more!"

"Be real, are you ready? Is your team ready? Is your product ready?"

"Of course … not!"

"And it's in two weeks," he said. "Two. Two. Like I said, TWO!"

He held up two fingers like a peace symbol.

He turned it into a thumb and index finger gun and shot himself in the head figuratively. Then shook his head.

"No peace between now and then."

Then he held up two fingers – thumb and pinky — like the surfer dude "hang loose" symbol.

"No hang loose, no shaka, no … this," he wagged his fingers in the "Relax!" gesture, making a big "Welcome to Hawaii" grin.

"Okay, okay, I get it. Two weeks and we're screwed," I said.

"Precisely," he said.

He walked away in the other direction in a daze.

"Wait man, come with me, I gotta show you this." I dragged Marshall down the hall back to our desks.

"The after-parties?" He knew just where I was going.

"Yes! I got invitations to about five hundred parties."

"Yep, scary, right? Last year, a bunch of us did a slumber party from 6 to midnight, right here on the floor, then went to all the after-parties."

"Let me get this straight. We are going to kill ourselves all the way up to Demo Day getting our presentations ready. Then we start at dawn that day going nuts the whole day, showing off our big pitch in front of hundreds of people," I said.

"More than a thousand this year, is what I heard," he said.

"Great! That makes me feel lots better," I said. "So kill ourselves all day and then there's five parties until the next morning?"

"Like Geek Prom Night sort of. I mean, like we were all supposed to have done in high school."

"But none of us did, because we were geeks," I corrected.

We were in front of my monitor and I was showing him my email.

"You little bitch, you have email from Scott Kirsner? Is he interviewing you?"

"I guess so," I said.

"What's that face mean? You should be jumping up and down, white girl," Marshall said.

"I just don't know what the hell to say to him," I said. "I'm going crazy, I don't even have time to talk to him."

"It's not about *you* having time to talk to *him*. It's about him actually having time to talk to you," Marshall said, opening my email. "I'll tell him you're too busy and he can talk to me."

"Stop!" I said, as he tried to open the email from Scott.

I pushed him with a hip check and actually knocked him over.

Roan sees this and comes running to our desks.

"Children behave!" he says, giving Marshall a hand, pulling him up.

"Wait, wait, here." I dive into YouTube and pull up that song.

"That's what they say," Marsh sings along very slowly.

"Tommy James and the Shondells? Is there any music you guys don't know?"

"The beating of our hearts is the only sound." Roan is going all karaoke on us.

"Bad case of Glee around here."

"Don't you love that 'tumble to the ground' part?" Roan says provocatively to Marshall.

He just rolls his eyes, says, "Now, Roan!" then wanders off.

"I do love that part," I say.

We listened to the song three times on YouTube, and then Roan runs back down the hall to his desk. I looked over to find my friend in a strange state.

Marshall was just standing there with a very far away look on his face.

"You okay?" I asked.

"No," he said, "and yes."

"Meaning?" I said.

He didn't talk right away.

"Nothing," he said. "So what about it?"

"That way you were talking about it. You know, that we are the whole show," I was thinking out loud.

"Yes," he replies.

"It's true, we are it. If we don't deliver, there is no Demo Day," I said.

"Shut. Your. Mouth. I told you not to utter those words! Those are the words … that must not be spoken!"

I sat. "I'll call it 'The Death Spiral' from now on, okay?"

"Perfect."

"You know you'll get money. People love your thing."

"And you already have money. You think the Alexandria crew isn't gonna back you?"

"After all the people pulling out thanks to my ex, I'm still don't know what to think."

"You'll be fine," he said.

He headed back toward the Ping-Pong table.

"Call Scott Kirsner at the *Globe* or I will," he said casually as he walked down the hallway.

Chapter 28

Practice

And now the days were rushing into Demo Day, or the Death Spiral, as I had renamed it for Marshall. What we'd all been waiting for and working for and hoping for, and imagining as a kind of nirvana, was now a dreaded date on the calendar that we all wished would go away. We wished everything would just slow down, so we had time enough to make our apps and products work just right. They needed to sit up like happy little puppies and beg during the so-called dog and pony show we were about to star in. And as those kinds of things go, of course, the apps were a total mess and even nice clean code base stuff that had been working was suddenly falling apart, crashing, next to impossible to fix and driving us all crazy.

You could choose to put all your time into your PowerPoint presentation *about* your product or you could choose to put all your time into your *actual* product. This was the terrible reality of accelerator programs. I'd heard about geeky founders with great prototypes that almost actually worked, deciding to go with their PowerPoint presentations instead and not getting the investments they deserved.

A few lucky people had apps that worked and even had adoption, nice little hockey stick graphs full of real-world users actually engaged in their brainchild. They'd crossed the river from idea to execution.

My teammates and I were just on top of one another now. We'd work endlessly at the Celery offices, go grab dinner somewhere, go home for a short time and then get back together online or at one of our apartments.

Suzy had to call a meeting of all the teams to stop this death march and force us to slow down and get some sleep. We looked like hell. She didn't need any of us getting sick or doing something stupid like falling off our bikes or walking into a bus because we were so tired.

It rained solidly for five days before Demo Day, which made it just about the worst time of all of our lives. I had bought a cute bright blue dress and nice suede shoes in a azure shade to wear for the parties, pretty light flouncy clothes like real people wore on a real warm day in May, but if the rain kept up, it would be a no go on the outfit.

Things started to move slow and fast at the same time, like a car crash of craziness. It was just the strangest thing. We all looked excited and exhausted.

J-C had gone to France the week before Demo Day and expected to be back in time. Suzy said she would throw him out of the program if he didn't make it back on time.

He had to go. There was a very good reason. The French government was actually interested in backing his company since the fashion and garment business was so essential to their economy. There was a new innovative investment group called "MoneyPenny" founded by a bunch of guys out of HEC, the French Harvard Business School, who had put together financing and they wanted him to be based there. But on the other hand, there were tax issues that could make it a bad idea.

Demo Day was a Wednesday and he was supposed to be back Monday for the first rehearsal at the theatre downtown. I knew before Suzy did that he wouldn't be back for the rehearsal. He missed that flight and wouldn't be back that day.

We rehearsed Monday afternoon in the cavernous quiet theatre. It was all going so well — for the first five minutes.

MortalWarriors showed up, did their thing and their CEO Adam decided to leap off the stage and amazingly for once, didn't ace the landing but fell in a heap.

He didn't move at first. His team rushed to see what was the matter. He was really injured. Suzy called for an ambulance and he was taken to Mass General Hospital ten minutes away. Long and short of it, he'd broken his ankle two days before the big day.

"You could wonder if this group was jinxed or something," I said to Marshall.

"Don't go there," he said, "No superstition stuff please. It's not good right about now."

"And here comes broken ankle number two," I said.

Irina was wearing her usual high heels – these were big cork platforms with gingham cloth ties. Instead of her usual sleek leopard wear, she wore a blue cotton dress, tight on top, big skirt on bottom, she looked like Daisy

Mae attending a 4th of July picnic in the actual town of Dogpatch.

Her team got on stage and did their thing. Slava and Irina got into a fight about something and Suzy, with her coach whistle around her neck came over to break it up. She blew the whistle for all to hear.

"Everybody on stage now please," she said.

A bunch of us crawled out of the creaky wooden auditorium seats, some leaping over rows, not bothering to walk the aisles. The guys from Barb's team summoned the rest of the teams who were out in the lobby practicing pitches. They even found a few smokers out front on the street and got the group assembled.

"It's Monday night. We are up here *live* on Wednesday morning. You all need to relax and sleep and be healthy for this. Stop practicing your pitch. I don't care how they sound at this point, I just want you all to walk through them on stage, so you see where the stairs are, how you get on and off, imagine what the audience looks like. OK, let's all go through one last pitch — no stopping — really quickly. We should be done at 7:30. I am ordering you to go eat some dinner, relax and sleep. No parties, no more practicing, no nothing," she said.

Tuesday morning at 7:15 my phone chirped with this text, "Hey *Globe* Girl", from Marshall.

There was a link to a story in *The Boston Globe*. There was a photo of me, Jean-Claude, Irina and Marshall and was a full-page story about Celery and great stuff about all our companies. I was glad the picture wasn't just me, since this can make people kind of hate you.

I dragged myself out of bed, looked out the front window, to find it was still raining, then got ready fast and out on the street to get a paper copy of the paper.

The old cigar store at the corner had a very creaky front door and stacks of newspapers, racks of magazines, every kind of lottery ticket and glass candy counters from way back. The pile of *Globes* was stacked inside the front door. The four of us were right there on the front page — it was bigger and seemed more real in the printed copy than the online version.

There was a line for Powerball tickets toward the end of the counter and I decided to get one for every team. It was silly, but we needed some good luck today I figured, after yesterday's crazy mess of a rehearsal.

I was getting more texts; I heard a beep in my pocket.

"Back," from J-C.

I texted "Thank God!"

"No, thank Lagerfeld's G-6."

Just like him to hitch a ride in a private jet from a famous fashion icon.

"U tell Suzy ur here yet?" I texted back.

"N"

"Do it."

"K" he returned.

I bought five copies of the paper, 10 Powerball tickets and started for the door. It was still raining, so I put everything under my jacket to keep it dry.

I dashed home and drew a bath, made tea, found some yogurt in the back of the fridge, which still had a shelf date before Demo Day on it. That date had been burned into my brain since January. Bath, tea, yogurt, I could handle this day.

"Celery?" I texted J-C.

"Will sleep now. B there noon," he replied.

He'd always been completely irreverent about the schedule at Celery. The rest of us jumped when Suzy set up a meeting or day full of meetings and never missed one, but J-C was just not that kind of animal. He was that way even on this particular day.

Most everyone arrived early to the Celery offices on Tuesday. Some were packing up desks with nervous energy. Most were joking around to hide their nervousness. It didn't seem possible that the next day was Wednesday Demo Day, an event we'd waited six months for and some of the teams were actually leaving on Friday, leaving for good. The Israelis' stuff was already packed and some of it would ship the next day.

There were occasional loud whoops and hollers that day – as startups heard from VCs or angels who had decided to give them money and expected to be part of the announcement the next day. There were journalists meeting up with different teams, or sometimes, journalist friends of Suzy's would come in, and she'd ask a few of the CEOs to come in and talk with them.

I walked around passing out the Powerball tickets, one to each team. The drawing was tomorrow. A guy from *TechCrunch* wanted to interview the women CEOs only and this got the guys really pissed off once again.

They were doing a photo shoot too with the females only, so a bunch of us girls slipped out before lunch to get fancy for the 3 p.m. photo shoot. This is why I missed J-C's arrival at noon.

Marshall texted me at 12:15. "Call Me."

I did.

"J-C just came in with a black eye," he said.

"What?"

"He's got a shiner. Something about a bar in Paris," Marshall said.

"Good God!"

"Better go pirate patch shopping!"

I got back from our downtown trip at 2 before we had to leave for the picture taking at 3. I found Jean-Claude behind his monitor like it was any other day of the week.

"What the hell happened to you?" I said.

"Your friend Dunhill," J-C told me. "I ran into him at Le Camping."

"Jesus." I dropped into a chair like my knees forgot to function.

"You should tell your lawyer lady," he said, "It's true. Your ex and Dunhill are really both working against you. One of the French VCs told me same thing you heard before."

"Risa was right."

"He sucks."

"What happened? What did you say to him?" I said.

"Dunhill's an idiot. He was with Nick at the American Bar and he said something about you not knowing crap about coding," J-C said. "I figured he needed someone to punch him in the face. I gave him a one-two punch. He came back at me, but don't worry, he looks worse than me, Madame," he said.

"Here," I pulled out an eye patch I'd found at the pharmacy on the corner.

He put it on.

"Now … I am a pirate king! Thank you and you look very pretty, Madame," he leaned toward me to kiss me.

"Don't," I said. "Not here."

"As you wish," he said and sat back down at his monitor. "I don't want to kiss you anyway."

"Really?"

"No, I don't. I rather sleep with you," he said.

"That might happen," I told him.

"I've fought for your honor, been wounded in battle, nearly fell off a mountain to my death and you push me away?"

"Be patient. Your luck may change. Wait till you hear what's going on around here." I told him about the Mortal team CEO breaking his ankle, and the rest.

We didn't have much time to talk and he seemed jet-laggy and exhausted.

His eye looked bad. "That hurts, doesn't it?"

"C'est rien." he said but winced. "And about sleeping with you … "

"You just need to sleep, not to sleep with anyone," I said, "And we'll both probably end up spending the night with our teams fixing things tonight anyway."

"Paris was beautiful weather this time. Very warm."

"Don't tell me how wonderful Paris was while we were all slaving away here in a week of rain. Not fair."

"You must go with me there with me. We will go."

"Maybe some day," I said.

We both worked all night with our teams that last night and no one was getting much sleep. The couches in the lunch room contained any number of Celery people flopped out in various configurations, a veritable battlefield of Ping-Pong paddles scattered among the wreckage of basketball sneakers, bike helmets, mobile devices and coffee cups.

Chapter 29

Demo Day

And then Demo Day was finally upon us and there was nothing to do but deliver your pitch and pray you got it right.

Amazingly, after all the rain, the day dawned clear, sunny and beautiful. That helped. We had to be dressed in jeans and team logo tees and head downtown to the old Art Deco theatre where we were presenting at 8:30 a.m.

"So why does the stage look so much bigger today?" I said to Slava, as we walked in, heading over to the main seating area of the auditorium. My stomach dropped in fear.

"Because we'll be up there in …. , " he looked at his watch, "forty-three minutes."

"Don't say that," I said, "Oh my God, look."

"Is that who I think it is?" Slava said.

"Yep, Zuckerberg and his sister Randi," I said. "Talking with C.A. Webb. She is so great."

"I need vodka," he said.

"Me too," I said.

We scanned the room, there were some other VCs we had seen before, the senior partners of certain firms who'd been sending their junior partners over to the Celery offices, but today was obviously different, so their whole team had turned out. Seeing the Zuckerbergs was cool, but even better was seeing local money moguls like Nicole Stata from Boston Seed, who was chatting with Don Dodge from Google and Aaron O'Hearne from Startup Institute. Even Bob Metcalfe had come back north from Austin to be here. He was talking with Dan Bricklin and Bob Frankston. The very tall Matt Lauzon was talking to the not so tall Sarah Hodges close to the front of the stage. These folks were Boston startup royalty.

"I wish there were a screaming room, where we could go and scream a little before we come out on stage," I said.

"Where they have many bottles of vodka," he said.

"Right, I hear you, wodka, wodka, wodka," I said.

Sonya came over with Irina, "They want all the CEOs backstage now," Sonya told me.

"Time to walk the plank," I said.

Suzy gave us a pep talk. Walt slapped our hands in a lineup like we were the Red Sox taking the field. The lights went up and it was show time.

Marshall and I had been keeping score for a long time, but today, I had to give everyone a 10/10 because they really did deliver.

The hat pick put MortalWarriors up first and as they rolled Adam on stage, in a wheelchair with his broken ankle and new cast, the house stood and cheered. When the noise subsided, he explained how he'd never been injured in Afghanistan, but the Celery program proved more dangerous. The crowd liked this and the team did their "Sir Yes Sir" presentation at the top of their game.

Next Irina and Slava went out and she surprised all of us by staying on her feet, not taking a dive from the high platform shoes upon which she perched. The Russians dodged all the difficult-to-pronounce words and made their startup concept clear and winning. I was proud!

The Israelis had decided to come running from four corners at the back of the auditorium and singing along with Queen's "We Are The Champions" played at a loud roar, to start their pitch.

Barb's more subdued and sedate MIT team had a big papier maché tree to show the difference between a normal tree and their Evergrow tree. It seemed be going fine, but then Barb turned fast and knocked over the normal tree, which got an unscripted storm of laughter.

We were up right after the Romanian team, so I can't remember how they did at all, I was barely watching their big data pitch. I heard it went well.

I stepped on stage and was happy to remember how the lights on stage blind you to everyone in the room. We'd worked out a routine where everyone on my team could hand a portable light bulb from one to the next as I introduced him or her. We pantomimed having all our phones go dead with no battery, then showed how BrightLight fixed that problem. A few very simple PowerPoint pages gave people a quick idea of the numbers behind our concept. We had decided not to announce the Alexander investment until we got a partner into the deal. We did mention Risa would be a board member.

The Aussies were next but with Chris still in the hospital, his geeky co-founder did the honors. He got through it well enough, but it was odd to hear Chris' pitch we'd seen him do so many times, now coming out of the mouth of his other founder. They made a short reference to Chris being on the mend from a climbing accident and how all of us at Celery got to learn what teamwork was really about when Jean-Claude and the MortalWarriors saved their fearless leader.

Marshall was after this, his team smartly dressed like him, in team tees but also nicely tailored jackets. His app looked cool and designy. His software worked. That's all he had wished for on Demo Day.

"You came for a demo. Let's do it," he said.

It worked well; I released a long slow breath. We all knew it had not been working the day before.

And last, but never ever least, was Jean-Claude, of course. He liked to make the biggest impression and he did. Not only was he wearing the pirate patch I'd gotten him, but he was dressed in full pirate attire. He'd talked one of the stagehands into letting him swing in on a rope.

He let go of the rope too high up and it looked like a disaster, but his team caught him in mid-air, which was even more dramatic than what they had planned, and they all acted as if they'd practiced it a thousand times. I don't think they'd even practiced it once. At least, none of us had seen it done on this stage.

He explained the fashion business and how they brokered fabrics worldwide. He showed off his app on the theatre screen behind him, about a hundred times larger than the actual Android version. There were no words on any of his slides — just his product after a few gorgeous graphics of fabrics, velvets, silks, leopard prints and calicos.

They were done quickly and got a great round of applause.

Marshall was standing with me. "It's over."

"I can't believe it," I said. "It went so well, it was almost boring."

"Boring is good. Boring and predictable attracts more money, even though they'd have you think otherwise."

All the teams filed out on stage once again. Everyone was jumping up and down and some of us were dancing.

"Now the hard part begins," Marshall said. "The mating ritual of money and geeks."

"Bring it on," I said.

They wanted us to pose for a group picture, as if it were a wedding. Jean-Claude arrived behind me out of nowhere, pressing up against me. It was reminiscent of another day he'd been bold enough to grab me from behind.

I turned and gave him a smirk.

"One, two, three … million!" the photographer from the newspaper said, as he snapped our photo.

The rest of the afternoon was a crazy dance of VCs, angels, reporters and all of us being romanced. Alexandria was so close and as I was talking to John and his wife, on the first floor, a scarf floated down from the balcony and I looked up to see the woman partner from Ventura Boulevard, a new firm out of L.A. Her name was Sandra McNamara.

John's wife looked up and yelled, "Macky Mack!"

The two women were hugging in a few minutes.

They did mostly entertainment and media startups but with all the dreadful news about climate change, they were opening an office near MIT that was all about green initiatives. Their Hollywood backers were keen on investing in that area and they had big bucks. BrightLight didn't quite fall under that rubric, but Sandra wanted to work with us and especially with John and Dot Alexander. The women had gone to Wellesley together. They hugged and chatted about B rounds and babies.

John looked over at them, then me, "Well, I don't think I can pull those two apart, so let me just say, they're in and we'll figure out the details with them later!"

"Awesome!" I jumped up and down.

Risa came over and we were all hugging one another. John stood there rather stiffly, looking more starchy than his shirt.

"Hey ladies, let's not get so emotional please! As Dot says, it's only money."

His wife actually kicked him for this comment.

"Do you mind if I go tell Walt and Suzy?" I asked them.

"No problem, but let's not tell the press until we work out the details," he said.

"Fine," I took off in the other direction.

I had really wanted to find Jean-Claude. He was at the other corner talking with the guys from Polaris. I just gave him a thumbs-up and hoped this would suffice for now, to let him know I'd closed my deal.

By the evening, we were exhausted, but so crazy happy about being funded. Jean-Claude had gotten money from Spark and Union Square. I had Alexandria and Ventura. Three of the other teams were funded as well and the rest had excellent prospects. The Russians were solid, the Israelis got a massive investment from an Israeli billionaire everyone but me had heard of and Barb with EverGreen was also working with Ventura and DFJ. Zuckerberg had shown interest in one company only — the shy Romanians' big data startup so Alex, Alexander and George were talking in an almost lively way, actually talking a lot and looking happy for the first time in six months.

At dinner, Jean-Claude and I got to sit together, holding hands under the table. This was the big party, then came the after-party, then the after-after party and a sweet, quiet post-prom time at the Celery offices at dawn, around about 5 a.m.

"It's officially Thursday morning," Marshall said as he poured orange juice and vodka into plastic cups for us. "Time for Drewscrivers!"

"Hey, if it's Thursday, they pulled the Powerball last night," I said, and did a quick search of the numbers up on my phone. "Hey, somebody in Cambridge actually won $256 million dollars!"

We all pulled our tickets I'd bought and checked them.

"Here you go." I read the numbers. Looked like none of us had won.

"There's other ways to make a million dollars," Irina said.

We laughed, wondering about all the ways our Russian friend might be thinking about.

"No, I mean legitimate ways – like founding a company, for instance! Hey, that's a good idea, maybe I'll do that," she said, standing up and then suddenly falling onto the couch by Sonya.

We turned to find Adam rolling down the hall in a wheelchair. "You guys aren't gonna believe this!"

He was holding up the Powerball ticket, waving it at us.

His teammates grabbed it.

"Crap, 4 numbers out of 5, it's a winner!" said his chief engineer.

"Listen to this. The ticket was in my wallet the whole time, but the wallet was in some bin in the nurses' office at MGH! It fell out of my pocket when they rushed me into the ER."

We all started jumping around and cheering. God knows where we got the energy.

"Listen, settle down. I'm sharing it with all of you, because it's no fun unless we all get a piece of it," he said.

"Some piece of nothing," his chief engineer said. "It's only worth $2000. How do they do the math over there at the lottery?"

"Okay, so we'll throw a big dinner. Irina's right, building a company is the right way to make a million and now we know how!"

We were high fiving and dancing, someone cranked up the disco music. Marshall got the disco ball turning.

We danced to about two songs and then all collapsed again.

Slowly, the vodka was gone and people started to leave. We'd all be meeting up for a Celery Send-Off Meeting, as

Suzy had called it, at 4:30 later that day and then a big dinner they were providing.

I was slumped on a couch with Marshall on one side, Jean-Claude on the other, my head on his shoulder, Sonya next to him and Irina next to her. We were getting philosophical and sleepy.

What I learned that long, long day, was quietly obvious to me in the morning light, after all the noise and excitement of Demo Day had died down. On the surface, it was a competition, this long five months, but in the end, you don't really compete with the other founders because they are the only ones who could understand what you'd gone through. We all knew the intensity of it, the feeling of being so in over your head, of constantly learning, of constantly yearning, of feeling at a loss most of the time, but going on, no matter. We knew the strange sensation of always falling and failing, but managing to land on your feet far more times than cats did, living many more lives than nine. We could comfort ourselves with the knowledge that the other founders were the cushion and the refuge and the safety net from being depressed and downcast about our losses. They were a bulwark against despair. Only they could lift you up and they are so damned good at doing that. And they were the place to celebrate the wins.

So when it comes to being competitive or jealous or combative with one another, founders surrendered their weapons at the door. Now that we were done, we knew that founders are *all* mighty warriors, fighting the good fight and so we refuse to do one another damage in this arena. We're here to learn how to wage the war, fight to win, win the fight, survive the obstacle course, learn to build the courage you need to believe you can do it. We share the experience, the lessons learned, on how to keep at it, how to work around anything, how to endure and how to create.

Chapter 30

Here Come the Brides

We were done. Most of us had slept for 18 hours just to get back to some sort of normal level of energy. It was hard to believe, hard to hold in your head. Demo Day was over. There was a lot to be thankful for, but just the experience itself was the most prized possession of all. A time, a place, a shared ideal and striving to make it all happen.

That first meeting in January was like a far away, long ago snowy, swirly scene in a story book, as if some mischievous child held us all prisoners in a snow globe, then shook it up and watched as we flew up and down against the Boston and Cambridge skyline, the Longfellow bridge on one side of the river with the MIT and Harvard buildings. On the other, you saw the shiny golden dome of the State House, the sharp shard of glass known as the John Hancock and the flat-hatted Boston pope, the Pru at Copley Square. There was snow blowing all around us, to cushion our landing wherever we fell.

And we were each like snowflakes blown about. All strangers blown together into a group of unique, creative, crazy, inspirational fast friends, joined at the hip after these five months at Celery. And soon we'd be going our separate ways.

It was late May and the only snow fluttering down on us was tiny apple blossoms scattering in a warm wind, parachuting from the trees above the courtyard veranda at the Cape Cod hotel, where two weddings were about to take place. The blossoms flew by like snow and might remind some of us of that January day we'd first met in a blizzard, but now it was over and it was a warm beach day on the Cape, out past the Chatham Lighthouse, where we'd spent the morning hanging out and getting wet and sandy before dressing for the wedding.

As evening began, we were all together one last time in fancy dress, young and pretty in handsome tuxedos and décolleté gowns. We even surprised ourselves with how wonderful we could all look, after a winter and spring covered in wool and windbreakers. Here on the terrace of the Chatham Bars Inn we finally looked like the start-up stars we'd been trying so hard to become.

Jean-Claude was headed for two weeks in Trento, Italy first, to visit another accelerator program there called Trento Rise. Then he was back to Paris to set up a new office with his team. Sonya was off to Brazil for her honeymoon. ABC of the MortalWarriors were already gone and doing business in Atlanta, thanks to their VC backing from a firm led by ex-Marines. Marshall and Roan were heading for New York.

Double wedding. Who could resist? It was like a double feature movie. The invitations might have confused the old-school attendees. Marshall and Irina. Roan and Sonya. That's what it looked like, but of course this was 2012, so this wasn't boy meets girl, but boy meets boy, girl meets girl, marriage Massachusetts style.

Marshall had apparently had a thing for Roan for a long time but they'd actually managed to keep it under wraps. Meanwhile, the tall Russian girl and my sexy Hispanic co-founder Sonya had let most of us in on it and anyone could see those two were falling for one another.

Marshall would be walking down the aisle with Irina, Roan would escort Sonya and then they would swap partners in front of the Justice of the Peace.

J-C had spent the morning helping the men get ready. He'd called a pal in Paris, (he always knew a guy to call) and somehow the perfectly fitted tuxedos had just arrived. They had Cole Porter panache, very 1930s but also very 2012. The men looked like something way beyond GQ, like a spread in *Men's Vogue Italia*.

I'd spent the morning with the ladies. Irina was already so much of a fashion plate; there wasn't much to attend to there. It was Vera Wang squared. They decided to do the showstopper, both wearing the same dress. On the tall, usually high-heeled Irina the crème brulée color sheath was a stunner, but to be fair to her partner, she actually came down to earth for the occasion and wore flats. Sonya, on the other hand, wore vertiginous high heels, something she never did and with the Wang wedding gown, it made her short curviness even more sumptuous and rendered the two ladies only a few inches different in height.

When the dressing was done and the wedding two hours off, I went downstairs and found J-C in the bar with three other Celery friends, chatting about when they were leaving and where they were headed. He looked so handsome in his full formal dress and tails. He even had a top hat next to him on the bar, and gorgeous grey pigskin gloves sitting next to those. Really made me swoon, that guy.

"Pal mal," I said, coming in.

"Not bad?' he pouted. "That's all I get?"

"Okay, you look very, very handsome," I confessed.

"And you look trés, trés belle, Madame," he grinned.

I bowed a "thank you" of sorts.

I wore a pale violet silk cocktail dress, cut like a Chinese Cheongsam dress, with silk frogs closures up the front, cap sleeves, pale almost white hose, pale purple high-heeled sandals. I had a wide-brimmed straw hat with a ribbon band of violet grosgrain. Irina had made the fashion choice, rendering this the rare wedding where a bridesmaid dress was something you didn't mind wearing on the big day and might actually wear again on a not-so-big day.

"I have some news. No more calling me Madame," I said.

He turned quickly. "You mean?"

"Nick agreed to the divorce. That girl Sendi wants to marry him. He's going to sign the papers my lawyer sent to his lawyer. Then it takes 90 days."

"C'est parfait," he said.

"Sort of," I said, looking at him.

"I know. I'm still married, but I'll see her in Paris next month. She wants to marry someone else too, she told me," he said.

"Nice for her," I said.

"And for us," he said.

"But you're leaving," I said.

"So come with me," he said.

"I can't do that," I said. "I have a company to run."

"You've got a co-founder," he reminded me. "Let Sonya work here and you do the EU office."

A few of the guys in the wedding party came in and the photographer set them up near the old mahogany and brass bar for pictures.

"Hey," Marshall called, "we need you for the photos."

"Let's go." Jean-Claude offered me his arm.

Marshall said, "Irina's mom is really something."

"She finally understood who was marrying whom this morning," I said, starting to grin.

"When you were all getting the brides dressed?

"Yep, she was going crazy saying you can't marry a black American man. Then Irina tells her, 'Don't worry mama, I'm marrying a yellow woman from the DR and Brazil.' You should have seen her face!"

"No wonder her mom keeps looking at me sadly," Marshall said.

I turned to see a group of wedding guests arriving in the lobby. There were some very big Russian guys in large mobster-like suits. Scary, but interesting.

We did some candid pictures with the photographer and Marshall said his quick good-bye to find Roan. Jean-Claude and I ran into Barb with her kids on the stairs, as I was on my way back up to the room where they were dressing the girls.

"This is Chester. And this is Mattie," she said.

"Hi guys," I said, and bent down to shake their hands. Two very cute kids.

"We saw the brides," Mattie told me. She was a flower girl and very excited at six years old to do the honors.

"It's pretty crazy in there, are you sure you want to go in?" Barb said.

"They needed something blue," I showed two blue garters I had for the ladies.

"Good luck, but I'd get in and out fast," Barb warned.

"I'll meet you at the back of the hall," Jean-Claude said and headed off. "We have an hour left before it really starts."

There was something about a wedding. You couldn't help think about your own life and becoming someone's wife. You had to wonder how you could have made make such a dumb choice on an equally beautiful day. The thought went in and out of my sunny happiness like a nasty sharp pain in the ribs. We'd gotten married on Stinson Beach, north of San Francisco; a friend of Nick's had an amazing beach house he loaned us for the weekend. Our guests sat on bales of hay, covered with dark red velvet pads, hand embroidered in gold with our names on them.

After delivering the blue garters, I went back down on the back staircase, away from the others. I needed a break. I was really sad suddenly to know it was ending and I'd miss all my friends when they headed out after the event.

I had to get outside, so I walked past the bar, to the back porch exit, along the row of white Adirondack chairs, mostly taken by summer guests, reading or glancing at us, wondering what event was happening at the hotel.

I walked down the stairs, into the road, toward the beach. I was crying. I put my sunglasses on to keep people from noticing. The wedding would start in 45 minutes and I was messing up my makeup and wishing I were somewhere else.

I couldn't walk in my fancy sandals, so I yanked them off once I was in the sand and started to walk barefoot. I had to get air, smell the ocean, remember there was more to life than the Celery, and more than starting companies.

There was a rock wall around the perimeter of the property, which I followed out toward the pier, wishing I could just walk faster and faster and somehow just disappear. Some guys were fishing at the end of the pier.

I was short of breath from crying and feeling lost. Tears were falling from below my sunglasses. My dress had little stains of tears all over the front of it. Tears and silk didn't mix well. Within a few days, I'd watch all my friends head off to every part of the globe, dissolving our group, as if it had been a dream, a mirage.

I don't know how Suzy found me or if Jean-Claude had sent her out to look for me, but she came out of nowhere, touched my shoulder.

"Remember that bet we made, that this 50/50 class of females and males would be the best ever?"

"Yep," I said, trying to remember back to the beginning. It felt so long ago.

"How'd we do?"

"I think we all won," I said.

"I agree, this class has the biggest investment total so far. But what's up with you? Tears?" she said, then stood next to me on the pier. We couldn't sit and mess up our dresses.

"Everyone's leaving," I said.

"Everyone?"

"Okay, *he* is," I said.

"So go with him," she said.

"I can't go with him," I said.

"Why can't you go with him?"

"I can't," I said, then I was crying more.

"You'd be surprised what you can and can't do when you love someone," she said.

I wasn't sure where she was going with that.

"My husband just showed me that," she said. "He kept me from making a big mistake."

She got up, gave me a hug and then kissed me on the cheek. We started back toward the hotel.

"Why not let Sonya run your Boston office and you go off to Europe."

"And be with him in Paris?"

"Well, we can't let these guys take us for granted. Maybe try Berlin, there's a lot going on there with start-ups and co-working spaces. Then Jean-Claude gets to keep chasing you. Make him take the train from Paris to find you."

"You're pretty smart, boss lady."

"Just been around the block a little longer than you. I can help set you up. I know some great folks in Berlin."

"Thank you," I said.

She hurried back without me.

I wanted to take a little time, so I wandered the long way around the porch and gravel drive. I entered the hotel, at the back door, to the sunroom foyer. They were already pooling there, in the back, getting ready to go in. I didn't see Jean-Claude at first. And then I did.

He had his top hat on. And the grey morning coat and fancy trousers. He looked great.

"That's all you should ever wear," I said.

"I thought you liked that other suit – what did you call it? My birthday suit?" He grinned.

"Yes, it's even better," I said.

"Shh! No talking, we're just about to enter," the wedding coordinator lady said. She pushed us into position.

He gave me his arm.

I took it, then looked in his eyes.

"Go with me. Be with me in Paris," he said.

"I can't go to Paris," I said.

The wedding lady came back to us, held her finger to her lips in the "shh!" gesture of librarians of yesteryear. She made big eyes at us, to say "No Talking!" She opened the door. The music poured out. The chords of the traditional wedding march began, sending a jolt through me. We all stood up straighter when we heard it and were at attention, ready to go.

We headed down the aisle. I never gripped anyone's arms so fiercely.

"Ouch!" he said and caught my eye, then winked slyly at me. "Mademoiselle, please, don't hurt me!"

We smiled for the crowd and there was quite a big one.

He was good at this. I felt a blush just feeling how much I loved this guy. It was the most confusing thing. He leaned toward me, whispering.

"Don't say you can't. You can. You can do anything you want. You showed us all that with your company," he said, just before we reached the front and separated in front of the justice of the peace.

He squeezed my hand.

I went to the right. He went to the left. I hated to let him go, even five feet away was too far. I could just see him out of the corner of my eye, but tried not to look. The groomsmen and bridesmaids peeled off one by one.

Suzy and her husband were the last before the brides and grooms.

Her husband was whispering something in her ear and she was grinning. They looked closer than ever. How much had she told him about falling in love with a handsome Australian who'd nearly fallen off a mountain?

At last, the grinning brides and grooms paired off, Marshall and Roan standing on the right, closer to the bridesmaids in pale lavender, then the two brides to the left of the groomsmen, who all wore pale lavender ties.

J-C held the girls' rings and I had the guys' rings.

A bunch of Hispanic women in the front row were weeping. One made a loud snort noise and I looked at J-C who made a funny face of surprise back at me.

I noticed it seemed like we were all holding our breath, as the justice of the peace started the slightly standard but mostly improvised wedding text.

"Do you Irina take this woman … " I heard parts of the ceremony, but now was just watching Jean-Claude for cues when we went up, when we did the rings. It was more like being in a play and trying not to blow your entrance and lines. It all came off smoothly and once we played our parts, it was over. I could breathe again and relax. I was looking at him in a kind of a trance.

I was not even aware it was done and we were the third couple to leave after the two newlywed couples exited. J-C was on it though and he stepped up to me, offering his arm.

I took it and we walked.

"Smile," he whispered. "Un petit effort."

I did.

"Much better," he said, gripping my arm.

There were lots of people taking pix, some doing videos.

Halfway down the aisle, he leaned close and asked again, "Will you meet me in Paris?"

I looked at him.

"Suzy wants to help set me up in Berlin," I said.

"Great city. That could work," he said.

"And Sonya could stay here, running the Boston office."

"But you must meet me in Paris first," he insisted.

"Will you wear that to the airport?" I asked.

"This? At CDG?" he said.

"Yes, I want to see you exactly in that," I said.

I always wanted to see him looking so handsome and happy.

"Okay, then yes, I will," he said.

"Deal," I told him.

About the Author

Halley Suitt Tucker is an early blogger, a TechStars alum, and a community moderator for the APE (Author, Publisher and Entrepreneur) community on Google+. She did a successful Kickstarter program to crowdfund her book. She's been published in *Harvard Business Review* and *Penthouse Magazin*e and appeared on Oprah!

The book cover was designed and illustrated by Susy Pilgrim Waters and formatted by 52 Novels.

Susy Pilgrim Waters is an illustrator, designer and painter. She has worked extensively in print advertising, book and magazine publishing as well as commerical licensing.

www.pilgrimwaters.com

52 Novels designs ebooks, getting manuscripts to play nice with Amazon Kindle, Barnes & Noble Nook, Apple iPad, and other e-readers. They also prepare books for Kobo, Smashwords, CreateSpace, and Lightening Source.

www.52novels.com

novels

Made in the USA
Monee, IL
13 September 2026

62981004R00193